CHAINED KNIGHT

CHAINED KNIGHT

A Tale of the Underdark

LILITH SAINTCROW

For the strange, the bold, the untamed

The best in this kind are but shadows, and
the worst are no worse, if imagination amend
them.

— WILLIAM SHAKESPEARE

I

EVENTUALLY BIT

NORMALLY THE GLARING RED CHECK ENGINE LIGHT PLUS billows of steam from under the black Oldsmobile's hood would be frustrating but solvable problems; the headlights cutting through dusk behind her could have been part of said solution if not for their red-and-blue flashing accompaniment.

It figured. If God existed he was a sadist toddler, never content to simply crush an ant when a few legs could be pulled off or a magnifying glass hauled out to focus sunshine. There were even zombifying mushrooms which could take over poor silly insects, forcing victims up to high places before they died in a puff of spores —which was the surest indication of the divine's fucked-up priori-ties *and* sense of humor Ariadne Millar ever heard of.

The road curved sharply ahead. She'd be out of sight for a few minutes if she could just nurse the car along a few more hundred feet, and if she was going to get away it would have to be now. They wouldn't chase her into the woods with night approaching and rain on the way, right? She'd only have to worry about starvation and hypothermia.

Risky, sure. Worth it, though?

She'd probably feel differently when she got hungry, but that was Future Ari's problem. Current Ari had all she could deal with right in front of her, especially since the Olds's overworked engine chose that moment to seize completely. Power steering failed, but she did manage to get the car onto the gravel shoulder. Tires crunched to a stop; multicolored lights had briefly disappeared from her rearview.

Running into the forest was a stupid move, yet in hindsight completely inevitable. Ever since she'd lunged for the gun on the nightstand, this was the only possible place she could arrive at.

Arrest, court, sitting in prison—oh, the Hardisons had more than enough resources to make the most of those opportunities. It wasn't even old Earl she was truly afraid of; Wanda Lee was far more dangerous by virtue of ambition, not to mention sheer venom per pound. Wanda would never forgive a daughter-in-law who had the temerity to say no and mean it, let alone one who had grabbed the snub-nosed .38 and put a stop to the beatings, the gaslighting, the thousand casual cruelties.

What you gonna do, Ari? Mike's perfect, expensively capped grin, because he knew she had nowhere to run. *Cry to the cops? My daddy owns this town.*

Well, wasn't he surprised now. And if she was going to die, she'd prefer it to be in the woods rather than a concrete cell.

Ari realized she was attempting to put the car in park, but the gearshift was frozen and the Check Engine light had been joined by a few others, all crimson and orange, none of them good news. At least she hadn't careened off the road; she stamped on the parking brake out of habit, though the Olds clearly wasn't moving under its own power ever again. Her right hand shot out, grabbed the back-pack on the passenger seat, and she had a bad moment tugging at the door-latch. Pawing at the lock's nobbin with clumsy fingers, she sobbed once before it chucked upward with a solid, comforting sound.

Why the idea of breaking a window to scramble out of a stalled car should be so much worse than anything else tonight, she had no idea.

Cool rainy air caressed her wet cheeks, temporarily soothing the puffing and bruises. Her backpack wasn't heavy; all she had were a few spare T-shirts and clean panties, a couple pairs of jeans, her mother's silver crucifix, a battered *700 Years of Western Visual Art*—her favorite textbook, its margins populated with many a doodle of feverish, staring eyes—plus a pathetically thin roll of cash she'd managed to scrape together with some dim idea of perhaps hitching a ride somewhere, anywhere else. The small roll represented months of careful, patient, tiny thefts from Wanda's pin money, and Mike's wallet on the increasingly frequent nights he came back near-blackout drunk from the Kittykat Klub over in Legeville.

Each time she hoped he'd either get stopped or into a Jim Beam-fueled accident, but he was the town's golden boy. If he was pulled over for weaving or running a stop sign the cops brought him home, apologetic, holding their hats in both hands while Wanda thanked them kindly. If she slipped a crisp, folded Grant or Benjamin their way at the same time, well, it was only polite to tip for good service.

Apparently Mike's guardian angel was a brown-noser as well, because even while wasted Ari's husband always managed to pilot his giant black-and-chrome truck home without major incident.

That particular celestial being had certainly been off-duty a short while ago. Ari could still feel the jolting in her palms, the gun trapped against Mike's chest bucking repeatedly as she squeezed the trigger over and over, until there was only a series of dry clicks and his fingers fell away from her throat.

She coughed, wiped at streaming tears. The back of her head throbbed, blood clotting as it dried in her hair. Steam from the dying engine smelled awful and her eyes hadn't stopped leaking throughout the whole ordeal; Mike had gone quiet before the first slap, and that was always a signal for the very worst beatings.

If he was yelling, things usually didn't go too far. But coming home so early, already drunk before he'd gone over to Legeville— she couldn't tell what on earth had set him off.

Did it matter? Wanda was at bridge club and Earl at an Elks dinner—she'd thought she had more time before they called the cops, the only reason she'd slowed down enough to stuff what she could in the backpack. She hadn't taken the truck because everyone in town knew it, and if they saw her driving... well, now it was too late to wish she'd stolen a vehicle with a more reliable engine.

The sky looked like a van Gogh or El Greco storm canvas, but there was no time to admire the light or take internal notes. On this side of the road was a high sheer wall of rock, a perfectly good mountain—albeit with its top flattened by assholes looking for coal —frowning at the pavement ribbon clinging to its flank. On the other, the slope fell away steep but not impassable, and though it had been clear-cut many years ago the trees had staged a helluva comeback. Heavy trunks crowded with undergrowth swallowed the rapidly fading sunset, and if she was going to run it had to be now.

I hate camping. It was just the last in a long line of things Ari despised but had to do if she wanted to survive. She wiped uselessly at her cheeks once more, settling the backpack, and jogged across two lanes separated only by a pair of faded yellow lines. More gravel crunched underfoot as she reached the shoulder, and a stitch gripped her side. Even that short burst of activity was a little too much at the moment.

She'd been hoping to get to a city and... what? Find a cheap motel, at least, and maybe get some real sleep for once. But not only had she killed her husband, she'd also stolen Wanda's old car to escape in, and even if she tried to explain about self-defense anyone in town could guess the foregone conclusion.

Christ Himself knew both Wanda and Mike said it more than once. *Nobody will believe you, you're just the wife. Shut up and do what I tell you.*

Ari snapped another glance down the road. No sign of the cop car just yet, just a white glare of headlights at the curve announcing it wouldn't be long.

Would it really be so bad? Arrested, put in handcuffs, attempting to explain to big-bellied good ol' boys who were already on the Hardison payroll—yes, Ari thought, it would be worse than what she'd endured so far, and that was saying something.

No water. No food but a couple energy bars. A few hundred dollars. That and her brains, overworked just as surely as the Oldsmobile's wheezing innards. She was vaguely surprised steam wasn't escaping from her ears too; a silly little art history degree couldn't prepare you for this nonsense.

Just as she stepped off the shoulder and onto steep weed-laden embankment, a series of loud crackles forced her to look back. Now the vapor from the engine was black instead of white, billowing ominously. Gasoline reek tiptoed across the road, further marring a soft spring evening. The hills muttered to themselves, trees brushed by an invisible hand, and the glow of not-so-distant headlights swelled, accompanied by vicious little dapples of bright color.

Not like a Turner painting, a moment of light-filled loneliness before catastrophe; the palette was different. More like Hopper, but there was no peace to be found in this isolation.

Ari staggered down the hill. She ducked between two vine-wrapped trees, heard the suppressed laughter of water running fast over rocks, and hoped she wouldn't turn an ankle. The bruised glow of evening was fading fast, and her blundering sounded loud as the heartbeat banging in her ears, or the sobbing gasps as her lungs heaved. A vine clutched at her arm, another at her ankle. Kudzu? She couldn't tell; she was hoping she wouldn't stumble through poison ivy or onto a snake just minding its own business.

Should've packed a machete. But if she had access to one of those she might've done something else before now. There was no telling how an animal would act when cornered. Plenty submitted, sure... but there were a few who eventually bit.

Well, she'd gotten a mouthful. A rancid one, to be sure, but at least she wouldn't be slapped anymore. Or kicked, or screamed at. Or choked.

Or thrown on the bed, attempting to muffle her sobs while the man who'd promised to honor and cherish grunted atop her.

Sure, maybe she'd feel different after a few nights sleeping in the cold, especially if her old nightmares returned, though Christ knew her waking life had turned into something almost as bad. Still, at that moment, all Ari Millar—she was taking her maiden name back, thank you *very* much—felt was the high savage exultation of escape.

Starving free was better than a gilded, horrifying cage. She just hoped she had enough willpower to remember as much once the hunger really bit. The wind freshened, pouring through treetops, and thorns on a long juicy bramble-branch scraped across the knee of her jeans.

Her mouth a pained rictus, her cheek and ribs aching, her throat on fire and her scraped hands outstretched, Ari plunged through bushes and low scrub, veering drunkenly between trees.

And of course, because nothing ever went her way, it began to rain.

❧ 2 ❧

PRESSURE AND CONDITIONS

At first it wasn't bad. Falling drops were caught in the canopy and a few irregular flashes of lightning showed just in time to steer Ari away from holes, cracks in the hillside, or vine-clots.

All too soon the treetops were saturated; heavy splatters thudded down all around as she crouched briefly in the lee of a hoop-skirted evergreen. The branches began to toss as the wind got serious about its work, and the lightning, now finished tuning up, commenced to baton in earnest, orchestral thunder obediently keeping time.

A half-glimpsed overhang promised some kind of shelter possibly free of venomous—or anxious—critters. Of course, it wasn't much; still, she was dashing across soft mud and hopping a small stream chuckling merrily slantwise on the hill before she could weigh up disadvantages. Her ankle threatened to roll, but she made it into comparative safety and stood blinking heavily, her left cheek a furnace, her neck throbbing, and her lungs working deeply, smoothly.

She was alive, Ari realized. Her heart thumped along, her throat was raw but plenty of air was getting through, her fingers and toes all worked. Even the scabs on the back of her head weren't sending warm trickles down her nape anymore. She was watching one of Mother Nature's finest light shows, fit for a Renaissance master to immortalize, and she wasn't soaked too badly.

She was also shivering and stood a very good chance of dying from hypothermia tonight, but at least she wasn't lying stiffly in bed waiting for Mike to come home, gauging how drunk he was by the sound of the bedroom door opening. The thunder was far nicer than Wanda Lee's syrupy drawl, and the cold was balmy compared to old Earl's paralyzing pale blue gaze.

All told, this was damn near a vacation. She'd been wise enough to grab her old hiking boots from the closet's depths along with the backpack; there was some utility in growing up poor enough to understand the necessity of good shoes if you could get them. That was a blessing, right?

Mom would be proud of her optimism. Rose-colored glasses were, so far as Sylvie Millar had been concerned, the only possible response to the world's cruelty.

Ari had her own thoughts, none repeatable in polite company. With the rain coming down in buckets, lightning jabbing regularly, and thunder a continuous grumble, the cops probably weren't going to be looking for her. *That* was worth feeling good about, right?

Her backpack wedged safely against the rear wall of the semi-cave, she stared at a silver curtain of falling water. It was hard to tell if lightning was getting closer, since the thunder-growls and bellows overlapped into a nearly continuous roar rivaling that of the deluge. The small stream was a torrent now, and she seemed to be standing in the only dry spot for miles around.

At least, *relatively* dry. She devoutly hoped other animals wouldn't also find it agreeable, or that if they did they were of a mind to get along instead of fighting over space. Ari pressed hard against the wall, something inside her pack jabbing at her lumbar region—maybe the textbook, the only piece left of her college life, but now she couldn't remember everything she'd packed. Had she taken the gun?

Now would be a good time to get rid of evidence. Yet she stayed frozen, staring at tossing branches lit by bright white bursts, the foaming stream swelling past its banks and tearing great chunks of dirt free. The noise was like standing in front of concert speakers, a deep throb pressing hard against skin, ears, bones. Rivulets fell from the overhang's lip, and the moment she noticed some bore chunks of rock and dirt was terrifying, sure.

Yet it was better than crouching in a bedroom corner while Mike raged. At least the storm wasn't really personal—then again, had her husband's fury been the same? A simple product of pressure and conditions, emotional weather she could have managed if she'd prepared better or been more of what he wanted?

You think you're special, city girl? Wanda Lee's hiss like a threatened cottonmouth, her nicotine-tinged breath brushing Ari's nose. *You're nothing. Mikey should get rid of you, just see if we don't.*

A massive white glare filled the world, thunder immediate at its heels. A tepid wall of air moved through the trees, ripping leaves and branches free, scraping past the overhang's precarious bubble. Ari screamed; the ground under her boots softened alarmingly.

Oh, crap. The whole hill trembled; had something divine noticed a woman whose hands still tingled from a .38's jolts hiding here? Wanda Lee went to church on Wednesdays and Sundays, nodding and smiling; maybe she had a few credits to spend on some vengeful smiting saved up in the ol' heavenly bank.

The world didn't care about bruises, swelling, broken bones. All it wanted were appearances kept. The Hardisons were champions at that game, a thin veneer over the truth like Victorian fixers dabbing fig leaves on Adam and Eve.

Ari wasn't truly surprised when the earth gave way. Another white flash, a brief starry flicker of *well of course it would end this way*, and the landslide tore free of the hill as thunder laughed like a portly sheriff who had just been asked to do his damn job. She fell, grateful it wasn't hunger or hypothermia after all, her backpack torn loose and her throat bubbling with a bottled scream.

But of course it couldn't be that easy.

❦ 3 ❦

POST-INCIDENT MORNING

HER LEFT HAND WAS COLD; HER RIGHT, PRESSED AGAINST AN exposed slice of belly since her T-shirt and flannel had ridden up, was warm. Her back ached, a fuzzy faraway feeling, and her throat was afire with thirst. There was a crust across her eyes, and something hard digging into her hip.

What the hell?

For a moment Ari thought Mike had finally slipped up and hurt her so bad she had to be hospitalized, but there was no smell of disinfectant or bleached linen. Maybe she had just *taken to bed*, as Wanda Lee would say with pursed lips, and the window was open? Her nose was full of fresh air, the scent of rain-washed earth, and a faint powdery goodness like mimosa trees in full bloom.

She didn't want to move. For one thing, it might hurt—she was used to discovering new damage the morning after Those Incidents, as she'd taken to calling the eruptions of Mike's rage. For another, it might alert someone she was awake, and they might start in on her again.

But the light spilling in through her clump-matted lashes was wrong—neither fluorescent nor incandescent nor LED, a lovely outdoor glow bearing a silvery tinge—and the flowery smell was wonderful. She heard a soft breeze through leaves, a phrase of sweet fluting birdsong. Slight crackles, like a small animal in underbrush. And there was no flat chill of air conditioning, either; a cool, entirely natural breeze moved over her from toes to tangled head.

Finally she had to twitch. The thing against her hip was a small round black pebble, and it shifted away without complaint. Ari found the crust on her face was dried mud instead of blood, which was a deep relief. But once she got her eyelids clear and her vision came into focus, nothing she saw made any kind of sense.

For one thing, the trees were absolutely wrong, straight grey smooth-barked columns, their interlaced arms freighted with heavy fanlike leaves instead of mimosas' lacy flutters. No kudzu, no blackberry or raspberry, indeed very few bushes at all. The loam was soft and mossy, and her hand was numb because it had rested just over the margin of a small circular pond, the water's surface shimmer-reflecting soft pale phosphorescence.

Ari rubbed at her eyes again and stared like a wondering child, mouth slightly open.

The pond rested in a clearing, and flowers spread from its banks to the forest's wall. Or at least the cabbage things were vaguely flowerlike, except that they held pearly globes, ranging from fist- to head-sized, in their central rosettes. Those glowed, and they were the source of the silver light.

What. The fuck. It looked like one of Rembrandt's disciples had taken up painting fantasy book covers. She might've thought she was dreaming, except for the coating of heavily plastered dried mud. Ari's scalp crawled, her hair matted with guck and her face aching. At least the mud would cover the scabs on the back of her head—her hands were scraped, too, and she felt every place Mike had hit her for the past two weeks as a separate note in an orchestra of welling discomfort. Her throat throbbed; she considered the pond for a long moment.

Standing water. Probably full of bacteria or parasites, and the glowing cabbage-pearl things were maybe some kind of fungus? She'd no doubt die of dysentery if she drank here.

But there was nothing else on offer and she was—in defiance of all odds—still alive, so Ari tentatively wiggled her fingers and toes. No bones seemed broken; she went down the checklist like she did every post-Incident morning. Everything hurt, sure, but nothing felt sprained or strained. It took a couple tries to sit up, then she pushed tentative fingertips through the hood of stiffening mud at the back of her head. Poking the scabs made her wince, but there was no fresh blood. She patted herself down and discovered her backpack was gone, most likely ripped free in the landslide.

Great. But she was too thirsty to care at the moment, and once she got her hands free of dirt the first few swallows of water were amazing. Clear and cool, without the taste of chlorine or dirt, it soothed parched tissues and calmed her stomach wonderfully. She continued dipping up palmfuls, drinking until—between one moment and the next—she'd had enough. So she scrubbed at her face with wet hands, rinsed, and finally sat back on her heels, looking over the clearing.

The woods were alive with various sounds, but that was usual— a lot of people who never went camping talked about wilderness peace and quiet, when it was just a different kind of ambient noise.

Yet the trees weren't dripping and there was no sign of the land-slide. Which was utterly weird.

There was also zero indication of her backpack in the immediate environs. She was positively caked with dried mud, and the thought of wading into the pool for a rinse was only moderately attractive since she was already soaked clear through, everything from jeans to shirt to socks and panties sodden and full of grit. Washing her clothes would raise the prospect of sitting around naked in the woods while they dried.

She hadn't struggled into a bra before fleeing. That was something small to be grateful for.

As a matter of fact, Ariadne realized, she was the very definition of *rode hard and put away wet*, her mother's favorite expression for utter dishevelment. A small, terrified giggle escaped before she clapped a damp hand over her mouth to trap it.

The cabbage-pearls brightened; the light was almost liquid, laying lovingly against every surface. A soft chiming joined birdsong and other tiny noises, dying away as her laughter did.

Dreaming, or something else? At least it wasn't her old nightmare of a haggard stranger's face staring into darkness. Ari decided against pinching herself; more physical misery wouldn't help. Maybe she was hallucinating, hit on the head and wandering the forest near topped-off mountains.

If the cops caught her before she died of exposure, would they stick her in a mental facility instead of jail? She'd never considered that particular possibility. Ari sank back on her haunches, gazing at the ripples spreading through glassy water, then examined the trees.

Nobody was screaming at her. There were no floors to wax or curios to dust, none of Wanda Lee's dissatisfied little verbal or physical jabs, no listening for the cordless landline's shriek—Mike wouldn't even let her have a smartphone, and God forbid she wasn't there to answer when he took it in his head to call home—or for Earl to say, *where's my cigarette lighter?*

Her father in law would stare at Ari while she clicked the ancient Zippo, and blow smoke in her direction when she was done. Never a single *thank you*, just a burst of acrid burning nicotine and the slight narrowing of his pale blue eyes, so like his son's.

No yelling, no slaps or pinches. No sudden searches of her dresser, no attempts to break her pencils or rip pages out of her barely used sketchbook. Nobody was expecting her, or watching her, waiting to seize a slight or imagined infraction to punish.

It was the happiest she'd been in a long time. Ari sat, tiny shudders passing through her in waves. Maybe her body just wasn't used to peace anymore?

Cool when it went down her throat, the water had turned warm behind her breastbone. A strange soft feeling of well-being spread through her ribcage, and when she realized she was rubbing her hands together like Lady Macbeth she stopped, examining them closely.

No blood, hers or... or Mike's. A few streaks of mud, but the bruises weren't so bad as she feared. The scrapes looked better, too. Her throat was still a bit scratchy, but her face didn't hurt so much now and the back of her skull wasn't throbbing. No trace of dysentery yet—of course, there was precious little in her system for it to work with, but she wasn't hungry. She didn't even long for the energy bars in her backpack.

Which she should probably find. It couldn't have been carried too far away, could it? Then again, she had no idea where on earth she could be; the vegetation was different than any hill or holler around the Hardisons' precious town.

And I thought it was like a Hallmark special. Another laugh caught in Ari's throat; her own naiveté was bleakly hilarious. Three years ago she'd been a starry-eyed young bride, ready for small-town life full of quirky characters and evenings on a porch sipping lemonade or sweet tea, maybe dabbing watercolors *en plein air* while her husband napped in the shade or readied a picnic. Possibly even running a small gallery for tourists, comfortably selling kitsch, crafts, and antiques, with a small but definite place among the local gentry.

Instead, she'd ended up... here. Wherever this was.

A faint snuffling pushed her up to kneeling again, looking wildly in every direction. Her neck didn't hurt as much as she expected, giving only a faint twinge as her head turned, and the light brightened a little more—probably from adrenaline roaring into her bloodstream, widening her pupils to grab every possible photon.

A small furry grey animal bumbled away from a knot of tree roots, nosing at mossy ground. It looked a little like a raccoon, except its tail was flat as a beaver's and when it lifted its head to regard her a pair of big, bulbous golden eyes held only mild interest.

It watched her for a moment, shiny black nose sniffing again, and its whiskers twitched gently.

What in the name of Darwin is that? It definitely wasn't a possum either; the creature visibly decided she was no threat and wandered up to a nearby cabbage-pearl, nimble paws patting at the broad, fuzzy leaves cupping the central jewel before it commenced nibbling at the edges.

The small sound of teeth chomping on something like crisp lettuce halfway convinced her it wasn't a dream. Were hallucinations always this vivid? Or was this some kind of native microhabitat she'd never heard of?

"Okay," a thin, terrified little voice said, and she realized it was her own. "Where the fuck *am* I?"

⚜ 4 ⚜

DEFIANCE OF RATIONALITY

THE NOT-POSSUM LOOKED UP, BLINKING FIRST ONE GOLDEN EYE, then the other... and continued chewing. Very much like a cow with a cud, in fact, and the slight pooching of its cheeks was yet another tiny, overwhelming detail. This entire place was full of such touches, damn near photorealistic.

Damn near real.

Fortunately the animal didn't seem to consider her a threat, or even very interesting. It continued its lunch—or perhaps its midnight snack, since no sunlight filtered through the branches overhead. The tiny sounds of chewing mixed with birdsong, wind, and other small noises. How many of these things were hanging out among the trees? Were they all docile?

God, I hope so. Slowly, Ari pushed herself upright and backed away along the pond's edge, her boots sinking into moss. The creature glanced up again. It didn't shriek or bristle, just watched her while nibbling, which was great.

The thought that other critters, maybe not nearly so relaxed, might be lurking in the woods at night should have kept her nailed in place. Maybe she'd used up a lifetime's worth of fear, though, because Ari was blessedly numb.

Well, she did feel something—faint curiosity, growing by the second. The pearl-cabbages glowed, their leaves softly fuzzed like lamb's ear, each individual hair lovingly crafted. When she passed close to individuals the sweet scent intensified. It didn't mean they were edible, but the water seemed fine. She could return to this clearing and at least not die of dehydration.

Isn't that a happy thought. She turned, hoping the not-possum wouldn't decide to leap once her back was exposed, and peered between trees, pushing at mud-heavy hair. Some people paid good money for this kind of spa treatment, right?

Of course, they didn't wear their clothes while getting it, but a murderer on the run couldn't be too hung up on the small stuff. And she felt far less battered than she'd thought—even her throat was a lot better.

Had she imagined the whole episode? Overreacted? *That* caused a faint twinge; maybe she was just as crazy as Mike and Wanda Lee always said. Had she done something else, something awful and irreversible?

Well, something *other* than shooting her husband? Was she criminally insane?

Ari stopped. The trembling was back; she had halted at the edge of the clearing and reached out blindly, her hand finding a tree trunk. Cool, smooth bark under her fingers certainly felt real. So did the mud, and the involuntary shaking. The light was strange, but no painter—no matter how gifted—could produce this kind of detail. No sculptor or set designer could either. Maybe she'd found a weird new kind of psychoactive fungus scientists would go gaga over if she managed to bring out a sample?

Well, she wouldn't be contributing to botany or biology just yet. Ari took a deep breath, squeezing her eyes shut, and opened them again, expecting to see pine and oak, or maybe hemlock since there was water nearby. She expected kudzu or multiflora rose, blackberry or raspberry, and all types of rhododendrons. She'd never been a big fan of botanical illustration before, but retreating to the woods and catalog-drawing for the rest of whatever life she could manage was a beautiful thought.

That was the trouble with hope. It kept creeping in, no matter the poison poured on its leaves.

No change—the same smooth grey trunks, the same lack of undergrowth. The faint silver glow from pearl-cabbages cast sharp, ink-black shadows. There was an answering gold-tinged glimmer in the near distance, a horizontal ribbon, and as she strained to focus she found it was a road.

But not paved. Or yes, paved, but not with concrete. Ari glanced over her shoulder. The pond and the cabbages were still there, still detailed, still glowing. Then she looked back at the road, squinting though she'd never had any trouble with vision—a little farsighted, childhood visits to the optometrist said, but nothing to worry about. Which was a relief; her mother had worn the same glasses since high school even if her prescription needed changing.

Blocks of yellowish stone, carefully fitted together. Unimaginable labor must have brought them, dumped them, and tamped them down; their edges were sharp and definite, forest moss not daring to creep onto the road's margins. It was also wider than she expected; Ari judged it at about three lanes, though there were no ruts or painted lines.

The highway just sat there in defiance of all rationality, faintly luminescent, secure in its own existence. Ari glanced up, gained a quick impression of thickly clustered stars scattered on a black velvet sky, their dry fires peering through wide fanlike leaves, and just as quickly focused on the ground again.

One thing at a time. She could worry about the fact that there seemed to be no streetlamps or orange cityglow later; even in the high hills on the way to Legeville there was the occasional collection of lights at a railroad crossing or where a few farmhouses clustered near a gravel turnoff.

"This is so weird." Her own voice startled her again, and she jumped guiltily. There was nobody around to hear but the not-possum and whatever else was in the trees, so she might as well vocalize if it would help her deal, right?

Assuming the cops hadn't found her and she wasn't stuffed in an institution already, having some sort of chemical nightmare administered by injection. Was this what a psychotic break felt like?

Now that she wasn't occupied with the problem of getting through the day without giving Wanda Lee or her precious baby boy cause for complaint, Ari's brain had its accustomed bandwidth back and was using it to... what? Create a seamless illusion of a forest full of glowing cabbages plus a yellow stone road?

What. The flying. Fuck. If she said that out loud Wanda Lee would purse her taupe-lipsticked mouth, or Mike might give a casual, stinging slap. He could cuss, sure, and his mother could let loose bursts of unladylike language at will. But Ari, not really a part of the family, was held to a much higher standard.

"Fuck that," Ari whispered, and a laugh boiled in her throat. If she was sedated and dreaming, it explained the altogether uncharacteristic sense of physical well-being creeping outward from her ribcage. There were still aches and pains, sure, but they seemed very far away, retreating toward finger- and toe-tips.

It was no doubt a mercy of short duration, and far more than Wanda Lee would say she deserved. When Ari woke up she would find herself in a straitjacket, but if she behaved maybe they'd give her art supplies? Even jails let prisoners scribble on paper sometimes. A public defender might loan her a legal pad. Of course Wanda and Earl had the money to make something happen to their errant daughter-in-law, even in a solitary cell... but that was tomorrow's problem.

She was racking up a lot of those for Future Ari. In the present, though, there was that strange road—ruler-straight, though it occasionally rose a few fractions and dropped afterward in gentle swells.

Maybe she should see where it led.

5

NOTHING FAMILIAR,
EVERYTHING REAL

SHE'D HIKED IN WET BOOTS BEFORE, THOUGH NOT IN CLOTHES covered with landslide mud. Each step made a soft squishing, almost lost between the stealthy movement amid the trees and a whispering breeze. The forest's grey pillars pressed close, but no roots dared crack or heave the road's surface.

Which was odd, but no more than the rest of this. Ari was just glad the swelling in her throat was going down and her eyes had adapted to starlight.

A road by definition went between places, so she would eventually get *somewhere*. With her luck she was probably taking the long way, but she was committed now. It felt good to walk, even with the chafing; occasionally, faint silvery light bloomed on one side or the other, casting long shadows across yellowish stone blocks. She caught a glimpse of more pearl-cabbages once, standing with her toes on the road's sharp stone lip, and decided more botanical observation could wait for daylight.

Whenever that would happen. And another thing—there was no sign of the storm, the topped mountains, the hollows, or anything approaching normal vegetation. She almost muttered *we're not in Kansas anymore*, but she had no terrier to talk to and dear God, she shuddered to think of what Mike would do to a pet of hers. The Hardisons didn't even have a cat, Wanda prized her expensively fake antique furniture too much.

He won't hurt anyone ever again. Grim, squirming satisfaction popped up inside her chest before being swiftly strangled; it wasn't right to feel that way after...

After killing someone. Ari couldn't even say she hadn't meant to do it, because the moment she lunged for the gun on the nightstand —for the past few months, he'd taken to habitually setting it there when he got home—she'd known one of them was going to end up shot.

The only surprise was it hadn't been her. She'd bucked the statistics, for once.

After an endless while of trudging along, she realized the trees were thinning. A faint rushing had replaced sleepy nocturnal bird-song; Ari also discovered the stars were winking out as grey mist rose, creeping alongside her. Still, she was almost startled when the forest decided to pull its arms away.

Ari halted, staring. The urge to rub at her eyes like a revivified Disney princess returned with startling intensity, struggling with sheer wonder; she outright gawped.

No moss, no grass. Instead, bare dry dirt stretched from a fringe of trees, making a softly undulating plain. A flat ribbon of paving arrowed ahead, taking a slight curve before ending at a soaring dark shape with high sharp pinnacles, the only hints of color a few brightly glowing... well, they looked like tall narrow windows. The chiaroscuro was fantastic, depth and weight given to every shadow —if an artist could capture even half the scene's complex shadings and values of grey the acclaim would be instant.

For the umpteenth time, Ari's lips shaped a wondering *what the hell*. The creaking intensified, and when she glanced away from the castle—it had to be, the golden-glowing window shapes were incontrovertible evidence, if merely a rock formation it was a damn uncanny one—she received another shock.

The trees were... moving? Thickening? Spindly saplings at the forest's edge swelled as the mist tiptoed among them, and the slight creaking sounds were their branches unfurling more fan-leaves. A deeper shadow-tinge inched down the hill, making its own subtle noise; nearby, Ari could see small blades poking up through dry dirt.

Grass, or something else? It certainly looked vegetative. She was deeply glad to be standing on stone, and weighed whether the castle-shape was likely to be something equally bizarre.

Or perhaps harmful.

Nothing had hurt her so far. In fact, the pond's water seemed to have helped more than a little. Maybe she should've taken that bath and done some laundry as well.

Where the hell was her backpack? And where, in God's name, was she?

Ari realized she had set off down the hill only because her boots still made soft damp sounds, though she wasn't as soaked as before. Mud dried, flaking free—she wondered about bacterial contamination, and how the people here would react to her appearance. Unless it was just a weird rock formation, which meant she'd have to start worrying about food, fuel for a fire, and the means to strike sparks.

She should have been shivering, teeth chattering. Instead, her soaked clothes were cool but not chilling. Maybe liquid dirt was good insulation.

So far, nothing seemed truly dangerous. Of course that was no indication, and she hadn't quite ruled out hallucination yet. Nor had she ruled out another possibility—the lightning strike had been massive, the landslide no joke.

If she was dead... well, was this hell? Ari was sure an agnostic who had shot her husband wouldn't qualify for the place upstairs, and if this was the devil's country, so far it was proving a lot nicer than the big white house on Hardison Hill. She wasn't even hungry yet, and hadn't had to step off the road for a pee break either.

The castle could prove to be worse than Mike and his parents, but Ari still plodded toward it.

There was nothing else to do, really.

The mist kept pace, and so did swiftly growing grass. Now she wondered about the sounds in the trees—critters like the little golden-eyed not-possum, or something else?

Before she was quite ready the castle loomed close, a towering wave of dark stone. It had snuck up on her, or she'd made far better time than expected. The place was massive, but the road led straight to an opening.

More precisely, it stopped at a lowered drawbridge over a dry ravine which had clearly once been a moat. The light had strengthened with the mist, but no dawn took this long.

At least, not where she was from. Ari studied the drawbridge— massive dark timbers, long metal chains bowing under their own weight, each link longer than she was tall—and the aperture it was meant to protect. An inner gate had been there once, now shattered by some unthinkably violent artillery.

Was the place empty? The lights in the towers said otherwise, but there was nobody standing guard. Or maybe they were hidden, just waiting for her to make a wrong move.

The mist didn't want to approach the castle. It hung back, thickening into a wall, and now she had to choose between waltzing through the gate or retreating into a screen of white fog. It was almost as if she'd been herded along the road, and Ari didn't like the feeling.

Did hallucinations last this long? Time was subjective, anyone who had taken Psych 101 or longed for summer vacation knew as much, but this was something else. So far, the theory that she was dead and in some kind of weird afterlife held the most water.

Purgatory, probably. Dante would have a field day with this. She tried to think who would best capture the scene—there wasn't nearly enough firelight for Caravaggio. Goya or Gentileschi would get the shadows right, but not the sharp edges of the castle's battlements, crisp even at a distance. The architecture looked near-Gothic; the spires were outlandish.

Frankly, the whole thing looked like Salvador Dali having a Pre-Raphaelite nightmare. Velasquez would get the colors, she thought, El Greco the *feeling*, except for its jarring, almost brutal surrealism. Nothing was familiar, yet everything was real, heavy.

And dark. Her eyes had adapted, but inside without starlight or the greyish glow from the mist...

Ari hesitated. One booted toe touched the drawbridge, a cat's paw warily testing the surface of a puddle.

Nothing happened.

Feeling faintly ridiculous, Ari pushed at her dirt-stiffened hair. The heavy mass rasped against her shoulders. Her face was clean, sure, but the rest of her probably looked like Swamp Thing.

She tested the drawbridge again, and edged onto its span. Solid as the rest of this strangeness, it held up just fine.

Hopefully, whoever had the lights on wouldn't be upset at her sudden appearance.

It wasn't until she had stepped cautiously through the shattered gate into a cobbled bailey that the worst idea in the world decided to show up.

What if it is *Purgatory, and Mike's here too?*

6

TO MOCK, OR TO KILL

MASSIVE STONE WALL, EQUALLY HUGE BUT SHATTERED GATE—
only a few twisted remains of wreckage hung on either side of the
opening, blackened metal and what might have been more massive
timber, like the drawbridge—with a wide plain of cobbles beyond.
At least it was open to the sky, shadowed but not pitch-black.
There was a long low gallery on one side, and on the other big,
shadowy barnlike structures. Another wall reared up at the far end,
melding with the castle's bulk; the edifice was the size of a small
city. It towered over her, a tsunami of carved rock like the ink drawings of Gormenghast in Mom's big double-volume edition.

At least it wasn't the house on Hardison Hill. Wanda Lee's
theory of aesthetics came almost entirely from glossy house-
keeping magazines, and she wouldn't let Earl put any taxidermy
inside the house—one small mercy, no furry corpses with glass
eyes needing constant dusting. The big white house had a library,
but the books were a hodgepodge of Victorian leftovers kept for
their decorative spines and color-coded interior designer remain-
ders bought by the yard during one of Wanda's many remodels.
Earl's family was old Dixie money, certainly, but his son had been

sent to college only to make connections and get blitzed at frat parties.

She'd thought Mike enjoyed how different their tastes and interests were, but that had changed almost precisely in the middle of their honeymoon.

City girl. Snotty snobby city girl.

Would luminous mist slip through the broken gate, lighting the frowning stone, the age-darkened wooden doors at the far end? The pillared gallery along the right side was full of rustling sighs, very much like the forest. Ari halted again, head tilted, listening intently. More faint noises descended into the bailey—metallic clattering, indistinct voices, the entire effect somewhere between static and faraway surf or traffic.

So someone did live here. It was the subliminal sound of an inhabited place, a drowsing hive. The sudden sense of *you're not alone* was immediate and terrifying, even if it held a faint comfort.

Then a clot of deeper shadow moved, a glinting in the darkness, and someone spoke.

"Step closer." A male voice, soft and terribly expressionless. "Have you come to mock? Or to kill?"

Ari's heart lodged in her throat, and the only thing saving her from an inelegant blurt of surprise was the obstruction. She staggered back, her boots no longer squelching—which was great—and almost tripped, which was very definitely not so good.

A pratfall onto cobbles would hurt like hell, and she wasn't sure if there were other analgesic ponds around.

The slumped shape was all wrong. Ari stared for a long moment, her eyes doing their best to relay data to a tired, overtaxed brain. Her grey matter shuffled through all available guesses, decided it didn't know what the hell, and was halfway to seizing up like the black Oldsmobile's engine on a sharp slope.

The Olds had been Wanda's car, not traded in for some reason when Earl bought her the powder-blue Caddy, and Ari couldn't decide if she was glad to have given it one last ride or sorry she'd forced it out of retirement. She also couldn't decide whether to scream, especially when the shape moved again with a slitherclash of metal.

Chains, she realized, and the relief was instant, though almost terrifying in its own right. The human mind hated uncertainty more than just about anything else, so it filled in the blanks with whatever was closest and called it good—plenty of artists, not to mention police interrogators, took advantage of that simple fact.

Shadows, highlights, and shadings snapped into recognizability. A stray gleam from the windows above suddenly became reflection on metal links, a large mound of iron topped by what she realized was a vaguely medieval helmet as it turned. A single horizontal eye-slit in the head-canister stared at her through the twilight; he was tall, and wrapped up like Marley's ghost. There was another glinting behind him—a boulder, with a stick jutting from its rounded top.

No, not a stick, because it had a crosspiece. The scene became comprehensible—a helmeted man loaded down with iron chains, next to a sword stuck into a big rock.

What the... Suddenly, the scene veered from terror to bleak comedy. What kind of fucked-up trip was this? "Chains?" she said, and could have kicked herself for sounding so stupid. "Oh. Hello." *Hello? Is that all you can come up with?*

Metal clashed and rang again. It seemed like an awful lot of noise in the deep hush, and she seriously considered retreating to the broken gate until she could figure out what the hell.

Maybe he sensed as much, because the entire pile went still once more. The suspicion that this was all an elaborate prank circled Ari's head briefly, fled when a nervous cough tickled her throat, and the shaking was back again. Her arms came up, crossed defensively; she hugged herself as her legs trembled.

Breathless silence stretched between them. The castle, humming to itself like an undisturbed wasp-nest, took no notice.

"Ah," he said, quietly. A long, soft syllable, like a mechanic under a raised hood seeing the problem, finding it was one he had the tools and parts for. "At last."

At last, what? "I'm sorry." The apology, tiny and squeaky, was dismally familiar. Occasionally it might mollify her husband, but usually it was just another landmark on the road to huddling in a corner, trying to sob silently and not set Mike off further. She took one blundering step back, and another; her left heel landed badly on a cobble and her ankle threatened to roll. "I didn't know, the door was open so I—"

"Don't. Don't go." Harsh now, command with a strange edge of pleading. "Please."

That was the moment she realized he wasn't speaking English. More distressingly, she wasn't either. The words changed as they left her mouth, mutating into something else—a rolling cadence very much like Spanish, but with the accents placed strangely.

Oh. Oh boy. Fortunately she was *thinking* in her usual language, but the sheer unreality of the situation softened her knees. Ari swayed, and the pile of metal links twitched as if he was startled by the sudden movement—or as if he wanted to catch her. A darker shape amid the chains was a gauntlet of dull metal, fingers outstretched, and the arm it was attached to strained under layers of imprisonment.

Ari couldn't get in enough oxygen. Go figure, she'd finally met someone else here and it was the Man in the Iron Mask, plus he was speaking in tongues. Absurdity warred with wine-dark terror, her heart pounding and the roaring in her ears hatefully familiar. "I'm sorry," she whispered, again.

And once more the words changed as they left her, into something more like *I ask your forgiving.*

"No need." He spoke much more softly now, and it struck Ari that he was trying to sound... well, maybe comforting, or at least nonthreatening. Something was translating the words as they hit her ears. "We have surprised each other, it seems."

That's one way to put it. "I didn't mean to." Hushed and conspiratorial, as if apologizing on the way to her seat in a crowded movie theater. Could people dream in foreign languages? She didn't know. The ragged edge between panicked laughter and hyperventilating fear was familiar, and she hated it. "I just got here, and I don't... I don't know anything."

"I see." Quiet and thoughtful, the voice also echoed hollowly inside the helmet. It sounded like a speaker trapped at the bottom of a metal well. "You have done no ill, my lady. Please, be at ease."

My lady? At ease? If this was a psychotic break it was an interestingly archaic one, both in aesthetics and linguistics. Something about the cobbled space and the gallery was naggingly familiar, lingering just on the tip of her brain. Had she seen the castle in a painting before, possibly in a textbook or a print? "I don't know if it's possible." Her shoulders hunched; at least if he was chained up he couldn't get mad and chase her.

Or so she hoped.

A strange, bitter sound echoed from the helmet. After a moment, she realized it was a laugh, deep and genuine, though pained. Her conscience pinched, but before she could find anything else to say he spoke again.

"Perhaps not." He shifted, but only a little; the chains didn't permit much movement, wrapped over and over in a weird cocoon. "Yet I must ask. Will you aid me?"

Oh, crap. "Um." The thought that whoever lived in this castle probably had this guy in a metal burrito for a good reason warred with empathy and the natural urge to help anyone in distress. Even in this situation she couldn't stop thinking about the absurdity of it all; maybe that was her original sin. Mike near-constantly accused her of laughing at him, of looking down on him. Maybe she had, unconsciously, and he'd known.

But this guy was *not* Mike, thank goodness. She'd recognize her husband's voice, even filtered through a helmet.

The silence turned even more ridiculous, and Ari realized he was waiting for her to speak. "Why are you chained up?" Her accent in the weird new tongue was different, shortening certain words and linking others together; she probably sounded like a country bumpkin.

"Because I did not care enough to gainsay those who did so." Still outstretched, the gauntlet relaxed slightly; he wasn't straining against the bonds now. Just holding his arm out, as if there wasn't a whole mess of metal draped over it.

Oh, is that all? Ari had learned the hard way that the only safe place for sarcasm was inside her own aching head, but still the words almost escaped. She swallowed hard, wishing for more of that cool, crystalline pondwater; it was weird that she wasn't hungry.

Then again, there probably wasn't anything edible in Purgatory.

"Oh." A ridiculous, simple syllable. The silence returned, awkward as the caesura after some embarrassing malfunction at a dinner party.

What were her choices here? Banging on the castle doors, covered in dried mud, and asking them politely why they had this guy locked up? If she was stuck in an asylum or having some kind of delusion in jail, he was probably a fellow prisoner. Which made him a question mark, but on the other hand...

She had to admit, she had no idea about the other hand. The distressing reality of this place bore some interesting, unwelcome, and entirely insane implications Ari didn't feel equipped to untangle at the moment.

"Those inside will not treat you kindly," he said, as if reading her mind. The chains made soft clinking noises as his arm dropped slowly, motion controlled at every moment like a dancer's stage-gesture. "Especially if they sense what you are."

"What I am?" She repeated the phrase, trying to pronounce the syllables as he did, hoping he wouldn't think it was mockery.

"Yes." The armor and chains were motionless again. Was there really someone inside the casing, or just blank space? "Will you aid me, then?"

She'd gone from being utterly alone on a weird forest road to holding lunatic conversation with a guy immortalized in a Dumas novel—although historically the Man in the Iron Mask had worn a velvet and silk face-covering, hadn't he? The images of a sprawled prisoner in a metal head-canister were propaganda, some very well done. This would make a beautiful acid etching if the artist was skilled enough to capture the mass of individual links, the rough matte armor, the different texture of cobblestones.

Why was whatever-this-was dredging *that* up? She hadn't thought about French literature or etching techniques since college, for God's sake. And she'd made him repeat himself. Men didn't like that, Ari knew.

"What kind of help do you want?" she heard herself say, and also knew she was about to make a huge mistake.

As usual.

7

ANOTHER POSSIBILITY

THE CHAINED MAN DIDN'T MOVE. HE WAITED, AS IF EXPECTING her to say more, but Ari was too busy hugging herself and keeping a nervous eye on the doors across the bailey. If one opened now and the inhabitants found an intruder... Well, this guy could be misleading her about the likely reaction, or he could be strictly honest.

There was no way of telling.

"Nothing much." The words echoed slightly. What did he look like under the featureless helmet? Probably deadly pale from lack of sun. How did they feed their prisoners in that getup? Or did they bother? "You see the sword, there?"

He twitched, the helmet tipping to indicate direction.

"Yeah." *I can hardly miss it.* Ari decided she had to believe there was an actual person inside all that metal, since the opposite assumption made a funny, squidgy feeling begin under her breast-bone, as if she would vomit or pass out.

"All you must do," he said, very quietly, "is bring it within reach."

That doesn't sound like a good idea. Or maybe it is, depending on who you are? Ari's legs had decided they might as well stop impersonating pudding since she might need them for continued survival in the near future, and the rest of her was trying to decide whether running away now or later was the better option. "Then what happens?"

He considered the question for a few heartbeats. "I enter the Keep."

Is that all? "Is that a bad thing?"

"It is... necessary. Do you not remember what happened?"

My dude, I just got here. Had he mistaken her for someone else—a native of this strange country, maybe? Did a lot of people show up covered in landslide? Of course, she was speaking his language, which was one more piece of evidence in the *this is a hallucination* category.

Or was it? Her head hurt; doubting your own eyes and ears was exhausting work. Ari glanced up, and her heart gave another nasty leap. Were there more lighted windows now? She hadn't counted before, but there *definitely* seemed to be a few extra narrow glowing shapes, very medieval, their tops tapered to sharp points.

Metal chimed. The helmet tilted; she wished she knew what era it was from. Maybe that would be the detail to tell her whether this was a bad trip on lunatic asylum drugs or... something else.

"They may have noticed a change and relayed the information to their master," he said. Urgency rode the words. "Bring me the sword, or hide. They must not find you here, not while I am still chained."

Really. That shed an entirely different light on affairs, so to speak. "What happens if they do?" Ari found herself edging past him, balancing nervously on cobbles. The rounded stones felt entirely real and individual, her hiking boots' soles gripping differently on each one.

Why was she believing this guy? The useless urge to help an animal in a trap even if it ended with getting bit, or was it simple dream-logic? What else did you do when you came across something like this?

"Nothing pleasant." He no longer sounded flat or robotic, but terribly grim. "And I would not remind you, if indeed you have forgotten."

Maybe she only imagined she understood his language, and they were both gabbling at each other with increasing incomprehension? That was a horrible thought, too. Ari peered at the sword, and swallowed a disbelieving laugh. *Oh, come on. I'm no Arthur, my friend.*

A good portion of the long, heavy blade seemed buried in a chunk of craggy igneous rock, like a needle in a horsehair pincushion. The hilt was restrained, beautifully functional, the quillons wicked talon-curves.

I've gone around the bend. Just as crazy as Mike always said. Well, that made things easier, didn't it? If this was insanity, it was a damn sight better than her usual reality.

Ari had to stand on tiptoe, reaching for the sword's hilt.

"I would ask you to hurry," the chained-up guy whispered, and she understood. The sound of weirdly modulated voices and footsteps was growing far more irrefutable, and there were also *definitely* more lighted windows above. Golden reflections filtered down to the bailey, light aggregating bit by bit.

I've had a helluva night, sir, and this is just icing on the cake. Briefly, she wondered what time it was—and what would happen if she pulled on the sword and it refused to budge.

Probably, in his words, *nothing pleasant.*

Her fingertips hovered uncertainly. A sharp clatter floated from above—it sounded like dishes breaking, or a drunken fist through a window.

Ari flinched. She hopped, awkwardly, and her hand closed around cold metal.

She expected to lose grip, fingers torn away as she landed, but the sword tilted as she pulled, its rocky prison giving a slight viscous protest. Her boots hit cobbles again and she staggered backward, unprepared for landing.

The sword followed, accompanied by a grinding rasp. Shining

metal slid free of stone like a hot blade through resistant styrofoam; maybe it was just stage-dressing, resin made to look like rock? The tip nearly banged cobbles, so she hopped back again, attempting to avoid slicing her toes.

The blade was heavy, but she didn't want to drag point or edge. Now that she had hold of the thing, the bright length looked wicked sharp, and one of the quillons touched her wrist, a cat-claw caress. Metal clash-slid behind her—the chained man moving but she couldn't spare a glance in that direction, too occupied with managing an unwieldy weapon as long as her leg.

"Careful." A curt, imperative word in that strange rolling language. "I will have to make another, if it harms—"

I am doing the best I can, sir. "Hold on," she managed, and was amazed at her own temerity. Men hated repeating themselves *and* being interrupted; she was storing up no end of trouble for Future Ari.

But he went quiet, probably deciding it was best not to pass up even this halfass help at the moment. Ari hefted the sword, turning so she could attempt keeping both him and the doorways along the rear wall in view. Her head swiveled, checking each direction as if gauging traffic on a busy street while already late for work.

The idea of just tossing the whole shebang in his general direction and hurriedly retreating was incredibly attractive, but that would make a lot of noise. If it was sharp enough to cut rock—assuming that chunk of craggy stuff wasn't some other odd substance—it would make short work of at least some of his chains, right? Or at least, he seemed to think so.

Good enough. Ari took a tentative step closer to the mound of metal. She was almost in reach.

He shifted. Two gauntleted hands rose, arms straining against webbed chains—how did he breathe under all that weight? Maybe the armor kept him from being crushed by the wrapping? Ari hesitated, studying the helmet's high crest, the blank sheerness over nose and mouth, the dark eye-slit.

What if the thing under it wasn't human but some kind of horror-movie monster? Sure, he *sounded* fine. She had also married a nice guy who held doors for her but turned out to be a cruelly violent piece of shit, which meant her ability to make good choices was clearly questionable. Again, she considered that maybe this guy was locked up for a good goddamn reason.

Still, it seemed needlessly cruel to imprison anyone under these conditions. She wouldn't wish being trapped under chains on Wanda Lee, or even Mike himself.

You don't have to wish it. Her palms tingled, feeling the jolts again. *You know what you did.*

"There is another possibility," he said, quietly. "You might strike me down, my lady. 'Tis sharp enough."

Oh, crap. Was that what her hesitation looked like? "I don't want to hurt anyone." The lie stung her tongue; she'd hurt Mike Hardison plenty, and Wanda Lee would be devastated even if her son was a brutal, lying asshole. Earl might even shed a tear; certainly his boy was the only thing that remote, faintly supercilious expression on his face ever altered for.

"I know." How could such a hollow, faceless voice sound so certain? "You never have, my kindness. We differ in that, as in nearly all else."

Kindness? Maybe he was mistaking her for someone he knew. She was, after all, covered with dirt; she could've been anyone. Ari took the last two steps in a rush, arms straight out, the sword a bright vertical bar dangling from her grasp. There was much more light now, not just from the multiplying golden windows but also the sky's vault, covered with grey mist instead of stars.

When had that happened?

One gauntlet closed around her right wrist, a cold iron cuff. The other found the sword's hilt, and as the fingers closed with a muffled clink a hollow sigh echoed from the helmet's depths.

Oh, Jesus and gin. Ari tried to step back as the weight in her hands lessened, but the ironclad fingers turned tight, trapping her.

Not painfully, but that could be because she froze, the instinct of three long years warning her struggle was useless and would only cause more damage in the end.

"Finally." The chained man's laugh was just as bitter, but lasted far longer.

Ari hunched her shoulders, trapped on tiptoe, and waited for the worst.

❧ 8 ❧

GAUNTLET, LOOSENED

A HAZE OF DRY, DEFINITE WARMTH SPREAD FROM THE METAL around her right wrist. A faint crackling filled the cobbled space, a heavy scent—musk-spicy and not unpleasant—lingering for a bare moment before the freshening breeze dispelled it. Ari shook her head, dark hair sliding against her shoulders, and flinched again as long ribbons of dirt rose from her skin and clothes, shredding into nothingness.

The now-familiar discomfort of muddy, drip-dried denim or clinging cotton T-shirt and flannel vanished; the relief made her aware of how awful it had felt.

Helluva way to take a shower. Ari gasped, and staggered when the gauntlet loosened.

The chained shape swelled, drawing itself up. The sword made a soft sweet sound, cleaving air and iron both; a spray of colorless sparks stung her dark-adapted eyes. Sudden, heavy metallic clatter filled the stone-clad space—she winced at the racket—and the helmet fell with a clang, in two neatly cloven pieces.

Chains rattled as he moved. His head was now visible, a ragged shock of inky hair, a haggard pale face rising from shadow. He didn't look as waxy and unhealthy as she'd suspected, so maybe he hadn't been locked in the helmet for long. Yet his cheekbones stood out startlingly, and heavy, slanting brows shaded coal-dark eyes, a fierce glitter in his gaze holding all the warning in the world.

Most of the chains fell free, hitting the cobbles and spreading with strange liquid twitches. A single layer remained, wrapping around his armor; iron links moved uneasily, as if something underneath bulged and flexed, attempting to break free.

He had a proud nose, an almost-lantern jaw, and he looked *seriously* pissed. She had doodled those eyes in the margins of her textbooks and lecture notes, drawn the face over and over while her mind was elsewhere, as if attempting to exorcise the image.

Which never worked.

It's the dream. Oh, God, it's him. The only mercy was that it wasn't her husband's face. Still, the familiarity was a fist to the gut, or a quick shot to her kidneys as if Mike was only moderately displeased; he didn't believe in face-hitting.

At least, not often.

Ariadne kept backing up. It seemed the wisest course. The armored man wearing a face from her old nightmares froze, a final layer of blackened iron ropes dripping from his arms and crisscrossing his torso, clothing both legs. Segmented armor boots clasped his feet, spurs clung to his heels, and if an artist had charcoal they would be able to capture the shades but perhaps not the sharp angles. Maybe they would have to work in ink, with quick hard strokes.

The chained man's long exhale ended, those terrible burning eyes half-lidding as the sigh turned into words. "Many thanks, my lady."

Oh, don't mention it. I'll just be going now. "That's all r-right," she stammered, as he took an experimental step. Metal chimed, the sound now soft and almost sweet, music in movement.

"Merciful as ever." The sword made another of those whisper-slicing sounds as its blade swung into place and halted, held point-down and slanted away. He handled the chunk of sharp metal like it weighed less than paper. "Do you recognize me now?"

Oh, God, please. I know I am a murderer but please, I didn't mean it, it wasn't my fault. "N-no." Would he hear the lie in her tone, as Mike always claimed he could?

If this kept up her heart would burst from sheer terror. Maybe it wasn't Purgatory after all, but her own personalized hell.

"Very well." One chain-draped shoulder lifted, dropped. Strengthening light played over every individual link. "Stay here, I would not have you see this."

What? Ari's throat closed to a pinhole. She nodded, trying to look accommodating, obedient, and harmless all at once.

The leftover mass of segmented metal snakes finished twitching, freezing into a shape very much like a burst cocoon. He stepped from the pile gracefully, and as soon as his booted foot touched down, the clanging and chiming from the cables still draped upon him stopped.

As if he *wanted* it to. As if he could have moved silently at any moment, and had just chosen now.

He paused, staring at her. What would that big, sharp, heavy sword do to flesh? How much did stabbing hurt? She knew she could take a punch, but this was an entirely different ball of wax.

So to speak.

The castle's hum intensified. Now footsteps were clearly audible, plus distorted, mechanical noises babbling with excitement. The sky was a grey lens, a ruddy tinge creeping in and shadows developing edges nearly keen as the sword's.

"Stay here," he repeated, in that weird rolling language. "This will not take long."

Please don't hurt me. Please don't recognize me, either. Ari nodded again, hoping her face was a mask.

He turned, and strode across the cobbles. His spurs struck more bright, colorless sparks, but made no noise. Silent as a hunting shark he glided toward the doors, and when he reached the largest one in the center the sword lifted, flashing once. Its gleam, oddly reddish, lingered as the blade swept down. Wood shattered, cringing aside.

He continued, unhurried, into the dark archway revealed by violence.

Ariadne spun, and pelted for the drawbridge.

9

HOOFBEATS, VOICES

SHE BARELY NOTICED THE FOG HAD REACHED THE CASTLE'S WALL, or that the flat featureless plain now held ranks of spindly saplings visibly stretching upward in fits and starts, fan-leaves springing free, growing with likewise jerks and small creaking sounds.

Ari was simply grateful for any cover as she fled, boots slapping huge, irregular stones fitted together so closely barely a whisper could slip between them. The mist was flushing crimson in one quadrant of the sky, and she supposed that was east—not that it mattered.

Nothing did, save escape.

She ran, and was also deeply, cringingly glad she wasn't filthy anymore. The dirt was gone; her jeans, T-shirt, flannel button-up, and everything else felt freshly laundered with only a tinge of that strange spicemusk scent clinging as each step jolted in her hips, her shoulders, her bobbing head.

Racing as she hadn't since grade school, fists pumping and hair lifting on the breeze, lungs laboring and heart threatening to pop as it pounded, ignoring the jolting and the hammering until her feet tangled together and she almost fell, weaving to the left side of the road, finally reeling to a stop. The saplings were taller here, pausing to thicken before each fresh burst of lengthening, and the soft creaking and cracking all around was the sound of their incredible fast-forward growth.

Hazy black flower-blots swam in her vision. A slim hard shape twitched against her shoulder, and Ari flinched away from the tree she had blundered against. It almost seemed to notice her touch; in fact, its creaking intensified. It shot up, taller than the surrounding ones, and she backed away, almost tripping again on the road's lip.

She could *feel* sanity stretching inside her head, a thin blanket stretched over a yawning, misshapen bulge. Maybe she had a brain injury from the landslide? There was no reasonable, rational explanation for *any* of this.

I don't have those dreams anymore. They stopped when I met Mike.

The worst part wasn't the detailed, seamless world in front of her, each tree distinct and individual. The closest sapling had yellowish splotches of lichen on its trunk, each whorl and striation in the bark like fingerprints, and the others all had differing patches. Another bore a scar where a branch had broken free and lay on grassy, mossy ground, the green mat thickening as she stared in horror. The road's pavers were each unique, their golden tint ever more pronounced as the light mounted. If she went to hands and knees, examining grass blades and moss-hairs, she was certain they would all be organic, flawless, each a marvel of natural engineering.

All that paled into insignificance beside one simple fact.

Do you recognize me now?

How could she not? She'd had nightmares about that face—the hollow cheeks, the cruel mouth, the strong jaw, the surrounding shadows she now knew were the gloom of a stone castle—all her childhood. The dreams had stopped during her last year of college, in fact.

The very same month she met Mike Hardison.

Ari suspected her legs wouldn't take much more punishment, so she set off down the road again, jogging when she could, walking when her body decided that was too much. A stitch threatened her side, and she pressed her hand below her ribs, pushing hard.

For all that, she somehow didn't sweat, which was a blessing but perhaps only a transitory one. The breeze was cool, not cold, and though exhaustion blurred along her limbs there was no actual pain. If not for the terror lurking behind her heart, a swelling boil pushing her to hurry, she might have been taking a pleasant stroll on a nearly level trail.

Whether she was sane or not, the only thing that mattered was the urge to keep moving.

By the time the mist thinned she was among taller trees, but couldn't tell if it was where she'd begun. Patches of violet sky streaked with white vapor showed through branches overhead; the light was reddish, as if the sun were lensed with wildfire smoke. The creaking, sighing, popping, and stealthy movement all around might have been more of those not-possums among the swell-growing trees, but Ari didn't care. She wrung her hands as she walked, finally stopping in the middle of the road, head tilted.

Hell. This is hell. Or she was crazy. Either way, it was a nightmare rivaling three years with Mike. At least in that fucking white three-story prison she knew what to expect.

Out here, she was completely helpless. Was she supposed to Rambo in the woods or something?

What's that? Ari listened, intently, and her eyes widened. She cast around, seeing nothing but trees. Even the silvery patches she'd passed on the way to the castle were gone, drowned by daylight. Plenty of undergrowth now—bushes with narrow dark-green leathery leaves, grass thick in clumps where the light fell or, in shaded patches, thinning to that springy deep moss. There was more fallen detritus as well, and everything looked a lot more... well, natural.

A real forest, instead of a dreaming approximation of one.

But the sound behind her was strange enough to send prickles down her back. It was rhythmic and purposeful; she stared at the nearest tree, her brain swimming through syrup. How long could anyone stay awake and rational under these conditions?

If she fell asleep again, would she surface in a cell or a hospital bed? It might be worth attempting to find out.

First, though, she had to get off the road. Because the approaching noise was hoofbeats, and they were drawing nearer.

One good thing about more underbrush was the ability to hide. Ari dropped belly-down behind a spreading bush, and found the grass smelled vaguely minty. She pressed herself flat as possible, not daring to peek at the road—she had no more mud camouflage and the light was a lot brighter. If whoever-it-was caught a glimpse of her, it would be immediately apparent she wasn't local.

The hoofbeats held a weird metallic edge, clattering past in quick, breathless tattoo. It sounded like a large group, individual beats blurring together. She sagged on surprisingly soft ground, the carpet of moss with bright green grass blades poking through incredibly detailed. It would take some time to draw each one, paying attention to their fine hairs, the curves and spikes, the gradations of color from dark-green to yellow to occasional grey.

Take a breath. You're okay for the moment, just be still. It felt good to stop moving and even better to have some kind of safety, no matter how precarious.

Unfortunately, stillness freed up energy for thinking about the chained man. Maybe his face wasn't really the one in her dreams? She was under stress—Christ, was she ever, another wild laugh rose inside her, was strangled, receded like a wave on a sandy shore—and human memory notoriously unreliable.

Hang on. Her ears tingling, she listened intently.

This time she was fairly sure there was only a single horse. The hoof-rhythm was crisp and distinct, approaching, cresting, and fading away. Each beat was almost musical, and the accompanying chimes reminded her of chains. Shudders raced through her. Ari buried her face in her arms, hoping she was invisible from the road.

Was she smart or even crazier if she suspected who the lone rider was? Had she unleashed something awful by retrieving his sword?

She breathed in the mingled scent of good damp earth and a hint of mint from the crushed foreign vegetation. Birds called and sang, different species and sounds than the stealthy nighttime movement; were there more not-possums around? What about spiders, beetles, raccoons, deer? Were there venomous snakes, or large predators?

One problem at a time. It was the most practical way to handle this, Ari decided, and was suddenly aware of just how exhausted she was even if her bruises, scrapes, and other injuries were fading. The landslide dirt had vanished as well, which was great—though both miracles were deeply unsettling in their own right.

She could credit the pond for the former, and the chained man for the latter. This might be marginally better than a jail cell, but Ari's nerves were well and truly shot. The forest's shade was temperately benign; come to think of it, she hadn't been cold since she woke up.

She could try to tease out the implications, or she could... what? Ari turned her head aside; the back of her skull was still tender. She rested her cheek on her bent arm, and tried to breathe deeply. If a mountain lion or a snake came along, she was just going to have to deal with it then.

Strange reddish daylight mounted as she fell into a thin troubled doze. Her breathing lengthened, her eyelashes fluttered, and around her the forest stretched and grew, bursting with fresh vitality. The light slanting through forest canopy changed its angle, stabbed straight downward, and shifted again. Birds sang; a long-legged creature with large golden eyes and velvety ears stepped cautiously through the undergrowth, disappearing into deep shade, paying no attention to a sleeping woman.

Her fingers twitched. Ari woke in stages, swimming upward through layers of restful darkness, and was finally jolted into stinging awareness.

She heard voices.

10

ROBUST THEORY

QUIET CONVERSATION, A MUTTER OF LAUGHTER. ARI RUBBED AT
her eyes; the wind was up, soughing through treetops. It was a
lovely sound, but a tinge of woodsmoke added itself to the minty
grass and damp dirt, the vast freshness of outside. That was another
strangeness—no breath of petroleum exhaust, discernible even in
the most remote camping locations. It smelled like this place had
never known an internal combustion engine.

But that was nuts. Certifiable. Of course, so was the rest of this
bullshit.

Her neck was slightly stiff, but other than that Ari felt fine. No
hunger, no thirst, though she wouldn't have minded more of that
clear cool pondwater. Her past self had managed a good decision on
that count.

Still, the voices were... concerning. They were male. And plural.
Cops, looking for her? Or people from the castle, maybe searching
for the chained man?

A nap hadn't returned the world to its usual dimensions, just
given her more to worry about.

Ari pushed herself upright, slowly and very quietly. She listened hard, and decided the woodsmoke was most likely a campfire. So, maybe campers? Or castle people—the chained man's warning could have been a bit of psychological fakeout to gain her help, and they might be perfectly nice.

Or not. And if they found out she'd set him loose...

Was she wandering around in a psychotic daze, unable to feel her body's demands? Should she take a look at the speakers, make herself known? They might be able to help her, true.

But they also might have entirely different ideas. Ari hugged her knees, staring at the jeans' denim nap. Faint grass stains showed; the chained man's magical laundry service was great, but apparently only a one-time deal. She lifted her head, blinking and shaking away dark curls.

Jesus, I'm a mess.

The same long glossy leaves on the shrubs, the same moss and grass, the same smooth grey trees with fanlike leaves. Now there were fallen trunks too, heavy with moss, providing shelter for small bushes and other flora. The birdsong was different once more, shadows lengthening. The light was still odd, reddish and falling in slants through openings in the canopy, dust and small winged things fluttering in columns of what had to be sunshine. It was sunset glow but at strange angles, and oil pastels would probably be best for capturing the view.

Maybe she could teach art classes or practice painting in prison, if Earl and Wanda Lee didn't pay someone to shank her in the shower.

Go ahead, Ari. Go to the cops. See what happens.

Even now she couldn't get Mike's hateful sneering out of her head. Maybe she should give herself up? But even if she was wandering around in a delusional, hypothermic daze, it was better than rotting in a cell waiting for the Hardisons to strike.

Or so it appeared to her at the moment. Which could be another symptom of hypothermia or insanity.

A short, crisp branch-break snap brought her head up with a jerk. Ari stared, and the man stared back.

He was dressed in green and brown, like a Hildebrandt illustration of Robin Hood—jerkin, blousy shirt, trousers, a long shape poking over his shoulder she decided had to be a bow, supple leather boots. But no illustration had hair so vivid Kool-Aid blue tucked under a dashing, broad-brimmed buckle-your-swash hat with a small black feather in its band, nor could it show the creases and folds of hard use on every piece of clothing.

Hazel eyes narrowed, and not only did his eyebrows match his hair but his lashes were tipped with cerulean as well. He was clean-shaven, lean and rangy; the glittering knob at his hip was a filigreed hilt, his fingers resting easily upon it, the rest of a sheathed rapier jutting behind him.

Ari considered screaming. Hauling herself upright to run away was another attractive option, even if the mere thought tired her out all over again. So she simply hugged her knees, hunched her shoulders, and watched him steadily, waiting for some indication of whether he was a cop, a hunter, a hiker, or whatever-the-fuck.

It seemed to take forever, but she had nowhere to be and maybe if she seemed harmless he'd leave her alone?

But that wasn't how the world ever worked. The blue-haired man turned his head slightly, pursed his lips, and gave a shrill whistle. The voices fell silent, and Ari decided she'd better be on her feet. She rose, slowly, not quite creaking in every joint but certainly a little stiff.

The man spread his hands, holding them up in the classic stance of peaceful intent. "Easy, my lady." He had a nice even tenor, and Ari's pulse jolted into overdrive.

Because he spoke in the same rolling near-Spanish language as the chained man, and apparently it hit the same invisible translator just as it entered her ears. There was an infinitesimal delay; the lag between what he said and the meaning arriving was like tiny differences in flooring between the rooms of an old house, tripping up even long-time inhabitants.

Talk or run? Ari couldn't decide, and in any case she was now surrounded. More shapes faded out of the forest, half a dozen men total, all in green and brown. One had flaming red hair—not auburn but actual crimson. Another was brunet, and two were platinum, nearly white-blond. Another fellow had bronze hair and deeply tanned skin to match; one of the blonds was pale and the other ebon-skinned. There was a vague similarity in their cheekbones and the shape of their eyesockets, and they all wore rapiers. Two had no bows though they carried quivers of dark-fletched arrows, and each regarded her solemnly.

At least they weren't shouting for her to put her hands up or get on the ground. But the silence was uncanny, and she kept finding new details that shouted *this is real, this is not a dream*. The tiny hits were cumulative, and who knew what would happen once she reached the end of her ability to absorb them?

"Well?" the dark-skinned blond said, finally, in a resonant baritone. "What is it, Jazarl? A breathing statue?"

"Strange cloth," the crimson-haired one added. "But no reek of his curst, rotting Law."

They both spoke the chained man's strange rolling language, too. Ari took a deep breath. None of them stepped closer, so that was all right. Could she get between the two to her right? Their ring was loose, but...

"Dazed, perhaps." Blue-haired Jazarl tilted his head, his hands still raised and relaxed. "We shall not harm you, lady, if you be not of the Bright King's servants. Can you speak?"

"Perhaps we should dispatch it, to be certain." The paler blond tapped his swordhilt with a fingertip. "Quick and painless to be merciful as well."

Oh, fuck. Ari snapped another glance to her right. There was a temptingly open space between the bronze one and the ebon-skinned blond who maybe didn't want to kill her.

"Pay no mind to Darjeth, my lady." Jazarl took a step forward; he was probably some kind of leader. And their names were strange, but that was becoming par for the course. "'Tis clear you are no servant of the usurper, no matter how odd your raiment."

I'm not dressed weird, she wanted to say. *You are.* But when in Rome and all that—and she was most definitely not in Kansas anymore.

Not that she had been in the first place, but it was the principle of the thing.

"Mortal," the crimson-haired one said, softly. "At least, very recently. Can you not tell?"

Now that was concerning. *Mortal*—did the word mean what she thought it might? Ari's brain attempted to process all this, but without a sane, reasonable framework for what she was seeing and hearing the effort was immense, Sisyphean, shoving a mental boulder uphill.

"Is that what that is?" Blond Darjeth's eyebrows raised. "But then, how..."

"Clearly she understands." The other blond caught Ari's gaze, his hazel eyes kind and warm; his smile was probably meant to be encouraging, too. "But she cannot speak if we chatter so."

Silence fell. The men regarded her expectantly.

How in the fuck did I get here? Maybe she'd been bonked on the head during the landslide, and everything around her was being passed through a weird filter?

"H-hello." The word trembled; it was clearly in their language. Her mouth shaped the syllables without any trouble, attempting to mimic their accent, and Ari hoped she didn't sound like a gibbering loon. "I'm... I'm not from here. I don't want any trouble."

"Well, she is no clockwork nor other foulness, 'tis clear." The stocky brunet smiled encouragingly as well. "In any case we cannot leave a lady unprotected, especially so close to the Keep."

Jazarl took another step. Ari stiffened, but there was nowhere to go.

There never had been.

"Come," he said, almost gently. "There is a fire, and you need fear nothing in our company. The Bright King's servants respect our blades, at least for some little while longer."

That sounded encouraging—except for the implications of *king* and *violence*—and at least they weren't handcuffing her. So Ari tried a smile, nodded like a good little girl who knew she had to propitiate authority to get along, and followed him.

The others surrounded her as they walked, and if the paler blond watched her narrowly, she more than returned the favor.

They listened to Ari's halting explanation—not the *I killed my husband* part or the *I got a guy out of a chain burrito* chapter, but a short, heavily edited *there was a storm and I ended up in a pond* version. And though they did indeed have a campfire—small, expertly built, near-smokeless despite the tang she'd detected upon waking—there was nothing approaching dinner. Which was fine because she wasn't hungry... but it was deeply abnormal as everything else in this hallucinatory place.

Between them and the chained man, she was wondering if she'd somehow stumbled into a RenFaire camping retreat and gotten a dose of heavy psychedelics to boot. If that was the case, she simply had to wait for the drugs to wear off. The idea was vaguely cheerful, a sign that she was thinking rationally.

Or at least, attempting to.

"The water did not gripe you?" Darjeth exchanged a meaningful look with Jazarl. If this was a good-cop-bad-cop routine, it was a reasonably gentle one. Maybe she was really in an interrogation room, and the strange foreign language was her scrambled brain putting a protective layer of fantasy over the whole deal. That was another reasonable attempt to understand what the hell was happening.

If only she could just get a single clue which prospect was most likely, even the tiniest indication, it would stop the sickening, spinning sensation of being unable to trust her own eyes and ears.

"No." Huddled on the ground, her back against a dry, moss-covered log—there was a lot more litter on the forest floor now—Ari tried not to look guilty. Now she was feeling bad that she *hadn't* gotten dysentery; it was ridiculous, but the reflex of shame had been ground into her for years and simply wouldn't turn off. "I thought it might, but I was thirsty."

The crimson-haired guy, Alzarien, piped up. "Could you find the pond again?" He was examining each arrow in a quiver, sometimes paring the fletching with a small curved knife. The blade looked very sharp and the hilt ended in an oversized pearl, glowing under reddish daylight.

The canopy was too thick to see much of the sky, but sunset was lasting a long damn time. "Probably not," Ari had to admit. "I... I thought I should look around. I found the road."

"Will none of you say it?" The stocky brunet was Sarle, and he finally spoke up again. "The forest is renewing itself."

"It does look different, even from when I..." Ari quickly looked at her boots when every eye settled on her. Served her right, opening her big mouth. She had no choice but to go along with whatever she understood of this place, but that didn't mean she had to be stupid about it.

"Indeed the change has been swift," Jazarl said, thoughtfully. "When did you arrive, my lady... Ari? Have I the name aright?"

Her name sounded nearly exotic in their rolling accent, but she nodded. "Last night, I think." She probably sounded like a liar, though it was strict truth. "The sun came up while I was running away."

Naturally, he seized on the important word. "Away?"

"On the road." *Make it a good lie, if you have to.* Her conscience pinched. "I heard hoofbeats." It wasn't really a falsehood, just omission, like letting Mike think she'd come straight home from the grocery store, or hiding the remains of a broken glass under something else in the trash can so Wanda Lee wouldn't start in on her.

Self-protection was reasonable. She hated it anyway, and the persistent sense of unreality, of spinning insanity, made it so difficult to *think*. She almost wanted to be alone in the woods again, even if they had a fire and presumably some supplies.

A charged silence, prickling with unheard static, surrounded the campfire. The wood burned normally enough; it looked dry and well-seasoned.

Where was the damp from the storm? Was it possible to wander for miles after being hit on the head with a landslide and then...

Jesus Christ, Ari, pay attention. She needed to figure out what was really happening, pronto. Had the entire world decided to gaslight her like Mike and his mother loved to do, or had Ariadne herself gone gratefully, entirely insane? Was she babbling to invisible people in an asylum's garden? She didn't think she was the type to get violent... and yet.

Dry clicks, the .38 heavy in her bruised, aching hands.

"Darjeth. Naithor." Jazarl still sounded thoughtful. "But carefully, using night as a shield."

"We shall leave now, then." The blue-eyed blond stood in one fluid motion, stretching with catlike grace. Like the chained man, they moved with dancers' economy; they handled both rapiers and bows with the ease of long habit, just as he'd swung that heavy broadsword. Tiny details threatened to swamp Ari again. "And creep in at dusk, like mice."

Bronze-haired Naithor followed suit, though his clear green gaze rested speculatively on Ari for a long moment. He finally nodded in Jazarl's direction and set off with the blond, both men fading into the trees almost immediately. Even with their funky hair choices—although the colors looked natural, undyed, and utterly real—they had great camouflage.

She wanted to ask where they were going, figured it was none of her business, and swallowed the question. But Jazarl answered anyway.

"They will see what is afoot at the Keep. The Bright King keeps a garrison there, and a prisoner who should be told of your arrival." He stretched out his hands to the fire, and Ari was suddenly certain that he had fingerprints. That they *all* did, whorls and ridges just as unique as the trees' bark-sheaths.

No way was this a simple dream or hallucination, or even a brain injury from Mike throwing her against the wall. The hell theory was still pretty robust, though there was no hint of brimstone. Simple insanity couldn't be this detailed and seamless.

What was left? Aliens? Another wrenching internal effort to pay attention, to find something reasonable to say, almost made sweat prickle under her arms, at her lower back.

"The Keep." Ari nodded. "Okay." Only what came out of her mouth wasn't *okay*, it sounded like a shortened version of their *very well*. The invisible translator was working overtime, and she wondered what would happen if she tried to explain the concept of steam engines or cell phones.

This place seemed pretty pre-industrial. It was a pity she didn't have the .38, but even the thought of threatening these guys with it if she had to escape sickened her as the pond surrounded by pearl-cabbages hadn't. She was a coward; maybe Mike was right and the world belonged to the brutal. Any empathy was a sucker's game.

"We should make haste to Gesthel." Sarle shrugged when Jazarl shot him a sharp glance. "We cannot care for a lady here, my friend. And if she is what you hope—"

"Do not." Jazarl's tone clearly said he wasn't having any of this *hope* nonsense, thank you very much. "So long as we are still in these woods, the garrison at the Keep is threatened and the Mere at least a little safer. That is our charge. And..." His sharp face softened. "And if *he* can be saved we shall spend our lives in the attempt, but we must use them well and that requires planning. In any case the lady must be weary and in deep confusion. Haring pell-mell along the Road will achieve nothing."

Gethsel. What you hope. She stored the terms away, trying to arrange all her questions in order of importance or, failing that, in order of those she could possibly get some answers for through careful observation. Ari hugged her knees, staring at the fire. So many had tried to capture the evanescence of flame. Artists largely had to paint around it, catching the effects and not the fire itself. There was always something lost in translation.

Or gained, maybe? You could peer through van Gogh's eyes at sheaves of wheat, through O'Keefe's at the desert, through Varo's at ruddy-tinted dreams with their own owl-faced logic.

She'd thought Mike could see the world differently through her, and vice versa. But he wasn't interested, the goalposts constantly shifting; Ari didn't even know what he wanted or she would have given it to him.

If he'd just asked instead of hurting her, seeming to delight only in her pain.

The shadows were definitely longer now, twilight instead of late afternoon. The trees didn't creak or grow in fast-forward anymore, and the sounds of wildlife had settled into a low hum. Her new acquaintances—or captors—spoke quietly, but she focused on the fire's voice instead. It was time for some heavy thinking, though she doubted her battered, stressed-out neurons were up to the task.

It wasn't Past Ari's fault. She'd had a lot to deal with.

Come on. Focus. Of course *the Keep* had to mean that huge, spire-topped castle. She could claim she had no idea why the chained guy was roaming around free, and maybe they would believe her. Was he the 'prisoner' they talked about?

She kept tripping over that word, *mortal*. Maybe the invisible translator had a false cognate, but it didn't seem likely. Ari huddled as small as possible, watchfully quiet, trying to look reasonably sane, considering her options.

None were very attractive.

II

GOLDEN ARMOR

No fog, no cloud, and though her astronomical knowledge was nearly nil it didn't matter since she couldn't see more than a few bright white diamond stars peeking through the canopy anyway. Night thickened between tall grey tree trunks; at first she thought the guys were going off for bathroom breaks and was glad her own bladder seemed to have forgotten all about her.

The worst part of camping was peeing in the woods. Just plain *undignified*.

Ari soon realized, however, that her captors—or protectors— were standing guard. They exchanged grim looks when they returned to the fire at intervals, and always left one of their number with a bow and two full quivers.

When she finally dared to move, raising her head from grass-stained knees and stretching as unobtrusively as possible, Majan— the darker blond, ropes of pale hair brushing his lean shoulders as he fed the fire—smiled in her direction, seeming almost pleased. "'Tis difficult to rest, when first arriving."

She used to know how to relax, it was natural. Just take a deep breath, settle down, and let it happen—but not anymore. Not after the white house on the hill, full of its tense colorless gas.

More important was that simple term, *when first arriving*. If it wasn't a mistranslation it could add up, with *mortal*, to something incredibly disturbing. If the problem wasn't inside her head, or with her perceptions... but that was indeed looney-tunes, and she needed all the sanity she could grab right now.

He was studying her intently, Ari realized, and was acutely conscious of being alone in the woods with a group of men. The fire was happily chewing at a heavy branch fallen from a tree that might have just been a sapling that morning, if the fast-forward growth was any indication.

"I am passing curious," he continued, sinking into an easy crouch with his back to the log she was braced against. "Do they still put dishes of milk upon the doorsteps, certain nights?"

What? Ari wasn't sure the question had been translated right. A vague memory from childhood reading and a long-ago Lit class popped up, though, and she decided old, literal fairytales were no crazier than the rest of this nonsense. In fact, they explained a lot of what she was seeing and hearing.

The relief of having a mental peg to hang all these events on, some classification that was at least consistent, was overpowering— if she could trust it. Her fireside companion was clearly waiting for an answer.

"In some places, maybe." She watched carefully for any sign the translator was breaking down on his end too, but he just nodded and looked pleased.

"Good. They should remember." He scanned the woods, a quick flicker of awareness. Firelight brushed his cheekbones, and his eyes gleamed from shadowed hollows. "You are very quiet, my lady."

Best way to get through this. Or anything else. Keeping her mouth shut had never been Ari's strong suit, but three years of Wanda Lee's gimlet eye—not to mention her husband's steady stare and son's escalating rages—would turn even the biggest chatterbox into a mime. Ari tried a shrug, hoping it was the right response.

He stiffened, nearly leaping to his feet.

A jolt of dark, hideous fear slammed through her, Ari's heart leaping high and hard like a fish at dawn. She shrank against the log, but Majan wasn't looking at her. Instead, he whirled and stared into the forest, head upflung, the green and brown of his clothing melding with shadows.

There was a click, a whir, and a yell from the woods. Majan hopped onto the moss-cushioned log, landing like a cat. The bow was in his hands; he nocked, swiftly drawing to his ear. A high hard *twang* accompanied the release of an arrow, whistling as it leapt into the night.

"*Stay down!*" he shouted, and his hands blurred. Another arrow followed the first, then a third. The clicks and whirring were now accompanied by a discordant metallic clamor, and Ari stared uncomprehending at the darkness.

A gleam swelled between two trees. Firelight ran wetly over something big and reflective; when it staggered into the small circle of visibility she couldn't even scream. The shapes her eyes relayed to her brain refused to make sense.

A plus-sized suit of golden armor, easily eight feet tall and topped with a horned helm, wicked gilt-painted curves coming to high sharp points. Broad spiked shoulders swelled above a barrel chest sheathed in metal, columnar legs ending in segmented boots, massive arms and gauntlets very much like the chained man's but bright mirror-polished gold instead of dull iron.

Did he get cleaned up and come back? No, this thing was too big; the chained man been very tall and broad-shouldered, but unquestionably of human dimensions. This thing was definitely super-size, and the way it moved was wrong too—terribly fluid where it should not be, and jerky-disconnected in certain other places.

Majan's bow spoke again. The arrow flickered, burying itself in the dark bar of the visor, but the big bright thing didn't stop. Its head turned slightly, and the quivering back end of the bolt's fletching pointed unerringly at Ari.

As if someone trapped in the armor was looking at her, despite the arrow buried in his face. Its bright-gauntleted hands held a massive broadsword, the blade glowing-gold, and the razor edge clove soft evening breeze with a low ugly whistle.

The sword's tip also pointed right at her now, and the thing took a stamping step in her direction. Another arrow bloomed in its neck, sticking with a *thuk* sound like a steel bit punching through sheet metal. She hadn't heard that particular noise since high school shop class, but it was horridly familiar all the same.

"*For the Moon!*" Another shout, and Jazarl appeared from the darkness. A solid silver arc was his rapier, singing as it swung, and the thin flexible blade bent as it sought the tiny space between the big golden thing's horned helm and gorget. Sparks sprayed, not colorless but bright yellow; a deep grinding noise filled the small clearing as the thing shuddered to a halt. Its arms jerked, a parody of puppet-motion, and there was a popping mechanical *ping*, something critical hitting the underside of a car hood.

That sound always meant trouble; the last time she'd heard it the Oldsmobile had started spewing curtains of steam. A trembling glitter buried in the thing's eyeslit, right next to the arrow, was exactly the same color as a Check Engine light.

No. Hot acid bile burned the back of Ari's throat. *Please, God, no.*

But God had never been interested in her pleading. Not when she got that terrible phone call about Mom's accident, not during any of Mike's rages, and not now.

Jazarl landed, whipping his sword free with a thin bright sound of metallic strain, and more shouts echoed from the woods, accompanied by a cacophony of clanging. The armored thing's bright broadsword wove in midair, sharp-shining length running with wet firelight.

Majan hopped down from the log, landing cat-soft once more and bending to snatch the second quiver. It was on his back in a twinkling; he leaned further down, his hand closing around Ari's upper arm. "Up," he said crisply, in their rolling foreign language. "As you love life, lady, *up.*"

Ari's legs, numb from terror or sitting, unfolded like springs. She collided with the platinum-haired man, overbalanced, and nearly toppled into the fire. He saved her with a neat, graceful tug on her upper arm, the bow in his other hand held well away.

The big yellow thing's gleaming horned helmet turned, the arrow's feathered hind end following her again. Oily crimson fluid dribbled from the gash between gorget and helm, running in a thin rivulet down the expanse of armored chest.

It wasn't quite blood, but close enough. Metal ground and strained as the thing took another heavy, clumsy step toward them. Hellish forge-clatter surged through the forest, the night alive with banging and the screech of tearing tin.

It didn't look like the monstrous mechanical armor-suit was going to stop. It tottered, lurching with nightmare slowness.

Jazarl was somehow past it, skirting the campfire in a quick-shuffle two-step. Majan dragged her sideways, a bruise-hard grip on her right arm, and then they were running, Jazarl behind them, Ari doing her best to keep up. Trees reared on either side, a piercing whistle rose in the darkness.

No firelight meant she was temporarily blind, but Majan didn't falter. The world spun, confused motion on a turntable, another hand closing on her left arm, and between the two grips she was lifted bodily over unseen obstacles. Her hair streamed on the wind of their passage, and if there had been anything left in her stomach Ari might have brought it up in a painless hot rush, adding to the festivities.

Chill breeze on her cheeks, her right boot touching down and nearly torn from her foot, a violent yank and she was flying again. Her legs dangled, her heart strangle-lodged in her throat, hot tears squeezed from her eyes, and when the wild motion ceased she hung limp between twin vise-grips, wondering if she was still alive.

Faint silvery light filtered from above. Her feet touched soft loam and her knees promptly gave out, arms nearly yanked free of their grasp as she reeled.

I don't care. It was enough that she was away from the lurching, grinding metallic armor-puppet.

"Peace," someone said quietly, and the nightmare wasn't over. The word held a sibilant in both English and their strange language; she recognized the voice as Jazarl's even on such short acquaintance. "Peace, my lady, we are safe for the moment. Majan?"

"Here," the other man said grimly. "It came for her, even damaged."

That does not sound good. She was too occupied with not throwing up or screaming to worry much about anything else at the moment, but suspected the thought would come back soon.

"Aye." Jazarl exhaled sharply. "Alzarien? Sarle?"

"Curst clockworks," someone growled. "Alzar?"

"At least three of them will trouble us no more." The fourth and final guy was obviously all right, and Ari was dimly grateful.

She'd been worrying about being alone in the woods with strange men, but they hadn't left her behind. Which was nice, and she was glad they were all right.

Nothing about this is all right. A shapeless sound escaped, despite her longstanding habit of keeping her mouth shut on any whimper that might drive Mike into even deeper rage.

"How fares our lady?" Sarle, urgently. "Is she—"

"It was damaged." Majan's hand loosened slightly. "Yet still it turned in her direction, Jazarl."

"Yes, I saw." Jazarl's breath came in deep hard swells, like her own, and he finally let go of her. Ari squeezed her eyes shut, swaying against Majan's grip. She didn't quite want to break free; she was just a ship pulled by the tide, straining against a hawser without intent of its own.

I'd really like to wake up now. She thought she knew every tint and shade of terror, but this was something else. "Not people." She tried to find another specific word for *human* in their tongue, but it wouldn't come. "Those... those *things*..."

"The Golden." There was a soft sliding sound—Jazarl's rapier, returning to its sheath. Then his hand found her shoulder, patted awkwardly. "The Bright King's clockwork horrors, enforcers of his rotting Law. Worry not, my lady Ari. We shall not let them take you."

That's good, I guess. She had the idea being 'taken' would be very uncomfortable; if this was the Bright King's police force he was probably nobody she wanted to meet. More strange terms to add to the list in her head. Something had to start making sense soon.

I'm being very optimistic. Mom would approve. Ari found her legs were shaky, but they would now do their job reasonably well. She tried to straighten, to let Majan know she didn't have to be held up like wet laundry; maybe he understood, because his fingers gentled.

"We must make for Gesthel," Sarle said, heavily. "If Darjeth and Naithor do not find us they will go there, to tell the Grey Lady."

Another new term, *Grey Lady*. At least it sounded better than *Bright King* and *enforcers*. Ari didn't like the theory taking shape inside her aching, ringing skull, but at least it explained everything going on with distressing neatness.

"But what if *he*..." Alzarien's tenor was ragged. There was a slight sound—cloth tearing, and he hissed in a breath. "Would the prince have the strength to travel?"

Prince. Add that to the list. Ari's eyes continued adapting, the world filling in with chiaroscuro. The light filtering through branches above was definitely not sunshine, but it was far more intense than simple starlight.

"He will find it." Jazarl sounded certain. "How bad, Alzar?"

"A mere scratch," came the answer. "Have no fear, I will not slow our flight. But how is our lady?"

Silence. Ari realized they were waiting for her to say something else. Jazarl leaned close, peering at her face; on her other side Majan was tense, holding her upright, and the faint sense of living warmth from both men was comforting even if she had no idea what the blazing blue fuck, as they used to say in college.

"Where are we going?" she whispered. *Please don't leave me behind. Not with those things in the woods.* The hideous way they moved, that dribble of oily red fluid... no.

Nope. She wanted zero-none of *that*, another aphorism from her youth.

"To the Grey Lady," Jazarl sounded relieved. "Her joy will be hardly less than *his* at seeing you, my lady. Can you walk? If not, we will—"

"I can." Ari hoped she wasn't lying. The idea that someone in this weird place would be happy to see her was intensely ridiculous, but if these guys were heading away from the big golden robots she was more than happy to tag along. "Just point me in the right direction."

A soft laugh. "By silver," Sarle said, quietly. "I did not believe, and yet."

"Let us not linger." Majan was now all business. Though his grasp gentled further he still didn't let go of Ari's arm, which she was distinctly grateful for. "Dare we risk the Road?"

"Not yet." Jazarl's hand fastened on her other arm again, and he took a cautious step; Ari did her best to move with him. "Very good, my lady. And the rest of you, keep hand to hilt. The night is young, and the Moon has returned."

ARISEN ONCE MORE

STAGGERING IN DARKNESS BETWEEN TWO TALL ARMED MEN WAS another new experience. Ari was just glad no more of those huge robot-things were in view, and all she had to worry about was putting one foot in front of the other. The thought that she was being dragged along by a quartet of male strangers, with no idea of destination or route, paled beside the relief of still being alive—not to mention having a working hypothesis about this place and its inhabitants.

She was too busy staying upright and conscious to spend many brain-cycles on it, but the very presence in the back of her mind was reassuring.

Unless they happened across something that upended the theory, of course.

The group walked swiftly for a long while, until a silvery smear widened before them, tree trunks transformed into vertical black bars fencing soft light. The men veered slightly toward this new illumination. It was a familiar glow, and when they reached the clearing she was almost happy to see a few scattered pearl-cabbages, their big soft-furred leaves cupping globes which brightened as the group passed, sending up streams of that delicious, powdery mimosa-tree smell.

"By the Moon," one of the men—it sounded like Sarle—said in a hushed, wondering whisper.

Nestled in the center of the clearing, a mirror-smooth pond reflected more pale light. It couldn't be the one Ari had started at —this pool was larger, its rim starred with smooth white stones at irregular intervals. Her head tipped back, and she gazed at the sky.

There were stars, too. But hanging among them was a white plate, pearly and perfect. The ripe silver disc held no scars, no craters or gouges; stainless-bright, it gazed somberly at the forest below.

"Oh, God," she said, a long despairing breath. Perhaps she just had to be at her wit's end before she could speak in English—or they had no approximate word for *God* here.

Dante Alighieri had put a frozen lake and all sorts of other fun stuff in his *Inferno*. If this was her own personal hell, why was it so... well, so *pretty*? No, the hellfire and brimstone theory didn't wash. Even a Jungian-coded breakdown or swelling hematoma pressing on her grey matter didn't cover this.

Were all of her new companions native, or had they 'arrived' from elsewhere? If so...

The guys were suddenly all business. Jazarl let go of her arm and approached the water cautiously. He sniffed, catlike again. "I cannot tell. Sarle?"

"Is it my turn?" The stocky brunet approached the pool and bent, thrusting his hand quickly into the liquid before yanking free with a muffled splash. Ripples spread, dying almost immediately as if the water was heavier than it should be. He sniffed deeply, grimaced, and his nose wrinkled as he straightened. "I would not, my friend. It burns, and the *naryin* are scarce."

The word translated into *pearlflower*. Ari swayed; Majan's grip tightened.

"I'm fine," she said, and his hand fell reluctantly away. "Is something wrong with the water?"

"'Tis tainted." Jazarl sighed. "Were it not, we could fill our flasks. The flowers have not been seen in a long while and the Moon is returned; soon enough this place will be hallowed. But we cannot linger."

"Let her try." Alzarien had turned, intently watching the woods they'd just left; Ari had a horrible suspicion of why. His left sleeve flopped, a rough bandage knotted around his arm, and he was pale even in this ghostly light. "It does little harm."

Try what? But Ari suspected what had to happen next. Once she ruled out the impossible, the thing remaining—even if absolutely bonkers—had to be treated as fact.

Or at least, tested.

"No need." Sarle shook his hand, hissing a little as if it stung. "And in any case we should not risk injury to a lady. We are still knights enough for that."

Ari took one step, then another. "Try what?" The reflection on the pond's surface was almost warm, the light far nicer than reddish sunshine or the vicious reflected darts from bright yellow robot-things. "The water's bad?"

"The Golden seemed to be after her, but..." Jazarl hesitated. "My lady Ari, do not. There is one who could purify such things, and the *naryin* will in time. No need to risk a burn or griping."

She stopped next to Sarle, and took a deep experimental breath. It smelled just like the other pond—a mix of mimosa cabbage-flowers plus a trace of minerals, as if from a well. The water's surface ruffled again, expectant or simply brushed by a stray breeze.

Well, no time like the present to find out. Ari's knees were none too steady anyway, so it was no trouble to kneel. She reached out, ignoring Jazarl's short exclamation.

Her fingertips met coolness. She pulled back, expecting something like a chemical burn, but there was just a bit of damp on her skin. Ripples intensified, overlapping, and oddly, the reflection on the water brightened. A faint breeze rustled the pearl-cabbages; she found she liked their word for the plants. *Naryin*, pretty and fluidly accented. It was certainly more musical than *cabbage*.

She sniffed at her fingers. Nothing but the faint unscent of water—no chlorine, no other chemical tang.

"Should it hurt?" She craned to look up at Sarle; the stocky man was tense, peering down at her. "Did it burn you?"

He knelt beside her, and she caught a hint of leather from his clothing, a breath of male-smell oily and slightly acrid with hard exertion, though clean enough. He turned his head, his dark gaze locked with hers, and plunged his entire hand into the pond once more.

"Fool." Jazarl strode toward them, halted as Sarle raised his arm.

The dripping was very loud, and the stocky man shook his fingers. "Moon guide us," he said, quietly.

Then he bent and, quick as a wink, carried a palmful to his mouth. He drank, and Ari was suddenly afraid she'd just tricked him without meaning to, and into doing something awful.

So she bent and cupped her hands, drinking as well. The water was cool and fresh as before, sliding down her throat and warming as it settled behind her breastbone. A strange haze of well-being spread in her chest, and now she suspected the stocky man been playing a prank on *her* instead.

"No." Jazarl descended on them, reaching down to grip Sarle's shoulder and squeezing. "Are you crazed, or worse? Stop!"

"Sweet," the man beside her said. "By silver, Jazarl, she... Fill your flasks, my lords. There is nothing unhealthful here, now."

A slight sound echoed the words. The pearl-cabbage *naryin* brightened. Ari blinked, reflected silver light filling her head like the glare of headlights on a rainy night.

The fear fled for a single glorious instant. It would return, certainly... but for a moment, she was without its weight, and the relief was intense enough to make the crashing disappointment when it flooded back seem small by comparison.

For once, she'd guessed correctly and nobody was hurt. It was enough.

They took turns filling oddly shaped leather waterskins and drinking like parched camels. Alzarien dabbed at his arm with the wet bandage, his cut sleeve flopping heavily as it soaked up excess, and let out a sigh. "Finally," he breathed, and Ari almost gave a guilty start.

He sounded a little like the chained man.

"Perhaps Darjeth and Naithor have met with some success as well." Sarle kept stealing little glances at Ari, and she wasn't sure she liked the renewed interest. "Do you think *he* will..."

"Best not to wonder." Jazarl took a long drink from his canteen and sighed, a satisfied sound. There was a bubbling noise as he refilled, and a faint squeaking as he capped the waterskin once more. "They might find the remnants of battle, and track us. Or meet us in Gesthel."

"The Fox will be glad of this. His lady may speak again." Majan grinned, looking at Ari like she should share the joke. "Even in strange raiment, the gift will delight her."

Gesthel, Fox, Bright Prince, Grey Lady. She recited the names inwardly—a place and three people, or ceremonial titles. She was a slow student, but a thorough one; Ari just wished she could take notes. Her backpack was probably lying under half a hillside, buried in mud, but she'd been thrown somewhere else, a place obeying fairytale rules. Nobody was offering her poisoned apples or glass shoes, so maybe she could simply continue being quiet and watchful, gathering every bit of context and inference possible, avoiding any truly horrendous mistakes.

It was a good goal, perhaps even an achievable one.

Ari's hands glimmered, pale in the moonlight. Maybe it was just the water; she rubbed at her forehead and touched the back of her head gingerly, glad that the chained man had done... whatever he'd done, to remove the landslide filth. All in all, things were going far better—though weirder—than she could have dreamed while jamming clothes into her backpack and trying not to think about the crumpled shape on the bedroom floor that had once been...

"My lady?" Jazarl, tentatively. "What ails you?"

She was shaking, Ari noted with almost clinical detachment. The trembling passed through her in a wave, and her lungs threatened to seize up. *Oh, a panic attack.*

Her heart thundered, but no sweat greased her skin. "Nothing," she said, dreamily, in the cramped little voice that was all she could manage when Wanda asked, *again*, who she thought she was. "I'm sorry." The words were English, sounding harsh and unhelpful after their lovely rolling tongue.

"What does she say?" Sarle sounded anxious. "Is it the water? But—"

It figured, just when she was feeling halfway competent her body had decided to register a complaint at all the bullshit she'd put it through. Still, this could be a good sign. Lungs and heart didn't usually go wonky on her until the worst was over. All she needed was a few quiet moments, but there was no bathroom door to lock —even one with Wanda Lee cawing on the other side would work, or Mike banging because he just *had* to have her attention all the time.

Maybe her husband was afraid he'd vanish if someone wasn't looking. Who knew?

"Hold her steady." Jazarl was good at managing things. He sounded a little like Mom when there was a crisis to deal with— firm, calm, no-nonsense. Someone had Ari's shoulders, keeping her upright, and at the moment she didn't care that she was alone with a group of strange men.

If they were going to do something awful, now was probably the time. She could just disconnect, let whatever would happen wash over her.

"*He* would not like this," Sarle commented darkly. "I swear to you, the water was—"

"We all drank, 'tis not the water. You see the light as I do, my friend." Majan, quiet and practical. "She is but recently mortal, and bore the appearance of the Golden with much courage. No wonder she is faint—but we should move. I like not how quiet it has grown."

Recently mortal. Golden. Thank goodness for the invisible translator, Ari thought, dreamily. If she had to resort to drawing pictographs, this entire situation might be even more bizarre, not to mention terrifying.

Though it was certainly winning awards on both fronts. The real question was if this was truly better or worse than what she'd left behind?

And would she be catapulted back if there was another rainstorm?

What a gruesome thought, thanks. Another wave of galvanic shakes poured through bone and muscle, her heartbeat blurring like hummingbird wings. She tried to focus on breathing, achieving steady sips of cool, night-fragrant air.

"The forest renewed, the Moon arisen once more," Alzarien weighed in. His voice was near her left ear, so she knew who was holding her up on that side. "The faithless accursed will know what has happened as well. He does not lack eyes."

Silence. Ari fought to even out her breathing, telling herself there was enough oxygen, she just had to keep dragging it down her windpipe. Thankfully nobody was yelling at her. In fact, they all seemed to regard being a bit shaky as a reasonable response to current events, which was... nice, she supposed, if not exactly comforting.

"We make for the Road, and Gesthel," Jazarl said, heavily. "We will hear the abominations if they approach. Our aim is not to offer battle but to protect our lady. If she cannot walk we will carry her."

That would be so fucking embarrassing. Which meant Ari had to force her eyes open, finding a moon-silvered clearing, a ring of anxious faces, the sound of wavelets lapping at a pond's shore, and a breathless hush among the tall grey pillar-trees. "I can walk." She had to say it slowly so the invisible translator would work, and the words slurred as if she'd been at whiskey shots instead of pondwater. "I'll go."

Being left in the woods with those metal *things* was too much to contemplate. So she stiffened, leaned into Alzarien's grip, and told her legs they were just going to have to get with the program, however outlandish it turned out to be.

This entire lunatic situation was indeed better than what she'd escaped, Ari finally decided.

But not by much.

KNIGHTS OF THE KEEP

Stone blocks glowed yellow in moonlight. The vista could be a landscape print hung in a spare room—if guests didn't mind a persistent sense of unease, either from the slight alienness of foliage or the eerily flawless silvery orb hanging above. Or maybe it was only current events turning a pretty view into something far more sinister; Ari couldn't tell.

Jazarl waited for what seemed an eternity, crouched and staring at the road from behind a screen of leather-leaved bushes, before motioning them all forward. Walking helped; Ari was finally able to breathe deeply again, and each lungful of cool clear air put a little more of the terror and uncertainty behind her.

Maybe having other people around helped as well. Humans were tribal creatures, and there was a certain comfort in being part of a group. She'd almost forgotten—for so long her world had been that awful white mansion, the town simply enemy territory she had to navigate with an apologetic smile and quick steps.

That's Mike Hardison's wife. Got her in the big city, she don't talk to anyone. Stuck-up, I guess.

Christ, she would be glad to never see or even think of that shitty whistle-stop burg ever again. Like any wish, though, it carried a terrible price tag. At least big, shiny, murderous robots didn't pretend to be friendly.

The guys traded off positions, keeping her surrounded—one on either side, one before, one behind, as if she was some kind of VIP to be ushered along Secret Service-style. Unease at being hemmed in warred with cautious relief, especially as the big blank-faced moon sank gently to the horizon.

When the sky was half-full of grey and traces of mist crept between the trees, Jazarl called a halt. Off the road, safe behind a screen of undergrowth, they offered her more water from their oddly shaped canteens.

Ari turned it down as politely as possible, and they were back to hiking shortly afterward. Then, at dawn, came another shock—the daylight here, bright but reddish, turned out to be that way because the sun was a giant exhausted crimson orb.

There were limits even to doubting one's own perceptions, Ari discovered; the big gold-armored robot was one, and the sun was another. Was it a red giant, on its last hydrogen legs?

Now she had to worry about the sun going out, too. *Should've gotten a degree in astrophysics instead*, she thought, and couldn't restrain a tired, hiccuping chuckle.

"My lady?" Majan's forehead wrinkled. He was trooping along on her right again; her arm still remembered his grasp during the wild flight from the robots. The feeling was familiar, a bruise deciding if it wanted to rise to the surface.

She'd had far worse.

"Nothing." Ari's fingers tingled; she found out she was picking at her flannel's buttons. The woods were full of birdsong and the movement of small creatures going about their business, taking no notice of human-shaped interlopers. "Those things. The... the clockworks."

"The Golden." He nodded, as if he'd expected her to ask. "Servants of the Bright King. We know not from where he brings them, or if he builds them in his Mirrored City amid the Blight."

He sounds like a laugh a minute. Now she had other terms to add to her list as well. Were these guys a resistance faction, a sort of fantasy Free French? Maybe they were just garden-variety bandits, she couldn't assume. She belatedly realized at least a polite noise was required on her part to keep the conversation going. "Oh."

"He is faithless, and accursed." Alzarien was on her left now, and his steps landed at exactly the same time as hers, his stride artificially shortened. Maybe he was making a game out of it, like elementary school kids walking in line. "Now that you are returned—"

"We should not mention that upon the Road." Jazarl, from behind. "The Grey Lady will explain, in a manner befitting. Our task is different."

"Hannixe does not speak," Sarle said quietly. He sped up a little, drawing away in front of them.

That put paid to all further chitchat, but Ari had at least a little more information. *Mortal* was still the biggest question mark, but *returned* was also a strange term.

Now, in daylight, she could attempt thinking about the dreams. The *nightmares*, starring the haggard face of a man wrapped in chains. They came in waves, for as far back as she could remember; even Mom had been puzzled by the strength and duration of her daughter's night terrors. The shock, three months into dating Mike, that she hadn't suffered one since meeting him had turned into a source of quiet exhilaration.

The last time Ari visited her mother's grave, she'd whispered, *I think I've found the guy, I don't dream anymore.*

Would she ever see her mother's headstone again? Mike had gone off the last time she suggested a trip up north to visit. *Waste of time and gas,* he sneered, and when she persisted—oh, very cautiously, in her softest voice—he'd slapped her. A bowl of popcorn had gone flying, and that got her an additional shot to the kidneys. Then she'd endured a lecture the following day from Wanda Lee, who found a kernel Ari had missed.

The road was nice and level, but she was afraid of stumbling anyway. Time wore on, the big red sun mounting, and at least she wasn't sweating. Her stomach didn't growl, another blessing.

What was in that water? She wasn't big on caffeine, but a cup of tea sounded wonderful right now. So did buttered toast, even though she wasn't truly hungry.

Would she ever eat again? Nobody had mentioned breakfast, lunch, dinner. Maybe it wasn't polite to ask, as in certain cultures used to food instability. The only thing saving her from making some kind of giant faux pas was keeping her mouth shut, always the best strategy no matter one's surroundings, but...

"Hist." Majan halted—he was in front now, the bow strapped to his back bobbing. He held up a hand. "Alzar?"

"I hear it," the crimson-haired man replied from Ari's left.

Jazarl hustled them into the underbrush. A few days ago—Ari's sense of time had grown slippery, which she supposed was only to be expected—she'd been obsessively re-tidying the Hardison mansion after the housekeeper left each day, smiling fixedly as Wanda Lee spewed her venom, waiting for Mike to come back later and later each night reeking of liquor.

Now she was a murderess crouching in weird flora with a group of strange men, trying not to breathe too loudly and hoping whatever approached wasn't big shiny armor-clad robots.

It turned out to be Darjeth and Naithor, both nearly breathless. The pale-skinned blond took a long swallow from Sarle's leather canteen; his companion leaned against a tree nearby, eyes half-closed and hand locked around a rapier hilt, his ribs flaring with deep soundless gasps.

Darjeth exhaled hard, lowering the canteen. "The Keep is dark," he said, as if reporting on the passing of a foreign monarch. "The sword is gone, the fetters broken. I went inside."

"I cautioned against it," Naithor hurried to add, as Jazarl's blue-tipped eyebrows rose nearly to the hairline. "But he was determined; I could not let him do so alone."

"And?" Sarle prompted, shifting in his crouch. He glanced at Majan, who was busy watching the road through a screen of foliage.

"There were Golden inside, and... other things." Darjeth took another hit from the canteen. "All dead," he continued. "Savaged. They will trouble the Underdark no more."

Stay here. I would not have you see this. Ari decided she could be glad the chained man had made that particular call. The big heavy sword, handled so effortlessly—far different from these guys' rapiers, and he probably had a lot of feelings to work out. Plus, the word *Underdark* carried some interesting connotations, if she had any energy or mental horsepower to spare for figuring them out. Just another term added to her list, which was achieving Santa Claus checking-it-twice proportions.

Did this place have a Father Christmas? Now *there* was a question.

Ari was back to hugging herself, elbows digging into her palms. Dusk in the forest was pretty. She probably would have enjoyed it from a hotel window, or even a nice RV with a reasonably clean bathroom.

Not that she'd needed the restroom since she arrived, but that was almost beside the point. Right now she was more concerned with keeping quiet and *not* letting these guys know she'd gotten the chained guy out of hock. It didn't seem like they'd be angry at her over the event, but it wasn't worth the risk.

Her instincts appeared to be working just fine now that she had a reasonable theory of what-the-hell, and they were telling her to be as quiet as possible. Maybe these woodland bandits or resistance fighters would even forget her presence.

Fat chance, since every man in the group except Majan was now studying Ari intently. Naithor's breathing slowed; he was no longer chalky under his deep coppery tan.

"So," Jazarl said, after a long pause. "*He* is free, and perhaps... My lady Ari, you said you heard hoofbeats?"

Oh, Christ, don't ask me anything right now. She nodded. Hopefully they thought her a dimwit, a stupid mortal without two brain cells to rub together, and maybe she could... what? Pick a moment to run off into the woods?

Well, if hypothermia wasn't a danger and pondwater was capable of keeping her alive, why not? The only problem with the plan was those giant shiny medieval-armor robots. If she came across those on her own, it wouldn't end well.

Plus, she didn't know how long the water would work. What if it was some kind of drug or appetite suppressant, with unpleasant side effects on continued use?

They were waiting for her to say something, not just make an affirmative headwiggle. Ari swallowed, hard, and wished she hadn't turned down a shot from the canteens. "I heard a group of horses, I think. Then a little while later, a single one."

The men exchanged meaningful glances. Nobody asked how she could be sure, or questioned her ability to differentiate how many were on the road.

"*He* must have seen the Moon arisen." Sarle shifted again; Ari realized he wasn't fidgeting but moving so his legs didn't go numb. The others did the same at intervals. All in all, they seemed very comfortable with hiking.

"The traitor, too. And the Golden speak to their master somehow, that much we know." Jazarl rubbed callused palms together, thoughtfully. "They were already after her."

So this Bright King was some sort of traitor, or usurper? Well, these guys were dressed like Robin Hood illustrations; she could assume a King John with little trouble. Was he a mad scientist building robots in some castle like the Keep? It wouldn't put a dent in her theory, but it was certainly an interesting fillip.

None of that answered why the robots would be after Ari. Had she heard that bit correctly?

"We hunted at least half a dozen near the Keep before finding your trail." Darjeth looked a lot perkier after some hydration; the blond man handed the canteen back to Sarle. "Each alone, and moving in search-pattern. They will serve the faithless and his Law no more."

Sarle unfolded, shaking dark hair out of his eyes with a quick flicking movement, and offered Naithor another drink. "There is plenty," he said, quietly. "Our lady purified a spring surrounded by *naryin* as the Moon rose."

More significant looks. Darjeth was still studying Ari as if he expected her to grow another head or make some kind of embarrassing bodily noise. "Then I ask her pardon for my words upon our meeting," he said, finally. "We are bound for Gesthel, I presume? The Grey Lady will be overjoyed."

I hear the words, and the translator seems to still be working. And I really don't like where this is going. The robots couldn't be after her, she'd just gotten here, for Chrissake.

Maybe it was time to speak up, despite the danger. "Excuse me." It was a variety of their *I ask your pardon*, but her accent was different than theirs; she could write whole papers on this language back home.

Too bad she wasn't in school anymore. Naithor accepted the canteen and began quaffing, but his green gaze rested on her as his Adam's-apple bobbed.

"It seems like you have a lot going on," she continued, squeezing her arms more tightly. Would she bruise? And if she did would pondwater cure the wound, like it seemed to have helped her throat and scraped hands? "I don't want to be in the way, so maybe I should just..."

Five pairs of eyes stared at her; Majan still didn't turn from watching the road. The set of his shoulders said he perhaps wanted to—a subtle movement, but one she was used to decoding. Sometimes the only warning a woman got was a twitch, half an irritated breath, a flicker in peripheral vision.

"I do not quite understand." Now Jazarl's blue eyebrows were drawing together, his forehead puckering. "What are you suggesting, my lady?"

"Well..." She tried her softest, most reasonable tone; it sometimes worked on Mike. Not often, but a girl used what she had. "You'll travel faster to this Gesthel without me. I'm a stranger here, and there's no reason why those things should be—"

"A stranger?" Darjeth glanced at Jazarl, as if his own invisible translator was on the fritz. Were they all speaking different languages, a reverse Babel? "By silver, my lady, what do you think will happen if *he* finds us and learns we were so craven as to let you wander alone?"

"I don't know who *he* is." It was easy to lay the same stress on the pronoun, she found out. And it wasn't a lie—they could be talking about someone other than the chained man.

Right. You don't even believe that yourself. Ari longed for a sketchbook, a few pencils, and some uninterrupted time to think about all this absurdity. But she was miserably certain she'd find herself attempting to draw a strong-jawed face with burning dark eyes, the picture unreeling from her fingers without conscious volition.

Mom had been so proud of her sketches, and thought Ari should go to art school instead. But exposing that part of herself to strangers for grades seemed like the worst thing in the world, at least until she got married. She hadn't really had time to draw since just before her wedding, and she missed it.

A lot.

"A mortal, newly arrived..." Alzarien made a helpless gesture. "You must remember something."

Whatever they were expecting, it wasn't happening. "All I remember is the storm." It wasn't really a lie, she only had a series of half-baked assumptions and a working theory. "And I mean it. You should just go on without me."

The big shining robots couldn't truly be after *her*. If they were simply chasing whoever happened to be with resistance fighters, though, she was a liability. Her urge to escape, to get away from strangers and find a quiet corner to curl up in, was overwhelming.

It was like attempting to politely exit a frat party right before its voice mutated from the roar of simple drunken fun to the subliminal buzzing of predatory intent. Ari had just hit the limit of her ability to deal with current events. A hole or a handy fallen log to cower behind while the rest of this brave new world ignored her sounded downright *fantastic*.

"We cannot leave you unguarded, in woods hunted by the Bright King's servants," Jazarl said, stiffly. "We may not look it now, my lady Ari, but we are knights of the Keep. Such a thing would not be fitting."

So the huge dark spiny castle was indeed their home. A lot more made sense now, but unfortunately she'd probably pissed them off with what was meant to be a helpful suggestion. An uncomfortable silence reigned for several long, excruciating seconds.

"Night comes," Majan said, without turning. "Are we making camp so our lady may rest, or continuing onward? We may reach Gesthel by sunhigh day after tomorrow, if we do not linger."

"We move." Jazarl said. "My lady, we will not abandon you. Should you falter we will carry you, and ask forgiveness later. Majan, Sarle, you will be our lady's close-guard for now. Alzarien, give Darjeth a fresh quiver; his is almost empty. Take heart, my friends. If *he* is free, all else will follow."

At least she'd found out they weren't going to let her go, though that didn't answer the question of why on earth—or wherever this was—the Golden robot-things would be after her specifically.

She had the distinct idea she wouldn't like the answer, whenever it happened to trundle 'round the mountain. So Ari put on a facsimile of an accommodating smile, and tried to think of what to do next.

Unfortunately, absolutely nothing sprang to mind.

❧ 14 ❧

FINDING NO REST

A HAZE SPREAD AS THE HUGE, EERIE RED SUN SANK. CLOUDS thickened, pink deepening through maroon into violet and royal purple; the breeze sharpened, heavy with the good green scent of petrichor. Jazarl called halts more frequently, usually after a worried glance in Ari's direction; she was doing her best to keep up, but suspected it really didn't matter.

Inadequacy was her natural state, as Wanda Lee so often pointed out.

Had she found her son's body and called the cops? Ari's heart gave a terrible twinge, imagining an old woman's grief. For all her venom and nastiness, Wanda loved her child. Maybe Earl really did deep down as well, it was hard to tell.

The first few drops pattered on the road, small puffs of dust rising as they hit. "Rain," Darjeth muttered grimly. "Of course."

Ari had to suppress a weary smile. It was exactly what she'd been thinking, with a side order of wondering if a storm—or even a shower—would send her back to the normal world. Was this fairy-land, a different planet reached through some kind of temporary wormhole, an alternate dimension?

She decided all three pretty much amounted to the same thing. What mattered was the theory holding up; she'd really been thrown *somewhere else*, and having that settled was so comforting the decision turned her knees to overcooked pasta at regular intervals.

Relief could be indistinguishable from terror, given enough intensity.

The trees crowded even closer here, if that were possible. Jazarl turned aside and plunged into undergrowth; he had a genius for finding hidden thickets which could nevertheless be used to keep a watch on the wide paved strip. This time was no different, and the guys spread out, clearly glad for a rest break.

Ari stood awkwardly in the center of their ring, breathing deeply and trying not to sway. Fan-shaped leaves moved in masses overhead, and she heard a low rumble.

Thunder. If a storm popped her back home, would she wake up half-buried in landslide, or on the side of the road with the crippled Oldsmobile? Would she surface in a jail cell? A hospital bed?

"If we had equines we could already be there." Alzarien leaned hipshot against a tree, his hat pulled low and his eyes half-closed in the brim's shadow. Broad-shouldered and long-legged, he could have been modeling for a book cover.

"Oh, aye, and if we had wings we would never stumble." But Darjeth smiled, the phrase clearly a proverb and sarcasm edging it in friendly instead of spiteful fashion. "Dare we risk a fire? 'Tis cheersome, and our lady looks near to foundering."

I'm fine. But Ari couldn't say it. When they weren't moving she needed all her concentration for not sinking into a heap. She had to stay braced for a sudden jolt back into a world she understood, and that required carefully shepherding what little energy she had at the moment. Anticipation was almost worse than a beating.

Almost.

"Here." Jazarl uncapped his canteen, and his smile was no doubt meant to be encouraging. "Take a little more, my lady. 'Tis not the greater drink, but still is wondrous helpful."

Greater drink. Underdark. Bright King. She needed a thesaurus and a couple dictionaries to deal with all this; learning solely by context was exhausting. Which brought up another interesting point—were these people literate? "I'm all right," Ari tried to say, but the words slurred.

He thrust the canteen into her hands, so she had to at least take a sip. A few mouthfuls did actually help; she hadn't realized she was so thirsty.

"No flame so close to the Road," Majan weighed in. "Perhaps we should build a bower for our lady, and pass a night on guard."

Another roil of thunder walked across the sky. Ari tried to suppress a shudder, and failed miserably.

"The storm is far off." Jazarl really was trying to be helpful. He looked more anxious by the minute. "We have no mantle for you, but the trees are thick and will keep the worst of the rain at bay."

"I'm fine," Ari insisted. The translator turned it into *I am well enough*, and she wondered what they thought of her accent. They were clearly too polite to tell her if she sounded like a backwoods hick.

"Hist." Sarle gazed through moving branches, his shoulders stiffening. "I see a gleam in the distance, and do not think it friendly."

Now Ari heard something else—a rolling of hooves, a different timbre than thunder. "That's what I heard before," she whispered, and her fingers were suddenly clumsy on the canteen's top. Chill air brushed her flushed cheeks, stirring her hair.

"Get down," Naithor said, urgently, and everyone crouched. Ari shivered, clenching her jaw to keep teeth from chattering; she could peer over Majan's shoulder, through a natural tunnel in the bushes. The sound drew swiftly nearer, coming not from behind but ahead of their small group. When the cavalcade galloped into view her right hand flew up, clamping over her mouth to muffle a sound of mixed fear, surprise—and disgust.

It was the brightly armored robots, but they had changed. Their legs were shortened and arms lengthened with insectile segments, horned helmet-heads bobbing above thickened shoulders. The sound wasn't true hoofbeats, then, but the metallic galloping of terribly distorted things, and the worst thing was that they didn't *move* like horses either.

Instead, their motion was a parody, part mechanical jerks and part weirdly flowing, neither in the way her gaze expected. It was vaguely akin to the jerking, twisting motion of a mechanical bull, but without the unspoken limits engineering placed on randomness. Everything about the movements was deeply, utterly wrong, and called up images of sharp-toothed gears digging into recalcitrant flesh, pistons hammering amid cringing muscles.

Even the most fevered painter of grotesqueries would have trouble capturing the utter alienness, the cringing lopsided bizarrity. They streaked past, glittering in low bruised stormdusk, and branches toss-sighed as the wind mounted afresh. A bone-white flash followed, and after a long breathless pause thunder hurried to catch up.

"They're horrible," Ari whispered, barely aware of speaking.

"Aye." Jazarl had gone pale, and his cheeks and chin bore blue-tinged stubble. They all looked a little rough, and Ari was sure she wasn't in the best shape either. Her hair felt tangled, and she didn't even try to finger-comb.

There was no point. If this kept up she was going to be a rat's nest on shaking noodle-bendy legs.

A wave of rain rushed earthward, the pavers' golden tinge dimming slightly as wet spots spread. "Faster on the Road," Darjeth said, as if someone had asked a question. "But safer in the trees. Unless..."

"Too dangerous to halt," Majan weighed in. "And we are still too far from Gesthel."

Alzarien was just as pale as Jazarl. "The Fox is canny, but he has his lady to care for. He may have withdrawn to the Mere. If we strike overland..."

"There is the Breach to think of, though, and the bridge may be watched." Sarle looked at Ari as if she should know, or maybe he was simply gauging whether it was worth getting rid of deadweight. "My lady..."

More stabs of lightning-light drenched both forest and road. Thankfully, the thunder's lagging said the true storm was some distance away, but that could change in a heartbeat. Ari found herself shifting uneasily, rocking back and forth as if to comfort a child or anxious pet.

"The Road." Jazarl clearly felt there were no good options. "At least until we are past the Breach. If we are attacked the close-guard will carry our lady away while the others offer what battle we may. My lady Ari, will you consent to such treatment? We have no mounts; our own legs must do."

I could just stay here, you know. Even if everything inside her went chilly and loose at the thought of running across some of those robots again, and alone. "You could leave me and—"

"Never." Darjeth didn't look abashed at nearly shouting, though a few of the others gave him clearly warning looks. "What? There is no reason to gild a truth now, no matter how unwelcome. We shall carry you to Gesthel and the Grey Lady or die in the attempt, my lady Moon."

It was either extremely chivalrous or there was a factor her theory hadn't taken into account. "I don't think that's neces—" she began, but Sarle hissed another warning.

This time her view of the road was blocked, though she heard the sound approaching—neither hoofbeats nor the mechanical roil, but a softer slap-paddling. The men crowded around her, pressing close, and each looked grim, their hands resting on rapier hilts as they crouched. Being in the middle of the huddle might have felt safe, except for the weird, chilling cries.

Whatever was upon the stone pavers now moaned as it passed. Irregular shrieks rose as well, sawing painfully through rising wind and shiver-rushing rain. Ari shuddered, clapping her hands over her ears, and Majan had gone chalky, blood draining from his dark cheeks.

The hideous groaning faded, then the wet slapping sounds. She found she was physically cold for the first time since landing in this bizarre alternate dimension, and even the living warmth of half a dozen other bodies in a small space didn't help.

"What was that?" she whispered, unable to help herself.

"The Bright King's other servants." Naithor's shoulder pressed against hers, hard enough to hurt. "Those corrupted and infected by obedience to his curst Law, finding no rest. He is searching for you, my lady—as if we needed more proof of what you are."

Look, I'm a stranger here, and I just... There were no words. The trembling was back, and while Ari didn't quite wish to suddenly find herself on the side of a mountain highway or under an overhang during a bad mountain storm, the prospect was far more appetizing than it had been before.

At least on her own planet she knew what horrors to expect.

"Enough." Jazarl turned slightly. "We go now. Stay to the side of the Road until we are past the Breach." He paused. "'Tis an honour to fight beside each of you. If the worst comes—"

"Do not summon ill luck by speaking of it." Darjeth rose, pale hair gleaming, and as if signaled the others did too. Majan had Ari's elbow, pulled her firmly and irresistibly up as well. "They are upon the Road, but *he* may be as well. All we must do is endure."

A few moments later they were in the rain, moving at a quick walk, Darjeth and Naithor now on either side of Ari as cool drops patted her tangled hair and bowed shoulders.

She'd never dreamed of this Bright King or his minions, and Ari was deeply grateful even if the fact called up reams upon reams of unanswered, progressively more disturbing questions. Had all her new companions been dumped here as well? From where? Were this king plus his Golden native to this awful place, mounting an immune response to expel foreign invaders?

Even if Ari had breath to ask, it certainly wasn't the time. She simply had to keep up, and try desperately *not* to think about what she hadn't seen running past on these very same rain-sluiced stones, moaning like damned souls.

🕸 15 🕸

AMBUSH

THE STORM NIPPED AT THEIR HEELS, A CAT TOYING WITH SLOW mice. It was embarrassing to be hauled along, the guys taking turns ducking under her arms, carrying her between them as they loped— or it would have been, if Ari had enough breath or energy for any emotion at all.

As it was, her head bobbed, rain dripping from long dark curls, and her booted toes hovered above the stones. Lightning strobed as she tried to think about dry socks, hot baths and big fluffy towels, a nice comfortable chair in a quiet room, the sugary richness of hot cocoa.

These are a few of my favorite things, Mom sang inside her head; her mother had loved musicals. If she'd been alive, would she have suspected something was off about Mike? There hadn't been any warning signs.

Or had there? Ari initially thought his clinging was romantic, his frequent allusions to his own mother charming, his protective-ness old-fashioned. He'd held doors for her as a matter of course, put the umbrella more over her than himself when it was raining, and gotten down on one knee to propose. He never let her pay for dates—but he took over their finances almost immediately after marriage and also accused her of wanting to cheat on him when she suggested she could get a part-time job in town during the first year.

I'll kill you, and the man too. The vein on his forehead throbbing, his blue eyes hot with rage...

"She's fading," Sarle said, anxiously. Drumming rain and splashing leaves underscored the words. "We should find shelter, or make it."

They had already been driven into the woods twice as terrible things ran past, the hoofbeat sounds accompanied by the shushing of tires in standing water—or maybe that was just Ari's imagination, apt to run away with her even at the best of times—and once again as *something else* did, those weirdly modulated moans and pad-slapping sounds accompanied by vile squelching.

She didn't want to look. The darkness of closed lids was no comfort either, since whenever her eyes shut for more than a moment the image of the bedroom rose in vivid detail, from the slight dimples of the white eyelet comforter to the spreading pool of sticky red under Mike's body on hardwood floor, his blue eyes open, twin searchlights in the stormy night.

You little bitch, you can't hide from me. The sound he'd made when he fell, the horrible bubbling, the clicking of the .38 as she pulled the trigger again and again, her hands no longer her own and blessed air once more rushing down her bruised throat...

I didn't mean to, Ari howled internally, but what else had she expected when she bolted for the nightstand? A mad scramble to get there first because somewhere deep down, she knew he wasn't just going to hurt her that night, oh no.

No indeed.

His silence. The fixed, glazed stare. His hands—they had been gentle once, caressing fingertips or skimming palms—flexing and releasing as if he already felt her neck in their grasp. The bubbling of his last breath.

If she hadn't reached the gun, would she be in a different place now? Because the longer this agonizing chase went on, the more she couldn't shake the feeling that instead of a separate dimension she really was in a type of hell, specifically planned and tailor-made.

There went all her relief at having a good, working theory.

"Do you hear anything?" Jazarl, urgently.

Alzarien's reply, hushed and tense. "Naught but the storm itself."

Ari was hearing plenty. The dry clicking of a hammer on a revolver's empty chamber. The last rattling breath leaving a body she'd slept beside for three and a half years. Her own horrified gasps. The hiss of steam from an overloaded car engine, rattling as it crested the last hill it would ever climb.

"*Ambush!*" Darjeth yelled.

Ari was yanked violently aside. Her eyes snapped open; lightning stitched the sky. The big robots boiled out of the woods, lit in pitiless detail. Branches snapped, splinters flying. Jazarl had her arm; her feet slid as if greased, digging through moss.

How much more strangeness could she absorb before going actually insane? A painting of this scene would be lopsided, the center of focus thrown off. Drops beading on the golden-armored things, an arrow stuck quivering in one's neck; Majan and Alzarien facing another, their rapiers glistening and Alzarien's hat pushed far back now, almost falling free, wood splintering as a heavy straight sword hit a tree—

Her feet tangled together; Ari staggered. Jazarl was suddenly in front of her, rapier flashing in a complicated pattern as he shuffled, lunging and parrying, metal ringing. It seemed impossible that one slim blade could fend off an armor-robot's whistling broadsword; the blue-haired man just barely avoided a massive pistoning gauntlet-punch. Majan shouted, and an arrow bloomed in the thing's eyeslit.

I should help. Now Ari was wishing she had the .38, even if the mere thought of using it was sickening. Would bullets hurt these things?

Jazarl was flung aside. A pointless, acidic scream filled Ari's throat. Somehow she had reeled across the streaming road, and almost tripped over a long, slim piece of deadfall lying on the moss-grassy verge.

Ari lunged, scooping up the branch. Her fingers closed around wet bark; she whirled and straightened, raising her new, deeply useless weapon.

The Golden armor-suit ratcheted after her, squirts of reddish oil dribbling from the underside of its horned helmet meeting rain-rivulets coursing down its shining chest. Its sword lifted, lightning scintillating on sharp steel.

When it killed her, would she wake up roasting in actual hell? Or near the pond surrounded by pearl-cabbages again? Or maybe she'd be right back in the bedroom, listening to Mike's dying breath rattling in his chest.

"*Hau!*" A terrible, thunderous cry. A vast chiming shadow thrust in front of her, sparks flying as massive blades met with a clang nearly lost in greater turmoil. Rain glistened on dull-black iron, dripped from a shock of dark hair. Broad shoulders strained under metal, and the chained man's left hand flashed out—not to punch, but in a gesture of command.

What. The hell. Ari fetched up against a tree, still clutching the soaked, heavy branch, and stared.

A length of dark dripping chain shot out, punching through one of the golden robots across the road with a heavy, nasty *thunk*. The tall dark-haired man broke free of *corps-à-corps* and swung with his broadsword in the same moment, his blade shearing through the arm of the robot bearing down on Ari; another lightning-glare showed heavy links moving as they wreathed the new arrival's dull, heavily spiked armor.

He stepped into the fray almost lightly, the massive sword whistling—Ari could almost feel its weight in her hands again—and snake-lengths of chain whipping in every direction. Naithor ran for Jazarl, pulling the other man to his feet before turning to raise his rapier, but there was little need.

Alzarien let out a high chilling cry as a flying chain whispered past him, shearing the helm-head from the Golden looming nearby like a red-hot knife lopping a piece of cold butter. Majan's bow sounded twice more, arrows blooming in bright armor before the chained man made short work of another pair of robots. Darjeth and Sarle retreated, their rapiers up and relief shining visibly on both faces; the duo gave quick glances to either side in oddly synchronized fashion, found Ari, and hurried in her direction.

Oily red ichor sprayed as grinding and metal-tearing screeches outdid the thunder for a few brief moments. Another lightning flash showed a massive shadow to one side—a black paper cutout of horselike shape, standing patiently in lashing rain. One hoof lifted, pawing at the road's surface; the thing's tail was a charcoal waterfall and its mane dripped heavily.

The last robot gave a grinding scream when the chained man's blade rammed through its chest. The new arrival ripped his sword upward, and a great gout of oily reddish stuff jetted high. The tree Ari was leaning against vibrated as the wind kicked up as well, foliage splattering wildly. Cold drops showered over her. She blinked, her eyelashes freighted with rain.

He turned almost mincingly, gracefully precise despite the heavy armor—functional, even festooned with spikes—and the extra load of metal links. The chains flung in every direction retreated, wrapping around him, but he didn't seem to notice the weight. Those burning, starving dark eyes glittered, and he stared across the road.

Straight at her. He swung into motion again, each step oddly soundless, strolling like a panther through long grass. Thunder boiled, the sky a bubbling cauldron.

It was the same face, though now much less gaunt—high cheek-bones, heavy jaw, straight dark eyebrows, proud nose. Rain dripped from strings of black hair, and even in the darkness it was obvious the strands bore a faint reddish undertone.

Oh, she thought, blankly, her fingers remembering doodling those features over and over on sketchpads and in textbook margins. *I shouldn't have used true black but umber, maybe. That's why the drawings never really worked.*

Clearly the robots were no more problem. At least fifteen shat-tered hulks starred the road and the verge on the opposite side. Ari clutched the wet branch, and waited for doom.

16

NO SHAME, ALL HONOUR

THE GUYS WERE HELPING EACH OTHER UPRIGHT, EXCHANGING low questions and exclamations, wrenching arrows free of robot corpses and returning them to quivers. Jazarl seemed okay, grimacing as he leaned on Naithor but moving with relative ease.

Which was great, but Ari's entire body turned leaden, unresponsive. The shakes were back, spreading from her bones. Her teeth chattered, then stopped as if they knew it was useless to protest.

Whatever was going to happen was beyond her control. As usual.

The chained man paid no attention to the men *or* the dead robots. He slowed, then stopped in front of her, also ignoring the intensifying downpour. He spared a single glance at the branch clutched in her hands.

Ari's fingers sprang open; she dropped the wooden bar. Its heavier end almost landed on her feet.

Looming, blotting out the wreckage and the rest of this baffling, violent world, the chained man stared down at her. Lightning painted every metal edge, running off his gauntlets, flashing on the sword held carefully down and away once more. Just as he had in the Keep.

Oh, God. Ari shrank against the tree. *Please. If you're going to, just do it. Get it over with.*

The big horselike thing tossed its strangely formed head, pawing the road again with a faint chiming sound. Ari's heart triphammered, roaring mounting in her ears.

He said nothing, just looked at her. Finally, she felt ridiculous. Her lips parted; his gaze fastened on her mouth.

As usual, all she could produce was an utter banality. "H-hello," she managed, faintly. For last words, it was embarrassing, but what else was new?

At least it gained a response. "My lady." Grave and quiet, but effortlessly heard through the storm-noise. "Are you hurt?"

A prosaic question, but she almost couldn't absorb the syllables even with the aid of an invisible translator. "I..." Ari couldn't look past him, and she didn't precisely want to.

But she should, shouldn't she? Figure out if anyone was wounded, though her rudimentary first-aid skills were probably worse than useless. She didn't have so much as a Band-Aid in her pocket.

"Tell me." The chained man took another deliberate step, a vast shadow swelling before her. "Are you harmed? At all?"

How should I know? Still, it was downright polite of him to ask. "I don't..." Maybe getting him loose had been a rare smart move on Ari's part. "I don't think so."

"Good." His left gauntlet rose, slowly, and Ari realized he was moving very carefully, as if trying not to frighten a wild animal. "Can you ride? We should not linger here." Each word very soft and distinct.

She would never have believed a tall man wrapped up in armor and whatnot, having just finished killing a bunch of armored robots, could sound so... well, almost tentative.

I don't see a bicycle, my friend. "Ride?" Her brain struggled to process this new outlandishness, the invisible translator working overtime. Fat leaf-collected drops tapped the top of her head; waves of smaller driplets swept over the road, made tiny hollow noises on the chained man's armored shoulders.

"I would not have you walk, my lady." The chained man paused, still offering his left hand. The gauntlet looked very big, the short curved spikes on its back wicked sharp; the palm was a dark hollow, and he held it cupped as if asking for change. "Come. You need fear nothing."

I don't think I quite believe that. Once again, she had no choice. Her only other option was taking off into the trees, and that was a highly questionable tactic at best. "I don't mean to be rude," she heard herself say, slowly, in the breathless high voice of a woman embarrassed at a dinner party. "But... who *are* you?"

Bad idea, Ari. Don't piss this guy off. You saw what he did to these robots, and he may have killed an entire castle full of them not too long ago as well, if you're understanding what the other guys said. You might want to play along for a little bit, until you can figure something else out.

But she had to, *needed* to know.

His mouth curved slightly, the expression too bitter to be a true smile. He left his hand out, hanging in midair as if it were perfectly normal to stand in pouring rain after killing a bunch of robots. Soft black flowers of hyperventilation-fueled oxygen deprivation bloomed around the edges of Ari's vision, and her knees decided there was a limit to the bullshit they could be asked to handle even if bolstered by magical appetite-suppressing pondwater and the relief of possibly, maybe not dying at the hands of giant armor suits full of red oil.

Wet grass and moss rushed up to meet her. The roaring in her ears swallowed her whole. Whatever answer he would have made was lost as she fled gratefully into a semidarkness spangled with silver dots and a strange, unwilling sense of comfort.

It didn't last nearly long enough, of course. Muffled thunder echoed, and a faint edge of woodsmoke intruded on the soft, restful blackness. Dry warmth enfolded her; the sensation was so luxurious Ari considered staying in the gentle numb fog of shock, leaving her body behind. A breathing doll, it could absorb whatever punishment Mike was dishing out, and she could creep back in later, bit by bit, assessing the damage slowly.

Sometimes he was repentant after an Incident, and would even protect her from Wanda Lee for a little while.

Orange and yellow light, a faint sap-bubbling hiss. Low murmurs of conversation. There was something springy under her, and her cheek rested on her bent arm. For a moment Ari thought she was about to open her eyes, sit up, and find Jazarl standing in the woods studying her intently again. There were movies about timeloops; being caught in one required solving a mystery and keeping your eyes open, learning bit by bit until you could do things right.

Except she was a very tired groundhog; she had no desire to repeat any single day in the past five years or so. Even the good ones like graduating college were tinted with the sorrow of Mom gone in that awful car accident, and the joy of her wedding had turned into breathless anxiety soon afterward.

"My lord prince?" A soft, cautious tone. She thought it was probably Darjeth, and he sounded utterly respectful. "We have a few flasks' worth, by our lady Moon's grace."

"I need nothing." A pause, a soft sound of metal sliding against itself. "Though I thank you for the offer. How fares Jazarl? And Naithor?"

"Both hale, and ready to serve." It was definitely the blue-eyed blond guy, though now not a single tinge of sarcasm tinted his tone. Ari liked him better when he was talking shit, but he probably—and very wisely—didn't want to mess with someone who could cut a giant horned robot in half. "Jazarl did all he could, my lord. 'Twas judged best to attempt reaching Gesthel with every possible speed, and each choice held more danger than the last. He—"

"And you entered the Keep to look for me, not once but twice." The chained man said it like he might remark it was raining, or a Tuesday. Thunder crashed, thankfully *outside*; Ari had rarely been so grateful for the bare concept of walls and a roof. "Brave almost to foolhardiness, the lot of you. And loyal."

"To the Moon, my lord—unto death, or worse. The faithless one and his Law find no friend among us." The words marched out like a catechism, or an allusion to some text Ari wasn't familiar with. "How fares our lady?"

"When she has regained some strength we shall strike for Gesthel; gentler care than ours is required." The chained man sounded thoughtful instead of angry, thankfully. "Though 'tis far better than I feared. You are to be commended, knights of the Keep."

"Will we return, then?"

"Once the filth is cleansed. Now go and rest. You may reassure your fellow knights that no shame is theirs, and all honour. Especially Jazarl of Atalan." The dismissal was plain, and there was the sound of cloth shifting, soft footsteps retreating.

Which left Ari with a choice—take a peek out at the world, risking some new terror, or stay tightly curled up inside her own head, safe but also leaving her body vulnerable? Either way, something was bound to go wrong. Even the effort of silently, internally brooding on her list of questions, terms, and implications was too much.

The silence was almost a living thing, the sensation of being watched undeniable. It could be felt on a crowded street or in a quiet college library, an atavistic tingle at one's nape, the lizard brain perking up through layers of evolution with a soft preverbal warning.

But she was so goddamn tired. All the shocks, strangeness, delirious detail—someone else could deal with things for a while.

Please. Just let me have a minute, even fifteen stupid seconds without anything else.

As if he had heard the thought, the chained man spoke again. "You do not remember," he said softly, conversationally. "It is a mercy, and my penance. Sleep, and fear nothing."

Ari sank into darkness, and did not dream.

17

A VERY LITTLE

THE SLIGHT SMOKE-SMELL WAS FROM ANOTHER EXPERTLY BUILT campfire, and the storm had passed. Their shelter was a small cave, hollowed from a rocky prominence covered with slim grey trees and thicker, darker ones which looked like evergreens, their bark rough and cedar-spicy. The forest glistened, gemmed with swiftly drying water under the same swollen red sun.

She hadn't seen a hill since arriving in this weird place, so it was both comforting and unnerving. The rock was black and looked at least part igneous, and Ari had to rub at her eyes because the forest now seemed old-growth. Great ferns had arisen amid glossy-leaved bushes, and there were new squat, thorny shrubs as well, their teeth exuding gummy red resin.

It was unexpectedly beautiful, especially with tracers of morning mist rising to a violet sky. No blue vault here, the sun was far too red.

Waking upon a pile of soft, freshly cut boughs in a small rock-walled chamber was one thing, peering around a craggy corner into a larger cave another. Finding Alzarien at the fire near the mouth of the outer chamber, humming slightly as he watched the fire and shifted arrows between a stack of quivers, was a relief. Ari approached tentatively. Her bootsoles sank into fine dry sand over the stone floor, and she wondered if the cavern's walls were carved or naturally striated. Faint glittering spatters like mica were trapped under the surface, winking cheerfully.

"Ah, there she is." The crimson-haired man grinned, fans of wrinkles creasing the corners of his dark eyes. He looked a lot fresher than he had the day before, stubble-free and downright perky. "Worry not, Jazarl and Majan are on watch outside, and the others have gone with our lord prince to collect equines. Indeed the forest is wondrous renewed, almost as before."

Judging by his tone, this was all good news.

"Equines?" At least her mouth didn't taste like morning. No hunger cramped Ari's middle, and she wasn't crusty from sleep. Yet the ghost of last night's storm-terror lingered in her arms and legs, echoes of thunder caught in flesh.

The Golden robots were bad enough, but the lack of needing a bathroom was far more disturbing once she really thought about it. She could almost believe she was in a catheterized coma, all this a vivid dream while her body shriveled on a hospital bed.

"Far better than walking to Gesthel." Alzarien rose, scooping up his canteen; it was the first time one of her new companions seemed, well, downright chatty. "The Grey Lady will be overjoyed, and her Fox hardly less pleased. Here."

The water still tasted good, and faint thirst retreated under its coolness. Ari was past wondering what the hell was in it—at a certain point, some shit was just too academic to worry about. There were far bigger questions, and it looked like this was her chance to ask a few. Ari studied the slope outside the cave-mouth. "So... everything's all right now?"

"Of a certainty. *He* is freed, you are returned. All that remains is the Bright King's fall."

So they really were a resistance movement, the chained man

their leader. There was, however, a new, troubling wrinkle. "Returned?"

Alzarien's cheerfulness faltered a bit. "Ah. Well, you see... that is, *he* says not to trouble you, since the manner of your leaving was..." A helpless gesture, hands spread, and the crimson-haired man accepted his canteen back with an anxious smile. "But there is no doubt. Your face is altered and your cloth passing odd, yet your silence is the same. Like speech itself."

Never been told that before. "Oh. Thank you." So they were mistaking her for someone else, or they had been waiting for someone from another world to show up? "Can you... can you tell me how I left?" Whoever they thought she was, it would be a valid question.

Or so she hoped. Ari eyed the hillside afresh. Two of the guys were outside, probably well camouflaged. That was good if there were more robots, very bad if she wanted to get away.

Was there anywhere safe to run to, though? She'd had a foggy plan for escaping the house on Hardison Hill just as soon as she could scrape together enough cash, but heading out into this wilderness was an entirely different proposition.

For the first time since she'd landed here, Ari was thinking clearly. Or at least, she *felt* clear, like the pondwater itself.

Alzarien's smile faded. "'Tis not a pleasant subject," he began, carefully. "Our lord prince said—"

Come on, dude. "Please?" She tried a smile of her own, hoping she wouldn't have to bat her eyelashes. If she could make even a single ally, maybe this entire nutso situation could be rendered at least workable.

As it was, the funny slipsliding sensation in her middle was uncomfortably akin to not knowing what the hell Mike was going to be mad about next, a sense that the eggshells she was walking on could turn to rattlesnakes at any moment.

"I should not." All the good cheer was gone. Alzarien looked wary now, dark eyes shuttered. His lashes were tipped with bright red, the detail too bizarre and well-executed for either painting or photo. "Enough that you have returned and our lord prince is saved, is it not?"

Saved? Well, that puts a different complexion on things. Plus, the chained man was the prince. She was getting more usable information, and that was great.

Sort of.

"I just got here," Ari persisted, in that soft, reasonable tone that sometimes worked. There was nothing to lose by trying. "And I'm confused. If I knew what happened, it would help me." *Please help me.* She held eye contact, earnest and nonthreatening, her very best social judo.

Alzarien's gaze darted to the cave mouth. "The faithless accursed killed our queen." The softly rolling language held inexpressible sadness, or maybe it was his tone, each word slow and pained.

Oh. Is that all? "The faithless accursed?" That sounded pretty awful.

"Ternek." The crimson-haired man's voice dropped to a mutter, as if the word was an obscenity. He regarded her steadily, the canteen dangling from one hand. "He strangled her on the shores of the Mere during the last Conjunction, and declared himself the Bright King. Our shock was great, our mourning even greater as his Blight spread. But now you are returned." His knuckles whitened; leather made a small creaking sound. "Do not ask me to describe it, my lady Ari. And please, in your mercy, do not tell anyone what I have said."

Well, she could keep a secret. God knew she'd had practice. "Thank you." Ari almost flinched, realizing she sounded prim instead of shocked. "I won't."

Strangled. Conjunction. Queen. Her entire list of new foreign words needed rearranging, and that would take some thought. Ari retreated from the red-sun morning, the forest, and the small campfire, which crackled merrily, without a care in the world.

Jesus Christ, what kind of fucked-up fairytale am I in?

The 'equines' turned out to be big horselike creatures with sharp hooves and mild dark eyes, though their teeth weren't even close to herbivore. Chestnut, dark grey, and deep brown, half a dozen of the critters grouped behind a slightly larger pure-black one; the only thing weirder than their fangs and tassel-tufted ears was the fact that they had saddles.

And bridles, too. Where had *those* come from?

Not-quite-horses, just like the not-possum. Ari hung back, sticking to the cave's mouth as the guys broke camp and moved among the mounts on the hillside, clearly pleased with this turn of events. Of course the huge black horse-thing was *his*, and it regarded her sidelong, ears perked and silken tail switching. Daylight flowed along the creature's curves, glistened on its hide, and showed every single link on the chains wrapping its rider.

The chained man still wore a layer of dull black iron links, criss-crossing his armored torso, sheathing his legs over cuisses and greaves, spiraling his metal-clad arms. A few hung free, swaying as he moved, and their faint chiming was a reminder that he could be silent when he chose to. The huge broadsword rode his back; every-thing about the guy was a little larger than life.

How did he walk with all that metal clinging to his limbs? He should have been clattering like a cartoon, but the chains seemed almost alive, testing the air and swaying independently. Last night was a confused jumble, but she remembered them shooting out like tentacles, shearing through huge gilded robots.

Ari had to admit magic was the best explanation for all this, which opened up a whole new world of questions she didn't feel nearly equipped to handle at the moment. Not after the morning's revelations, still turning round and round inside her head like a dog stamping down its bedding, refusing to settle quite yet.

Plus she kept getting distracted thinking of how an artist could capture the way the chains seemed near-sentient, supple as snakes. Maybe sculpture would be up to the task, but in what material?

Her few semesters of psych electives didn't make her qualified to judge, but she was fairly sure the distraction was a coping mechanism attempting to somehow keep her together after being dumped in the middle of a guerrilla situation on another planet, or dimension, or whatever.

The chained man looked much healthier in daylight, less haggard, rufous sunshine picking out highlights in his dark mane. Without the gloom his cheekbones weren't as startling, though those feverish eyes were just as hot and direct.

Ari cupped her elbows, feeling distinctly underdressed. Grass stains lingered on her jeans; her hair, though clean, was probably deeply unhappy with everything about this situation. It was a distinct blessing there wasn't a mirror around. Rumpled and unnerved, she gazed blankly at the surroundings.

This chain of events could even be grimly hilarious, if she looked at it the right way. Out of a frying pan into a forest fire. *Strangled on the shore of the Mere. Conjunction. You have returned. Our lord prince.*

Nuts. Bonkers. Crazy. Insane. If she started listing the synonyms aloud, how many would the invisible translator be able to handle? And the chained man kept *looking* at her, like he expected something. The black not-horse stretched its head over his ironclad shoulder with a very horsey snort, and a faint shadow of amusement crossed his face.

Just a flicker, there and gone. He patted the thing's cheek and stepped away, leaving the reins fastened to the saddlehorn.

"Oh, aye, now we may ache from riding instead of running." Darjeth was back to merry sarcasm; the sally drew a chorus of low male laughter.

"Next you will complain at sleeping in the saddle." Jazarl patted the neck of a brown equine, its mane and tail a much darker shade.

For all their ease, the guys were careful not to step within hoof-range behind the beasts, and clearly respected their teeth as well. "Now, if only we had armor..."

"Soon enough." Sarle's mount was a glossy chestnut; the stocky man fiddled with a stirrup, reins draped over his arm. "The *rukka*-bushes are growing, and there are signs of both *mja*-horn and pard upon the higher slopes. We shall have to be watchful."

It sounded like there were predators in this part of the forest, another unwelcome but dismally predictable development. There was no mention of other guerrilla detachments, unless this Grey Lady was a bandit leader—the prospect sounded both intriguing and terrifying at once, since Ari was expected to... what? Impersonate a figurehead? Was she being set up to Bonnie Prince Charlie against an army of robots?

Given how the chained man went through the big shining horrors, it sounded almost doable. But he'd been tied up in the castle. What would happen if he got put out of commission again? Ari's head hurt, attempting to sort all this out while wearing what was presumably the interested expression of someone who understood what the hell was going on.

"Easier from atop an equine." Majan laughed, settling his hat more firmly on his platinum mane. "The Fox will want a dappled grey for his lady."

Maybe the Fox was the main resistance leader, waiting for the rest to show up? It was a fine time to wish she'd studied more than art in history.

The chained man halted before the cave-mouth, visibly and scrupulously respecting her personal space. "My lady." The suggestion of a bow; no wonder he was a prince. "You will ride with me."

That's just great. "Are you sure?" Questioning him probably wasn't a good idea, but it was already out of her mouth and she watched carefully for any sign of irritation or displeasure, any twitch of an incipient punch or slap.

If he turned out to be like Mike, she was going to have to hit the woods no matter the other dangers involved. Nothing, no fantastical dimension or murderous fairytale landscape, would induce her to suffer that again. The prospect of running across robots, big carnivores, or worse was deeply unpleasant, but what else could she expect?

She was, after all, still alive. Perhaps that was the sin she was paying for.

The chained man regarded her levelly. "Would you prefer an equine of your own?" As if he could just pop down to the corner store for one.

Sorry, sir, my people ride Fords, Chevys, and cowboys, not thoroughbreds. She had to throttle a tide of dark, unpleasant hilarity; nobody here was interested in Ariadne Millar's Comedy Stylings.

So she simply shook her head, trying for a conciliatory expression. "I'm sorry." She was going to be repeating it in this new language too. The habit of apologies would follow her into the grave.

Now *there* was a pleasant and extremely lucky thought.

"No need," he said, gravely. The phrase was familiar—he'd used it before, from the echoing darkness of a steel helmet, and without the reverb he sounded almost normal. "We ride to Gesthel; your most favoured companion lingers there with her Fox. There will be much joy in the reunion, she also holds summat which belongs to you. Will..." He paused, dark eyes half-lidded for a moment. "Will you at least consent to ride, my lady Ari? They say that is your name, now."

It's always been my name. "Ariadne." The correction slipped out before she could stop herself; if they expected a plausible figure-head they were going to have to give her more information to work with. "But Ari is fine. Are you sure you want me to go along?" Inspiration struck. "You'll probably go faster without, um, someone new."

The guys were busy taking their not-horses downhill. Sarle swung into the saddle; naturally all of them would know how to perform the maneuver. Ari liked drawing horses or seeing them in paintings, but she'd never been atop one and didn't think now was any time to start.

Not if she could help it.

The chained man took a step closer; clearly she was his problem now. Dull black metal drank the light, odd glints escaping here and there. "This place pleases you so much, then? Or is it my company you dislike?"

Oh, God. "No, it's..." *Crap.* She realized, from the unsteady feeling under her breastbone, that she was pushing to see how far this man would let her resist. Her shoulder pressed against the side of the cave-mouth, rough rock against flannel sleeve.

Who made the men's clothes, or their weapons? Where had they gotten the saddles? Was magic a good enough explanation for all this? "I just don't want to bother anyone," she finished. *Lame, Ari. He's not going to believe that bullshit.*

But if he was going to explode, she needed to know.

His jaw set, a muscle flicking in one pallid cheek. Had he left his cloven helmet where it dropped, in the castle's thick shadow? He studied her closely, and Ari shrank even further.

Another day, another angry man. Even magic couldn't change that one essential fact of the universe.

"Ah." Quietly. "You are frightened of me."

I know what men are like. And you really are scary as fuck. "I don't know what's happening. One moment I'm..." Words failed her. "The next I'm here, and then there's a road and the Keep and..."

"You remember nothing, yet you freed me." His head tilted back, and that tiny flicker in his cheek was more pronounced as he stared at the hilltop, or the purple-tinted sky. "Too brave for my comfort, as ever." His chin drew level once more, those dark eyes scorching afresh.

Nobody's ever called me brave before. Except maybe Mom. Thinking about her mother was a good way to get even further distracted, and Ari needed all the wits she could scrape together for this.

Once they figured out she was just an inadvertent trespasser, what would happen? Those swords were awful sharp, and the arrows too. She was caught between a possible punishment from these people at some unspecified future date, or attempting to rough it in the wilderness while trying to stay far away from giant robots and those horrible, unseen moaning things splatting down the road last night.

Had it really been just last night? Time had come unmoored, and she was drowning.

The chained man took another step, with strangely diffident caution. He couldn't possibly be afraid of a woman less than half his size. "Come." Businesslike now, he held out one gauntleted hand again, palm-up. "Trust me a very little, as you trusted my knights. I will not lose you again."

'Again' is doing a lot of work in that sentence, my guy. The terror of her young nightmares vied with unwilling comfort, and the silent firework of a further realization dilated inside the jumble passing for her brain. "I don't even know your name." She sounded like a complete dope, but she couldn't look away. In broad—if reddish—daylight, he was a different animal.

Maybe she looked like one, too.

"It was burned out of me," he replied gravely. "I shall be granted another when it pleases you. For now, though..." A slight, beckoning motion.

He doesn't even have a name? Oh, this is bullshit, Ariadne. Run while you can, get the hell out of here. But she had no choice, and in any case, Ari was... curious? Was that the word?

There was only so much fear a human being could handle before she simply stopped caring. She had to try twice before she could loosen her arms, and finally laid her fingers against warm, supple leather. There was a thick iron strap crossing his palm as well, tanned animal hide and metal enclosing a hand that had killed, and killed again—assuming the robots were alive.

The gauntlet closed. Metal whispered gently, cradling instead of crushing. Sharp edges brushed her skin, refraining from puncture with exquisite control.

"I've never ridden an equine before," she managed. Even with the magic pondwater, her throat was dry. Thankfully, the sensation bore little relation to Mike's fingers digging in, or the dusty tight-lodged rock of panic when Wanda Lee hissed *just you wait until my son comes home, little missy*.

"You once enjoyed it," the chained man said. "Let us see if you still do."

18

THE BREACH

IT WASN'T THE MOST UNCOMFORTABLE SHE'D EVER BEEN, BUT ARI still might have preferred walking. She couldn't really think while busily pretending she sat on top of a massive moving quadruped every day of the week, ho-hum, nothing to see here, move along.

The chained man held the reins, strolling at the beast's head, while she clutched the saddlehorn and tried not to feel ridiculous. Downhill and through thick forest the group moved, then the road appeared through a screen of underbrush. The chained man didn't break stride, stepping onto its surface. More hills rose on either side, though the road somehow avoided any in its arrow-straight course; the slopes were all of the same stone as the morning's cave, covered thickly with vegetation, and not a single almost-mountain had been topped.

Jazarl and his guys seemed happy to have their big friend back, riding in a loose pack surrounding her and the chained man. Every once in a while a pair would peel off, ranging ahead or dropping behind according to some arcane schedule, and rejoin the group a short while later, melding out of the trees. The equines' hooves made happy chiming sounds on stone paving, and she decided they were definitely shod. Which brought up the question of just who had done that?

Their conversation was minimal, and mostly cryptic. The Breach. Gesthel. The Grey Lady. How happy she was going to be to see Ari. The Mere.

At least she didn't have to worry about where her feet were going, so she could gawk at the scenery all she wanted. Was it possible to draw on horseback? You certainly couldn't paint.

Watercolors would work for the near-violet sky, she decided, but the woods required colors which didn't bleed so easily. There were more and different plants now, in every stage of maturity. Maple-like trees with bright red foliage had appeared, as well as pale-barked almost-aspens, and near-willows with purple fingers. Ferns exploded, still wet with rain. Droplet-gemmed bushes thickened or thinned according to light through the canopy. No debris settled on the road; pristine and whole, it cut through the woods in merry defiance of its own impossibility. The stone blocks seemed more yellow today, somewhere between lemon and light amber, but maybe that was the particular cast of the tired red light.

Each leaf was distinct, every fallen twig unique. She glimpsed flutters that had to be birds, though not clearly enough to guess what they resembled, and other animals probably knew to avoid any sounds meaning 'human-like things'.

At least riding didn't feel particularly like a punishment, unless it was one of pure embarrassment.

"My lady?" Darjeth leaned from his saddle, offering her one of their oddly shaped leather canteens. "We may halt at any moment, for your comfort."

Ari didn't need more water, but she took the offer anyway—maybe she could get more answers. All she had at the moment was a contradictory half-mosaic; survival would depend on what role they wanted her to play. "Everything looks different."

"All is renewed, and heals apace. You need not worry, though." Darjeth's grin was broad and chipper, his wide-brimmed, very handsome hat pushed slightly back and platinum hair touching his shoulders. Even the signs of wear on his leather jerkin, the stitches on his shirt, and the nap of his trousers were startlingly clear; his rapier-hilt bobbed, glinting. "The pards will not trouble us, nor the *kaharak.*"

Well, she could almost be comforted if she knew precisely what either of those translated to. She was too busy with another question. "What about the..." *Robots. How do I say robots?* But they had a different word, one that arrived with a few moments' thought. "The clockworks."

Darjeth sobered, glancing in the chained man's direction—a flicker, nothing more. "If any appear, my lady, they shall be quickly dealt with."

What about the moaning things? Her courage didn't extend far enough for that particular question. She uncapped the canteen slowly, trying to organize what she needed to know.

There had to be a better way of navigating fairytale nonsense. She wasn't a lit major, though she'd read Grimm's just like any other kid. Go figure, she should have studied up on politics, Che Guevara, or separatists instead of major artistic themes in the late Renaissance or methods of sculpture from Michelangelo to Rodin.

Three whole years since she'd been able to sit down and read a book. She was free of Mike and his parents, but there didn't seem to be any libraries around. A pained laugh bubbled into her throat; she chased it away with a swallow of pondwater.

It tasted just the same—clear and cool, no trace of leather from its container. Now she wished she'd spent last night trawling through memories of literature instead of passed out from stress and overload.

"Keep it, if you like." Darjeth indicated the canteen with a brief, efficient motion. They moved so gracefully, and she was a gawky, waddling duckling. "We should reach the Breach before long, and Gesthel near sundown. The Grey Lady will speak again, seeing you, and perhaps afterward we shall break the faithless accursed's—"

"All will be accomplished in due time," the chained man interrupted. "And I doubt our lady wishes a mention of the enemy."

I wouldn't mind knowing a little more. But clearly it wasn't part of the agenda, so Ari just returned the canteen with a tentative smile. Darjeth looked relieved, but he also steered his horse away and didn't approach again.

Ari suppressed a sigh, and went back to studying the rain-washed landscape.

She was still thinking furiously when they reached the Breach.

Thin purple clouds stretched across the sky, moving gently with a steady breeze. The trees drew back as if afraid, revealing undulating green starred with more of the high rocky hills. It might have been a welcome change if not for the great jagged crevasse slashing across their route.

Even the flowers were vivid, white and deep blue roaming in bands over the hills, peeking through vigorous mint-smelling grass. But the tear in the earth looked fresh and awful, its sides sharp and a faint hollow whistle rising from its lip. It looked bigger than the Grand Canyon—that particular geographical feature had been on Mom's bucket list, one of the few items not crossed off.

The lemon-brick road ran right up to the brink. Ari rubbed at her eyes, once more not quite believing what pupils and optic nerves were passing down the ol' brain highway.

A massive long-dead creature had fallen across the canyon somehow. Either that or bones had been dragged from the huge animal's grave, because spanning the Breach was a long chain of giant vertebrae, faintly tarnished. Curved ribs rose, smaller near the chasm's edges and gradually larger as the skeletal wonder bowed near midpoint. The wind fluted through bony reeds, a long modulated moan, and Ari's stomach clenched as if every ounce of pondwater had suddenly turned toxic and was going to bolt for escape.

Oh, no. There was nowhere to go since hills and forest had sunk into a dark smudge behind them; she clutched the saddlehorn, leaning back as her entire body tensed, and tried to think of how to refuse this.

It wasn't so much the height, although she was uneasy as any reasonable person should be with skyscrapers and cliffs. No, it was the... the bones, the thought of walking over a corpse, something that unholy large plus the subtle but undeniable strangeness of the structure.

Even dinosaur skeletons didn't look this *alien*. Now she was glad she hadn't seen any of the forest's fauna, but that was no help in the situation. Atavistic shudders poured down her back.

The big black equine slowed, its tail flicking, and the chained man halted. Which meant everyone else did too, and the men exchanged glances.

"My lady?" The chained man turned, regarding her sidelong. Walking with all that metal piled on had to be exhausting, but it didn't show.

In fact, he was far less pale than he had been; maybe it was just being free of the helmet. His face had filled in a little more as well, though with that jaw he wouldn't win any modeling work. Still, he was arresting.

"I'm sorry." Another apology, she was helpless to stop making them. "That... no. I'm sorry, I can't."

Majan was to her left now. He eyed the bone-bridge, cocking his ivory-haired head. "It is quite strong, and larger than it looks. There is no danger, my lady."

He could even be right, but there was only so much of this strange new world Ari could take. This was her tipping point, everything inside her trembling on the edge of the small, definite *snap* which meant she could not be pushed further.

The last time that silent internal breakage had sounded, she'd lunged for a nightstand and the .38.

"I..." At least nobody had yelled at her to stop being such a whiny bitch yet, though Ari suspected that was a blessing of exceedingly short duration. "I can't. I'm very sorry, but I just... I can't."

"There are other methods of crossing." The chained man turned more fully, and iron-clad fingers lightly stroked the equine's arched, glossy neck. "I suspect you would like them less, though."

His tone was soft, as if it wasn't a threat. Ari's pulse ran thin and thready in her wrists, her throat, even her ankles. "I'll stay in the woods. Or I can go back to the cave." The mind-boggling stupidity of wandering around without anything to build a fire with or a weapon against giant golden robots was fully apparent to her rational self, but Ari didn't care.

"Sarle, Darjeth." The chained man's burning gaze focused fully on her now. "Would you like the honour of crossing first, to show our lady there is no danger?"

"Of a certainty." Sarle touched his hatbrim, smiling; he didn't look like he thought the task was a punishment. Ari opened her mouth to protest, but he and Darjeth were already urging their mounts into a canter. They drew away, the chiming of their passage thankfully different than the thump-thudding of gilded clockworks.

The rest of the group set off at a far slower pace, the chained man now at the big black equine's shoulder though he still held the reins. Ari weighed the advisability of trying to topple out of the saddle. Each measured step, by hoof or spurred boot, brought those terrible arches of bleached bone closer. The skeleton's strange geometry, just a few degrees off anything earthly, grew more and more apparent.

"What is it you fear?" The chained man looked up, eyebrows slightly raised and his tone holding only mild interest. For all that, those eyes were absolutely scorching. "I am still somewhat fettered, true. Yet I would never imperil my lady upon an unsteady span."

It didn't make sense, and Ari was helpless to explain. A giant interior framework of no creature she'd ever seen or imagined, its skull and bony hindquarters sunk deep in grassy earth—a small faint charity, that she was spared the rest of its nauseating insult to all rationality, but not enough. To top it off, the crevasse's true dimensions became more and more apparent with every moment, and that constant, faint moan-whistle said anything dropped in would fall for a very long time.

Please. Maybe she would have some kind of cardiac event, and this whole shebang would become academic? *Don't make me do this.*

Begging wouldn't help in the slightest; Ari had learned as much over the last three years. No-one cared, so she might as well save her breath. She watched the two riders, Darjeth's pale hair shining and Sarle on his dark-brown equine pulling slightly ahead as if he couldn't wait to throw himself onto the damn thing. The giant bridge was absurdly miniature in comparison to the rift stretching upon either side, but that wasn't helpful either.

The hoofbeats changed. Sarle's equine thundered up the slight rise, easily dwarfed by the smallest, floating ribs, and clattered onto stone-laced vertebrae. Darjeth followed.

Thankfully the edifice didn't sway, even minutely. But she still didn't like it, and cast around once more for some kind of escape. It was awful, watching the thing approach at walking pace—as if the riders were standing still while a vast bone-monster slunk closer bit by bit, humming to itself, contemplating an unwary meal.

"You see?" Jazarl, with an anxious edge to the words. "The Breach is wide, but the bridge has always been here, my lady Ari."

Please don't. Oh, God, please don't make me do this.

By the time the main group reached the bridge's near end, Sarle and Darjeth were halfway across. Thin rancid horror crawled up Ari's throat; the sides of the Breach were sheer, plunging down to billows of white mist. Creepers and dark vegetation clung in scallops to the rock walls, life finding a way even on near-vertical faces, and her skin prickled all over.

The chained man dropped back still further, his spiked shoulder very near her knee. Maybe he wanted to be sure she wouldn't make a break for it. If there were any lemmings around, they might well be hypnotized by both bridge and chasm, gratefully throwing them-selves into oblivion rather than suffering the violation of having to *look* at the damn thing or hear that awful fluting unsong from wind-caressed ribs.

Ari squeezed her eyes shut, but she still knew the moment hoof touched stone-bound bone. A faint vibration rose, or maybe she was shaking again. Even disassociating couldn't save her; she had to cling to the saddle. The horselike thing snorted, a dissatisfied sound, and she wondered if her tension was communicating itself to the beast.

"All is well, Ariadne." Softly, the accent of their strange language caressing her name. "I am with you; there is nothing to fear."

I really wish I could believe that. It would be nice, especially given the number of times after Mom's passing she'd longed to hear someone say just those words. There was always plenty to be afraid of in the world; growing up was all about finding out nobody could —or would—help.

Something warm and hard closed around her knee. Ari started violently, the saddle creaking as her eyelids flew open, and the black equine gave another short, unhappy chuffing sound.

The chained man still held the reins loosely in one hand, but the other rested on her jeans. His palm, not the spikes on the back, but still, metal brushed her leg and she was painfully aware of how sharp the edges of his armor were. Not to mention the dangerous chains, one falling from his forearm almost brushing the horselike thing's side.

He stared up at her, not watching where his feet were landing. Ari's hair lifted on the breeze, a curl falling in her face, and a scalding flush poured through her entire body.

"You see?" Was he trying to sound, of all things, *encouraging?* "Wider than the Road itself, my lady."

Which brought up another interesting observation. She hadn't seen a single intersection yet, just the endless stone-block highway.

But Ari had no time to tease out the implications of yet more weirdness.

She shut her eyes once more, did her best to keep her ears from registering the wind's plaintive siren hum, and shivered until the sound of hoofbeats changed again, the equine now plodding downhill. The Breach's terrible, randomly wandering lament retreated bit by bit. Though the prickles still washed over her, no trace of sweat rose on her skin, and that was almost stranger than the lack of hunger.

Eventually the hand on her knee fell away. Ari kept her eyelids firmly sealed for a long while afterward, her lips moving slightly as she prayed, a chain of words both hopeless and useless when faced with a world where animals with such skeletons had indubitably once existed.

Please, I take it back. I didn't mean to. Please let me wake up...

There was no answer, just the wind-moan dying behind them, the rhythm of shod hooves on stone, and the sense of being watched even though the chained man faced resolutely ahead.

19

LONG WAIT OVER

GESTHEL TURNED OUT TO BE A TOWN SET AMID ROLLING grassland starred with occasional streams and dark copses—or more properly a village, Ari decided, since it wasn't even big enough for a stop sign, let alone a light. Given that this world looked pre-electricity as well as pre-industrial it was a moot point, but her brain simply wouldn't stop zigzagging around, staggering drunkenly from one terrible, outlandish implication to the next.

She couldn't even recite the list of most important foreign words to brood over. They jumbled together inside her head, hopelessly tangled, and each time the wind shushed over rippling grass she had to suppress a shudder. The sun swelled still further as it approached horizon, sinking rapidly through thin indigo cloud-veils into a fury of orange, crimson, and ruddy gold.

She couldn't even be glad of figuring out the word for *west*— more properly, *place where the sun dies*—in their rolling tongue.

Thatched roofs over white-plastered walls decked with black trim, the houses huddled around the road. Smaller paved arteries now branched off on either side, as if her recognizing the lack of intersections had summoned them into existence. The houses had window-boxes holding riots of cascading green vines and orange blossom. Windows were all shuttered fast, heavy dark wooden doors tightly sealed. Faint noises wandered between buildings as if the place remembered being inhabited, but not a soul was in sight save small wildlife. Fenced garden plots were overgrown and deserted; small brown and white birds twittered under thatched eaves, hopping along flagstone paths. Something that looked like a bluejay swooped from one roof, wheeling past the group and streaking between two houses. Ari also glimpsed a pair of wide golden eyes and a flash of grey fur, probably another not-possum.

The animal life was reassuringly near-normal—maybe all the creatures shaped like the Breach bridge-thing were extinct? Still, the rest of the surroundings were so creepy she preferred the forest. Except that was crawling with armored robots. Maybe the castle would be better?

No good, the guys said there were shattered robot corpses inside now. Nowhere to rest, not even a closet with someone yelling outside.

The group stopped, all the guys rapidly dismounting before one of the last houses on the left—a structure larger than the others, its garden *not* overgrown but trim and well-weeded behind a low white-painted wooden fence. An arch covered with blue flowers on thick, ropy vines held a white gate. A thin thread of smoke rose from the cottage's chimney, and Ari was now faced with the problem of how to get down from the horselike thing with her legs numb and the rest of her not too happy either.

The chained man lifted his arms, clearly expecting her to know what the hell. She decided it would be least awkward to attempt mounting in reverse, since falling on her ass was more embarrassing but less painful than on her silly head.

Getting her knee up enough to hitch one leg awkwardly over the beast's massive rump was a problem, and letting go of the saddle to trust-fall on the way down was even worse. But her waist was caught and she was lowered, slowly and carefully, until her boots touched the road.

Her knees buckled, but he didn't let go. Ari found herself facing the warm living bulk of the equine with its faint scent of fur and fresh air, the chained man behind her, equally warm despite his metal sheathing. His chin dropped, breath touching her hair, and under the smell of sun-warmed iron was a tinge of spice and musk mixed with the odor of a big, clean male animal.

Oh, no. Panicked retreat wasn't possible. The thought of what Mike would do if he found out she'd been this close to another man swam through her, retreated on a wave of hot acid-blue fear.

"A day's easy jaunt," he said softly. "Though perhaps not for one who is unused to such things. Tell me, do mortals still ride?"

"It's my first time." Trying to explain cars to this guy probably wouldn't get them anywhere, though the distinct implication that others from Ari's particular world had stumbled into this one was enough to check off a mental box next to that item on her question-list. Would her hair start turning a vivid Kool-Aid shade if she survived long enough?

Ari took a deep breath, willing her lower half to shape up and do its job. As soon as she tensed he retreated a bit and she could turn, unsteady on wobbly knees.

But he was still far too close, looming over her. She froze, staring at the chains crisscrossing his broad, armored chest.

"Ah." Did he sound faintly amused again? How did someone so big, scary, and metal-clad manage that trick? "Shall I carry you, my lady? It would be an honour."

Oh, hell. Now he was mocking her. Ari shook her head, and to prove it she sidled toward the horse-beast's front end. That made her back brush against the animal's shoulder, but it didn't seem to mind.

The chained man stepped away, almost reluctantly. His gaze locked with hers, though, and the stupid flush was back, rising in her cheeks.

Maybe it was a side effect of the pondwater. She could do with
another shot right about now, but that was probably out of the
question.

A new voice broke the village's murmuring quiet. "And what is
this? Visitors, at such an hour."

A tall, dark-haired man appeared in the largest cottage's now-
open door, a pale streak glowing at his right temple. He wore a
version of the other guys' Robin Hood getup, but in grey cloth and
likewise indeterminate leather, no hat, and his boots taller than
theirs though clearly just as functional. Shadows moved behind
him, along with warm yellow lamplight rendered pale by rubescent
sunset; his grey gaze was cool and direct, his thin mouth set as if he
didn't like what he saw.

The chained man half-turned, glancing absently at the house,
and Ari peered under the equine's head, suddenly finding her
balance. The sensation was very much like being plonked on dry
land after a long ferry ride, and she edged from behind the big black
creature, thinking a little distance from both something with those
sharp teeth *and* the chained man's razor edges might be a good idea.

"My lord Fox," Jazarl called. "We come bearing good news, for
once."

The pale-eyed man might have replied, but the motion behind
him turned into the first woman Ari had seen in this place.

She was slim and short, only reaching the grey-clad man's shoulder, and pushed past him with no visible fear. At first Ari thought
she was elderly, since her hair was a wildly curling ashen mass, small
braids on either side of her heart-shaped face to hold it back, the
rest falling past her hips. Her dress was ash-colored as well, low-
waisted in a V, double sleeves with the underlayer close to her wrist
and the outer falling free, a hint of décolletage showing at the
square neckline. Her eyes were wide and dark, the lids swollen and
reddened as if she'd just finished crying, and her pretty, aristocratic
nose was pink.

This had to be the Grey Lady, Ari decided, and watched curiously as the woman hopped down two wide, whitewashed stone steps. The man followed closely, every line expressing protectiveness; his palm rested easily on a plain, functional rapier hilt at his low-slung leather belt.

The woman's hands raised to her mouth, her shoulders hunching. Her gaze was locked on Ari as she nearly staggered down the flagstone path, past well-trimmed mounds of greenery and red trumpet-shaped flowers. Other plants bloomed riotously on either side—blue, purple, white, and pale green like some species of hellebore—and one high-arched, succulent bush held spiny fruit looking amazingly like cactus.

Jazarl and the others moved aside, Sarle chirruping gently to his equine.

"Careful, Hannixe." The grey-clad man tried to get in front of the woman, but she was too quick and the gate under the arch squeaked slightly as she blundered through. Her skirts made a sweet silken sound, and heavily embroidered slippers—black thread on grey material—peeked from under the hem as she reeled.

Is she okay? Ari glanced nervously over her shoulder. The chained man did not move, his gauntleted hands held carefully at his sides.

The woman's pace quickened. She made a beeline for Ari, and there was nowhere to go except ducking behind the equine again. But the Grey Lady didn't look angry, just distressed, so Ari's hands moved on their own, lifting and spreading, an instinctive move to offer comfort.

"My lord prince." The man in grey made a perfunctory bow in the chained man's general direction, but his gaze never left the woman who let out an inarticulate sobbing noise and flung her arms around Ari, hugging tightly.

She was taller than Ari—everyone was, in this place—and her chin touched Ari's cheek; she smelled of a light floral perfume and sweet health, a lingering touch of green sap. Her breath sobbed in, out, and she held on like she was drowning. Ari hugged back, confused and wondering if the other woman needed some kind of rescue. Eight armed men, the odds were bad, but maybe—

"Oh, m-my queen," the Grey Lady stammered in a husky, broken voice, each word cracked and halting. "Oh, b-by silver, it is you, you have f-finally..." A huge, shuddering inhale, and her grip tightened again. "Finally. You have r-returned. Oh, blessed day, blessed d-day."

The grey-clad man's jaw dropped; he recovered quickly, and his next bow was not cursory at all but deep, respectful, and aimed at Ari. "Blessed indeed," he echoed. "The long wait is over."

The thatched house's interior was pure medieval cottagecore except for large metallic globes held in branching wooden stands or jutting from the walls, providing steady golden light. Ari half expected to see antique switches and outlets, but none were apparent; a prosaic wood-fueled blaze crackled merrily in the big stone fireplace. Three chunky wooden chairs with heavy overstuffed cushions sat nearby, accompanied by mismatched ottomans; long benches crouched on either side of the front door, the left with a row of pegs over it and the right under a heavily shuttered window with a thick wooden bar. An honest-to-gosh spinning wheel stood in one corner; a butcherblock table laden with bunches of herbs, a black iron cauldron, alembics and other paraphernalia lingered along the back wall, and every window, not just the front, was shuttered as well as barred.

Except for that little detail, it could have been a Pre-Raphaelite stage set. Especially with the inhabitant's graceful skirts and sweet heart-shaped face. Rosetti would have loved her, though she didn't have Siddons's lush mouth.

"'Tis homelike, at l-least." The Grey Lady coughed delicately, the back of one hand held to her lips; her cheeks glistened with fresh tears. "Oh, pay no m-mind to my weeping; joy is difficult after s-so much sorrow. Let me..." She threw her arms around Ari again, squeezing hard, and it wasn't so bad to have the shakes if someone else was trembling too.

"It's all right," Ari repeated, faintly. Why couldn't she have met this woman first? The relief of another female creature was almost as overwhelming as the fear. "I, uh... I don't know..."

"You must be so c-confused." She cleared her throat, and only let go of Ari to hold her at arm's length, stepping back and examining her from head to toe with swift thoroughness. "Recently mortal, our lord prince said? And arrived but a few nights ago. Come, this way."

The guys evidently had no problem having this lady deal with the problem Ari represented. A hot shameful burst of gratitude almost made her stupid knees buckle again.

A staircase reared behind a thick fall of heavy dark-blue cloth. The Grey Lady beckoned her along, and Ari found herself obeying with the dazed feeling of a good dream instead of nightmare. "I woke up in a pond." It didn't sound completely outlandish, which was great; still, if this woman didn't believe her, what would she do? "And I don't know anything. Mortal, Underdark, faithless accursed —they keep saying these things, and I don't... I don't..."

"Men." The other woman held her skirts with one hand as she climbed, an easy natural movement. Her voice was far less hoarse now, an instrument regaining flexibility after much-needed tuning up. "Once they s-stable the equines they will r-return, and Keners will bar the door. He is quite—but forgive me, I was never so ch-chattersome before. Come, come. You are d-dressed most oddly; we shall remedy that."

Oh, great. Ari had to keep a hand on the plastered wall since there was no banister, and she climbed slowly, getting both boots on a step before attempting the next one. "You're very kind," she began, diplomatically. "But I was thinking, maybe I should just—"

"And your accent is so charming! S-so quaint." The Grey Lady reached the head of the stairs and turned, almost hopping on slippered feet as she made balletic hurrying movements with her pretty hands. She coughed again, dryly, and Ari thought maybe *she* needed some magic pondwater. "We will have long ch-chats, just as w-we used to."

Used to? "I'm very sorry." Ari halted on the next stair, bracing herself against the wall. "But I'm not what you think."

For Chrissake, just play along, the voice of self-preservation howled inside her head. But she couldn't lie to this very nice woman, and if she was going to make any sort of move on her own instead of being dragged along in a fucked-up fairytale the time was probably now.

Like what? Come on, Ari. Just like her hazy fantasies of escaping the mansion on Hardison Hill, any attempt to improv against the script these people operated from was doomed to failure.

The scenery was different, but she was still trapped.

"You don't r-remember." The Grey Lady became somber, her big dark eyes glistening. The red rims of her eyelids looked as if she'd sobbed so hard something was permanently damaged, and a sharp thin pang speared Ari's chest. "That is n-natural. But you are our lady Moon. *He* would not b-be here otherwise." Funny, how the stress on a pronoun could make the subject so clear.

"All I did was get his sword," Ari mumbled, and immediately wanted to kick herself. She'd been so careful not to breathe a word of finding the chained man in the Keep—although it seemed faintly ridiculous now, since he could very much tell the guys himself.

Had he? The thought made her feel vaguely unsteady. Not so much as the horrible bone-bridge over the canyon, though. Her knees, not to mention her stomach, were *still* unhappy about that— and what else was lurking on this terrible planet?

She should be counting her blessings, really. What if the landslide had knocked her somewhere there wasn't breathable air instead of this terrifying, beautiful place?

"And do you think any but the Moon herself could have freed that blade?" The Grey Lady shook her head. "Come, m-my queen.

A few more steps, a bath, and then we shall have you in some more c-comfortable cloth. We are friends of old, and you will remember soon enough."

Will I? When was the last time she'd had a female friend? She and Mom had moved so often, then graduation and Mike had separated her from college roommates. Women weren't automatically trustworthy, of course—look at Wanda, for example. But still...

Ari hesitated, and the Grey Lady stepped down once, twice. She reached for Ari's free hand, cradling it in both of hers, and had to hunch slightly to do so, slim shoulders curving inward.

"I am Hannixe," she said, in that husky, broken little voice, gazing into Ari's eyes. "I have n-not spoken since you left. Do you think I would now, if I did not r-recognize what you are?"

Ari's mouth crumpled. *Oh, crap. Don't cry, don't you dare cry.*

But it was no use. The tears came anyway, and she let the other woman draw her up the final few steps.

❦ 20 ❦

HAVE THE HONOUR

A BATHTUB OF BRIGHT COPPERY METAL CROUCHED IN A SMALL tiled room, and though Ari would have never believed it, the house seemed to have enough plumbing to bring hot, faintly floral-scented water from a curved pipe set in the wall when Hannixe pulled a chain.

The other woman even turned politely away while Ari struggled out of every stitch—jeans, T-shirt, flannel, underthings, socks—to clamber into the tub. At least she hadn't had to put up with an underwire during all this, and the chained man's magic laundry-and-shower service meant her socks weren't overly ripe. Her hiking boots looked sadly battered; even though high-quality they were also old, and had seen service she was certain they hadn't been designed for.

The Grey Lady settled on a small three-legged stool beside the tub; Ari sat in silken-hot water, hugging her bare knees. How long had it been since she'd taken an actual bath? The copper container was luxuriously deep, but she still felt... vulnerable.

"'Tis good *he* did not see these." Hannixe peered at the healing bruises on Ari's arm—some from being yanked around during the fight against the clockworks, the dim shadows of older ones layered underneath. There were more up and down her ribcage and on her thighs; apparently the magical pondwater eased pain and sped healing, but couldn't completely erase damage. The back of her head wasn't tender anymore, though, and no scabs met her questing fingertips when Ari poked under her hair. "And on your throat, I did not notice those before either. The mortal realm is cruel."

This one seems pretty violent too. "It was an accident." The lie was reflexive, even in their strange language. "Did you... Are you mortal too?"

"I was awakened in the Whispering; some of your companions are thus. Others were found in the mortal realm long ago." Hannixe's large dark eyes, thickly lashed, widened a bit. She searched Ari's face, and her expression was like an emergency room nurse who knew very well what had happened but was constrained from comment.

Okay. So some are native, and others are... well, at least we're all bipeds. Ari quickly shifted her gaze to her wet knees, bearing their own ghostly healing bruises and scrapes from God alone knew what. Making her own face a mask to fend off interest or sympathy was an old habit as well. Water lapped the tub's sides as she shifted. The heat was delicious, soothing faint aches and threatening to turn her into a puddle.

It was the nicest thing about this place so far. But the question of just precisely where she was—another planet, an alternate dimension, Tir nan Og—wouldn't go away, a nagging pebble worked into a sandal's sole. And the term *found in the mortal world* was thought-provoking as well.

If the wormhole or fairy door was two-way, that was certainly a new piece of information. She couldn't decide if it was comforting or terrifying.

"Well," the Grey Lady said, finally. Her stutter, like the hoarseness, continued to ebb. "You are here now, and our lord prince will n-not allow further misfortune. He is your first companion and eldest servant."

He what, now? "Ah." Ari wished she could press a rewind button on the invisible translator. "Maybe he should find a different job?" The final word was more like *occupation* since there didn't seem to be a term approximate to *career*.

Hannixe's laugh was bell-like, beautiful as the rest of her, echoing against the tiles. Why didn't they nominate *her* for the position of whatever-the-hell? She was certainly more equipped than one tired, battered runaway murderess.

It was self-defense, Ari told herself. The enormity of what she had done hung over her, a wave ready to crash at any moment. Of course, guys who carried bows and rapiers were probably a little more forgiving of her desperate act than, say, a county judge.

Hannixe's merriment faded; she tilted her head slightly. "Do you think that would please him?" A few small beads of steam-moisture clung to her glossy grey hair. "But let us speak of other things. How has the mortal realm changed? It has been long indeed since we rode to find new companions, or even simply for our queen's amusement. I wonder at their dreams—have they gone sour?"

Sweetie, you have no idea. "It's really different than here." Ari tried to imagine any of these people seeing a car for the first time, or a high-definition flatscreen. A smartphone.

Now she really wished she hadn't lost the revolver. Jazarl and his guys would probably be all-in on gunpowder, assuming it would put a dent in the big robot-things.

"Well, no matter, there is plenty of time to find out. The Underdark is renewing, and when you visit the Mere..." Hannixe's broad, happy smile was a wonder, even if her cheeks were still damp and eyelids swollen. "But before that, we must make you comfortable. I have a gown that will suit, brought from the Keep. I have also kept something for you, and will return it anon."

"That's really kind of you." If they started giving Ari heirlooms, it was going to get super awkward. This wasn't the first mention of the 'Mere', either, and apparently something was supposed to happen in that vicinity. Maybe some sort of guerrilla gathering? "But all I need is..."

What? What exactly did she want? Well, staying in this bathtub forever would be a good start, though hardly rational or achievable.

"I can barely believe it." Hannixe's fingers were cool and dry, brushing a wet curl resting on Ari's shoulder as if touching something precious. "So long, waiting and never speaking. How could I, with my queen gone? And in such t-terrible circumstances; there is not a sword sharp enough to p-punish the faithless accursed for what he has done. But I suspect our lord prince will find one to suit, and you need only stay with us. S-say you will, my lady Ari." Her eyes shone, and her accent on the name was slightly different than Jazarl's. "Do not leave us again."

They kept using the word *queen*, and Ari was good old-fashioned melting-pot American, not a drop of blue blood in the entire family tree.

When these people found out, what would happen? Could she afford to let that be a problem for Future Ariadne, who was already looking at a whole tsunami's worth of trouble?

"I'll try," she mumbled, and also tried not to see Hannixe's brightening, like a child promised early Christmas.

The dress was far paler than Hannixe's though sewn on the same lines, and both too loose in the bust and too long in the skirt until the other woman bent, her fingers flicking. A burst of strange musky non-perfume, a humming sound, and suddenly the hem was at Ari's ankles. Another soft thrum, and the bodice became closer but not overly snug.

If it wasn't magic, it was so close as to make no difference. Or maybe it was an incomprehensible technology, like steam engines or silicon chips might be for these people? Except if there was an entrance-or-exit and companions were 'found', had anyone fled into *her* world to escape the Bright King and the Golden?

Were there old stories about the hills near town? The Hardisons would never have talked about such things except to scoff and Ari hadn't had time or inclination to research local folklore. Imagining Jazarl or Alzarien strolling down Main Street might've been amusing if not for the likely reaction of cops to rapier-bearing strangers with Kool-Aid hair.

Even the underlayer and shift Hannixe bundled her into were comfortable, and Ari wished she'd taken a few history-of-fashion classes. It would be nice to know if this was from a particular era; the V-waist looked medieval and the square neck was lower than she liked. Still, it was pretty, tiny pearls sewn in patterns along the neck, hem, and the long belling oversleeve cuffs. A few more bursts of that shower-and-laundry magic, Hannixe's brow furrowed with concentration, and the gown fit as if it had been tailored.

Actually, the dress was flat-out lovely. The only problem was Ari couldn't believe it looked even close to reasonable on someone like *her*. The urge to spin like a little girl in a princess costume, just to hear multiple heavy skirts move with that soft sweet sound, was overwhelming.

She quashed it, ruthlessly.

"There," the Grey Lady said, nodding sharply. The two thin braids framing her face swayed with the motion, and this close Ari could see they were tied with grey ribbon matching her dress. "Slippers for my lady queen, too. First, though..."

A small table—it looked very much like polished rosewood— next to a pair of scarecrow-armed clothing racks held a dark wooden coffer, opening under Hannixe's slim fingers. A bright silver gleam burst free, casting sharp shadows on the heavily timbered ceiling.

It was a necklace—or more properly, a torc. A restrained silver curve held a single large clear gem full of white light; Ari's jaw felt suspiciously loose for the umpteenth time since landing in this dimension. The piece looked heavy, plainness of design barely saving it from overdone barbarism. Yet only that weight could possibly balance the jewel's glow, not merely throwing back available light with magnificent prodigality but luminous in its own right, like a star caught in crystalline glass.

"It's beautiful," she managed, accents finally falling in the right places.

"The Carcanet." Hannixe's smile was nearly as bright. "Let me have the honour, my queen?"

Of what? The question was answered as soon as thought, for Hannixe turned to her, hands raising, and Ari couldn't restrain a flinch.

The other woman paused, a shadow crossing her heart-shaped face, and waited.

Every girl was supposed to like jewelry, diamonds being a woman's best friend and all that. But something this pretty, so heavy, so... so expensive-looking? No. Ari didn't even wear her own engagement or wedding rings; they were kept in a box on Wanda Lee's dresser.

All the same, she stared at the necklace, almost longing to touch. What would it be like, to settle something so beautiful against her skin? They kept saying *queen*; this was probably some version of crown jewels.

"'Tis yours, I cannot keep it." Hannixe's eyebrows rose, and her mouth turned down slightly. "Please?"

Oh, God. Ari had to shut her eyes as metal, strangely warm, touched her throat. Fortunately, the reminder of Mike's strangling grasp was brief, and the torc was oddly light—the weight was even, she thought, vaguely enjoyable. A spot of heat dilated under the gem, resting lightly against her breastbone, and the only thing more frightening than the sweet silk-sound of fabric moving as the shakes returned was how natural and strangely *right* a single piece of jewelry could feel.

Like Mom's silver crucifix, no doubt now irretrievably lost. Getting dressed up was probably necessary at this point—you couldn't have a pretender to the throne in Levis—but now Ari wondered if they'd give her regular clothes back at some point, or if she'd be returned wearing a ballgown.

"There." The Grey Lady stepped away, tilted her head, and viewed her work with visible satisfaction. "Now for your slippers, and would it please you to descend? The knights will be waiting to partake."

Partake of what? The bath's heat lingered but tension returned anyway, stiffening Ari's shoulders. "They're waiting?"

"As is their honour and privilege. So few remain, though. Once we filled the Keep, your companions fair and fell, all merry and wild." It sounded like a song, or poetry; a faint trace of huskiness remained in Hannixe's voice. "Many were lost the night you suffered misfortune. The shock was too great."

There it was again, talking about Ari like some kind of reincarnation. Was it just lip service? Either way, it was dangerous as Wanda Lee's pointed little trap questions or Mike's louder, fake-cheerful ones when he'd already decided to hurt her and was just looking for an excuse.

The torc warmed even more, a subtle pulse spreading from its contact with her skin.

"Forgive me." Hannixe paused, the backs of her fingers briefly touching her mouth, a pretty little mannerism. "It must distress you to think upon. Come, your slippers."

Slip-on shoes of creamy velvet with heavily embroidered silver uppers and very thin leathery soles, no match for Ari's hiking boots but at least now she maybe sort of halfway looked like she belonged in this weird place despite her hair turning into a cloud of curls, no makeup, and the rapidly fading yellow ghosts of bruises hidden by long sleeves. There was no mirror to check if the marks on her throat were still visible, or to see how ridiculous she appeared next to Hannixe's easy, unstudied beauty.

"There." The Grey Lady straightened, clasping her hands. "Oh, I have longed for this; I should keep you to myself, but that would be s-selfish indeed. Shall we?"

Clearly, there was no way of escaping whatever came next. Ari nodded, and hoped nobody would bust a gut laughing at the sight of an interloper wrapped in borrowed finery.

21

EVENTUAL JUSTICE

Low, half-familiar male voices filled the cottage's downstairs. Hannixe held aside the curtain at the foot of the stairs, beckoning Ari through.

Do I have to? But there was no escape.

"—the Mere," Majan was saying. "Leshe is serious in her charge; indeed I think 'tis the only thing she is not careless of."

"There is a Conjunction soon." The chained man sounded flat, uninterested. "If missed, simply waiting will suffice."

"Another ten thousand mortal years?" Jazarl was audibly having none of this.

Ten thousand what now? Ari paused, trying to figure out if her invisible translator had burped, but Hannixe was waiting.

"She is returned. It is enough." A slight edge to every word, the first brush of killing frost. "If need be we will stand guard twice or thrice as long, and count ourselves lucky to have the chance."

Ari braced herself, stepping through the curtain.

A couple more plain hard wooden chairs had been found to crouch near the three overstuffed ones, but the downstairs room was hardly crowded. Half a dozen men in green and brown. One in grey, his pale gaze finding Hannixe and sharpening. The chained man was at the fireplace, ruddy flamelight running over blackened armor and strings of links; did he sleep in the iron getup?

Now *that* sounded uncomfortable.

The window shutters remained tight-closed and barred; a heavy beam rested in brackets across the front door's blank inner face. Golden glow from the globes in branchlike holders brightened as the chained man stepped away from the stone hearth; one by one, Jazarl's men rose. The grey-clad fellow with the stripe in his hair was already on his feet, leaning easily against the wall; his rapier-hilt gave a smart, cheerful little winking gleam.

Thick silence, broken only by the fire mutter-crackling about its business. Ari shifted uneasily, her skirt swaying, and a faint edge of silver touched the room's light.

Christ, I probably look like a clown in RenFaire dress-up. But the stitching on the gown was exquisite, the material of excellent quality, and every item in the house had begun to look distressingly, utterly normal.

At what point was she going to start considering her life before waking up in the pond a multicolored nightmare, and this the reality? Human beings were adaptable almost to a fault, but if Ari started believing she was what these people had been waiting for, she would no doubt overlook some tiny, crucial clue.

The consequences would be drastic, if not violent. Just because these folk didn't know about cars or phones didn't mean they were stupid, and their laws and norms weren't hers. She was a foreigner, and couldn't forget as much even for a moment.

A shadow loomed before her. It was the chained man; somehow, he had crossed the entire room. "My lady." Quiet, and grave. "The Carcanet is returned. Will it please you to partake, and hear our counsel?"

I am so not ready for this. Was she going to start dropping *thee* and *thou* like a drama kid finally getting a soliloquy chance? These people sounded sophisticated; she would simply stumble, falling flat on her verbal face. "Will it help if I do?"

"More than you may ever know." No trace of sarcasm in the words, that feverish gaze fastened on her face. It felt almost indecent, to be studied so closely. Once more he offered his gauntlet, the right this time, palm-up. "Soon it will feel natural."

I'm not betting on that, my dude. Still, Ari laid her fingers in his hand, and was grateful all over again when the iron glove didn't snap convulsively shut. A strange, unwilling feeling settled on her, impossible to name.

Was she losing English? It was hard to tell, and the very concept of misplacing her own language was too terrifying to contemplate at the moment.

He led her to the biggest chair in the room, its almost severe lines softened by cheerfully threadbare pillows. Ari hoped she wasn't taking anyone's seat. It was fantastic to get off her feet, though, and even better that the skirts hid her legs.

Hannixe set off for a row of wooden cupboards along the back wall; stripe-headed Keners hurried in her wake. Everyone else remained standing, watching Ari, and she began to get the idea she should say something.

Thankfully, the chained man piped up. "Take your ease, knights of the Keep, so long as our queen is at hers. To all present that signal honour is granted, and shall endure so long as Underdark does." He arranged himself at the right hand of the chair, a bare foot away, and while the hovering was faintly comforting it was also scary as fuck.

She was all dressed up and a formal meeting was about to start; go figure, it was equally anxiety-producing in this world *or* the one she'd left behind.

It took a few seconds for the guys to sink back down, and the rule of human behavior that said everyone stayed in their first-chosen seat—even if getting up was part of the program—apparently held here too. It was just like the beginning of a middle-management bitch session, except with everyone in old-timey Eurotrash drag.

I'm definitely feeling better. A hot bath and new clothes did wonders for a girl's equanimity.

"I have but a s-single tray," Hannixe said, "though thankfully you shall not have to share cups. But 'tis less mannerly in the forest, I wager."

Sarle and Majan shared a glance, eyebrows up, speaking without words. Jazarl shook his head, Naithor stretched out his legs with a sigh, crossing his arms high on his chest.

"I had half forgotten the sound of your voice, Grey Lady." Laughter ran under Darjeth's tone. "Or confused it with a fox's bark."

"If I speak for my lady, Darjeth, 'tis only because she has little patience for lackwits," Keners shot back.

"Oh, aye, and you have more?" It was impossible for the pale blond man to smile any wider, the expression of a class clown with all of lunchtime to perform in. He rubbed at his cheek with callused fingertips, and wrinkled his nose slightly. "Well-matched you are indeed."

"Soon Hannixe's tongue will be sharp as ever," Alzarien draped himself on the bench near the door; he had slicked his crimson hair back and his boots looked suspiciously like they had been polished. "And you will be too occupied in crying mercy to remember when 'twas silent."

"Crying with laughter, perhaps." Darjeth was having a *grand* time, one knee twitching as he lounged.

Ari couldn't help but smile as well, and looked quickly at her lap to hide it, letting her hair fall in a damp curtain. At least the dark curls weren't frizzing; they hung sleek and well-behaved, probably because Hannixe applied the comb.

Who would want to disappoint her? And it had been... nice, Ari decided, to have someone mess with her hair. She listened intently, ready to soak up every possible clue, hint, and inference.

"Pity Leshe is not here." Majan interlaced his fingers, stretching out his legs from another hard wooden chair set at an angle to the others. He settled his shoulders, clearly arranged for deep thought and serious conversation. "She would enjoy the contest most roundly."

"And complain we could be riding instead." Jazarl dangled his hat from one capable hand as he sank into one of the cushioned seats; a full quiver leaned against its leg. "Speaking of wagers, I believe I have won one, Darj."

"Oh, aye, and when we return to the Keep the item is yours." Darjeth made a dismissive gesture with one hand. "If the Golden did not smash it, that is."

"Do not speak lightly of such filth in my lady's home." Keners came back into view, carrying a wooden tray bordered in ornate scrollwork. Hannixe hovered behind him, cradling a dusty green stoneware flagon. "We have a bottle of the greater drink. A full measure for the ladies and a scant for every knight, unless our lord prince finds it best to observe the prohibition."

"Madman," Jazarl muttered. "Steal into the Keep for a single bottle."

"My lady was determined to rescue some small effects." Keners halted with the tray, handling it easily despite its thickness and the load of glassware and goblets clustered at its center. Each piece looked distinctly handmade. "Could I let her go alone?"

"Four Golden slain that night," Sarle aimed the words in Ari's general direction, as if she could be expected to know all the in-jokes. Or as if he was inviting her inside the popular kids' holy circle, a bit of social mercy. "The entire place in uproar, the Bright King's servants riding every direction for days, and later we find 'twas because the Grey Lady wished a visit and a few trinkets. We did not dare test *her* hospitality for some while afterward."

So the stripe-headed guy was good at killing clockworks, which made sense. Were there other small groups hiding elsewhere? Maybe at this Mere, with this Leshe. That was good to know.

"They were taken by stealth, not overmatched in strength." Keners shot an uneasy glance Ari's way as well. "But still, the purpose was served."

The chained man stirred, one of the cables hanging from his arm rippling. "My lady's handmaiden was well-guarded," he murmured, and that seemed to be what everyone was wanting to hear.

"Oh indeed, Keners fusses endlessly." Hannixe presented the flagon in the chained man's direction. "My lord prince, if it p-pleases you?"

He didn't move. Yet there was a sharp cracking noise of break-age, and Hannixe smiled as if answered. She turned to pour, concentrating and biting her lip gently while filling a wooden goblet. It had a twin, sitting companionably close, but the other four containers were smoked, bubble-streaked glass, all shot-sized.

However, she only filled the one goblet, swept it from the tray, and presented it to Ari, sinking into a graceful curtsey. "My queen."

You guys have got to stop. This is ridiculous. But what did it matter?

The bath had maybe sluiced off some of her old life. Her working theory had been admirably proved unless something better came along. The chips and cracks on much-used items or plaster walls, the individual hairs, the creases and small worn spots on clothing—there was no way she could come up with a vision or delirium so detailed.

Ariadne was stuck here, for however long. The problem now was impersonating this queen of theirs; could she claim amnesia forever? Hannixe seemed to believe, but who knew what the others truly thought? Ari's position depended on the chained man, so she had to keep him happy.

More disturbingly, she didn't want to go home. This was terri-fying and bizarre, true. But it also felt... strangely comforting? And at least the dangers were overt.

Unless she just didn't know the real ones yet.

"'Tis the greater drink." Did the chained man sound faintly

anxious, or was it her own uncertainty projected onto his flat, just-the-facts-ma'am tone? "It will not have turned as mortal vintage does, nor is it harmful. And your companions may this time share the blessing instead of waiting for the lesser, or the slow restoration of clear water."

Maybe she was supposed to chug since it was her first time at a party? Ari took the goblet, and didn't wait.

There was no point.

Cool liquid, vaguely spiced though she couldn't untangle all the different components. The drink poured down Ari's throat in a rush, hit her stomach, and spread in a warm velvet haze far different than the burn of alcohol. An almost-stinging thrill expanded all the way out to fingers and toes, and her scalp tingled as if her hair had joined the party and was attempting to speed-grow.

Ari lowered the carved goblet, exhaling in wonder. The remaining liquid trembled, clear as water, but faint hints of cinnamon, capsaicin, and cardamom simmered in its scent. "Oh, wow," she breathed, but thankfully the invisible translator swung into operation. "What's in this?"

"'Tis a mystery. Perhaps Leshe knows, but will not say." Hannixe beamed, turning back to the tray. The stripe-headed guy held it steady, watching her closely as she poured again—half-filling the other goblet, and dolloping splashes into the collection of small glass containers. "I know 'tis not a knight's duty, Keners, but will you carry to—"

"Of course." He didn't even wait for the rest of the question, and no hint of irritation was visible at all. "An honour to perform such service, my lady."

Wow. He's really gone over her. It was nice to see romance wasn't dead, though Ari would have to watch carefully to see if he was really even-tempered as he seemed. She took another hit off her drink. *Good Lord. This would make millions back home.*

Each guy took a shotglass, raised it gravely in her direction, and toasted Hannixe as well before tossing the contents far back. The other woman curtseyed once again before sipping steadily at her own goblet matching Ari's. Keners settled the tray on a small table near the stairs and went through the motions, lingering over lifting his drink to the Grey Lady and watching her while he swallowed.

The chained man simply stood there, making no move to down a slug.

Ari decided she shouldn't swill the rest of hers just yet. "Aren't you going to have any?" A completely uncharacteristic sense of well-being swamped her, along with fresh unease.

Nothing that felt this good was legal, or lasted very long.

"Pleasant, but I do not require." His dark head tilted, a listening look. "We shall tarry here long enough to regain your strength, then travel to the Mere. It will be easier, now."

That's good, I guess. Ari held the goblet up, an offering to his looming; her arm didn't want to shake. The drink burrowed in, much more filling than the pondwater.

The good feeling of being full, warm, dry, and reasonably safe had to be transitory, but at least she had a breather. "Are you sure? I don't mind sharing, and you're probably..." Would he take *you're probably tired* as an insult? She didn't know the rules well enough; this was a risk.

The offer earned her a long considering look, his chin down and that strange, hot gaze resting first on her outstretched hand, then moving to her face. It was unsettling, being watched so closely.

"If my lady offers," he said softly, "I cannot refuse." His metal-clad fingers closed around the goblet, brushing hers, and it was also super strange that the armor wasn't cold but instead skin-warm.

Did he ever take it off? Or was he burning with fever inside its embrace?

He turned the cup slightly, and Ari had the bizarre idea he

deliberately rested his lips where her mouth had touched the rim. A single swallow, those dark eyes half-lidding as his throat moved, and he returned the goblet to her numb hand—which had forgotten to return to its proper place, just hanging in the air.

"My thanks." His mouth curved, a smile blooming, and it was official, she was transfixed.

Wow. No doubt she looked completely ridiculous. Ari's cheeks were flaming hot, and she couldn't blame it on the bath or the drink. "You're welcome," she managed, faintly.

Everyone was silent, as if embarrassed for her. She stared into the cup's depths, and the longing to be invisible was a familiar half-friend, half-enemy.

At least the chained man didn't let her suffer long; clearly, it was time to get on with business. "A Conjunction approaches," he said, gauntleted hands crossed before him, all sharp edges and dark metal amid the softer shadows and more organic textures. If this were a painting, he would definitely be the cynosure; the artist would have to be at the corner near the stairs to arrange each element properly. "I intend to be at the Mirrored City to meet it, which will break the last of the fetters placed upon me after the... misfortune. Of far more importance is our queen's renewal of the Mere, and the traitor will do all he can to deny that event. Upon every knight present rests the duty of giving him no success in further blasphemy."

Renewal of the Mere sounded like a religious ritual. *Mirrored City* was new—no, wait, she dredged a mention out of memory. That was where the Bright King lived.

The traitor who had strangled the real queen, Ari's predecessor. Clearly this wasn't a constitutional monarchy with largely ceremonial duties. She continued staring into the remainder of her drink. Was she supposed to know about the Mere thing? Should she down all of the extra she'd been given, or pour a bit out for the gods of this weird place? Was she required to transubstantiate?

Hannixe set her goblet on the tray. She approached the big chair with a rustle, and sank onto a small ottoman to Ari's left, a breath of sweet perfume spreading from her skirts. Then, as if it were quite natural, she touched Ari's elbow. "Come, my lady." Her eyes sparkled and only a bare trace of huskiness remained in the words. "A little more, if it please you? It will do naught but g-good."

Now Ari had to finish the goblet. She was very aware of the stares while she took down more spice-smelling medicine—or was it a wine? These people didn't seem to eat.

"He will send many Golden," Jazarl said. "And other, fouler things."

"Mere dolls will not trouble us overmuch." The chained man didn't quite give a dismissive wave, but Ari suspected it was close. "Of far more concern are the restless dead of his Law, for he has gained some slight puissance. They must not be allowed to approach our lady in any wise."

"Restless dead?" Ari didn't mean to interrupt, but the phrase was disconcerting. Especially when it called up the memory of those wet slapping footsteps and cold, despairing moans.

Like damned souls, she'd thought, and didn't it just figure she'd be right about the most horrifying possibility?

"Our old companions." Keners was back to leaning against the wall near the door, new color in his cheeks. His pale gaze rested on Hannixe, and his hand on rapier-hilt. "Not all, though. I think some of them unlucky mortals; Sarle disagrees."

"I do." Sarle stared at the fireplace, tense even while seated. "But wherever they hail from, they are dangerous."

"Only one fetter remains upon me." The chained man's tone remained even, businesslike. "While it does, there is some small difficulty in dealing with those particular abominations."

A series of alarmed glances exchanged between the men. Even Keners looked a little taken aback. Ari tried not to stare, but their open shock was thought-provoking.

"They are infectious," the chained man continued, as if not noticing. "So you must take care, and above all do not let them near her."

"My lord." Jazarl shifted uncomfortably. His seat squeaked a bit; the small noise was another reminder of this place's terrifyingly detailed reality. "Should you miss the Conjunction, there might be... further complications."

"In that event, we will retreat to the Keep and stand a siege." The chained man didn't sound particularly worried at the prospect. Nobody mentioned the 'ten thousand mortal years' thing again, so maybe that was a figure of speech. "This is not the first war I have fought, my friend."

Well, that's comforting. Sort of. Ari's fingers creaked on the goblet. Hannixe was still watching her, a worried line between dark eyebrows. Was the grey in her hair natural aging, or the result of lingering stress? The rims of her eyelids remained red and faintly swollen. At least her cheeks were soft and unmarked now, and her nose wasn't pinkened-raw. She still looked way too young for that hair.

"A little more," the Grey Lady pleaded, quietly. "Please, my lady Ari."

Even a magical drink couldn't erase the lump in Ari's throat. "This traitor—the Bright King, right? What exactly did he do?"

Alzarien studied the floor. Maybe he was grateful she was playing dumb. Even the fire was hushed; the expression *could hear a pin drop* didn't quite work in their language, but Ari could think it in English.

That was a relief.

"He placed violent hands upon my lady Moon." The chained man's tone could only be described as *forbidding*. "The fault is mine; I was not present to stop him. He laid his plans well, giving report of a strange irruption near one of the doors to the mortal realm—"

Now *there* was a piece of news; she'd been operating off the assumption of a single wormhole or gap. Ari didn't quite sit bolt-upright, but she certainly stiffened. "There's more than one entrance?"

It was also confirmation that her theory was entirely sound.

Folklore and fiction were full of the idea—openings to fairyland, alternate dimensions, whole other worlds. There were historical reports of people visiting *other places* and sometimes returning, and where there was smoke fire couldn't be far behind.

This still could be a completely different planet, and Ari wasn't sure about all the stuff that seemed to be magic. Advanced technology couldn't be ruled out. Did these people only *look* human? If they were an alien species...

Worry about that later. The reassurance of finally, for once in her life, having guessed right when it counted was so intense she downed the rest of the goblet; when the drink hit her stomach its warmth could barely compare to that consolation.

"There *were* doors, yes." The chained man turned his head, gazing down at her, and he sounded almost pedantic. "The... misfortune closed them, and more cannot occur without a truly blasphemous effort."

So this Bright King had murdered their queen, and now they'd nominated Ari to take her place. That explained some things—but not how she'd managed to arrive, and not the damn dreams.

Where was the instruction manual for this kind of thing? "But..."

The silence warned her. Ari realized everyone was looking at her, and hastily dropped her gaze to the empty cup, her fingers tightening on its stem.

Hannixe, however, wasn't about to let her off so easily. "Something troubles you, my lady?"

"No," Ari said, hastily, and wished she'd stayed quiet. "I was just wondering how I got here if all the doors were closed, that's all."

"There is no door which will not answer *you*." Fortunately the chained man still sounded professorial instead of irritated. "If Sarle is correct and the faithless accursed is indeed using mortals to create passageways—and his abominations—it is simply one more crime he shall be brought to account for in due time. The fact remains that I rode to investigate his tale, and so was not present to gainsay his foul purpose."

This Bright King guy was sounding worse and worse. No wonder they were resisting; at least Ari could be reasonably certain she was on a morally justifiable side. "So he planned pretty carefully, is what I'm hearing." She almost winced at the banality of the observation.

"He was ever of a thoughtful bent, while one of your knights." Hannixe shook her head, the twin braids moving gently to brush her shoulders. "I will never forgive myself, that I did not see his treachery."

"He misled us all," Keners immediately objected. "The fault was not yours."

"I didn't mean it that way," Ari hurried to explain. The subject of mortal doors, as well as figuring out who had already guessed she was an ersatz substitute for their old queen at best, could wait until she had some time to think. "It just seems to me that he probably has some kind of plan now, too."

Wanda Lee would have scoffed. *Oh, it seems to you? A stupid little city girl should probably keep her mouth shut.*

Ari was no great shakes at coping, but at least she was adjusting better than she could imagine her mother-in-law doing.

Focus on the bigger problem. It's how you'll get through this. Ari's head ached, a swift crunching pang vanishing almost as soon as it arrived. Maybe the magic drink was a variety of interplanetary aspirin.

"No doubt he does." The chained man's nostrils flared and his mouth turned down, his forehead wrinkling slightly. "It will avail him less than nothing, my lady. His defeat only required a single event, and that has occurred. All is done save eventual justice."

If you say so. "That's good, then." The last thing she wanted was to argue with a scary metal-wrapped prince, who might even turn out to be the legitimate ruler with their old queen gone—but in that case, what did he need her for? Just to grab his sword, or as a figurehead? Hannixe called him a servant, but that had to be some kind of mistranslation; Ari couldn't imagine this guy fetching bonbons. "So, we start in the morning?"

"Unless the traitor's forces invade Gesthel tonight." Jazarl hurried to smooth the waters. "Though they have a healthy respect for the Fox's disapproval of such visitors."

"I will be more than happy to stand guard." Keners stiffened, drawing away from the wall.

"No need." The chained man shook his head, a short, very nearly regal movement. "Tonight is for what rest we may gather. There will be little once we leave this place, until I tear the traitor into pieces and consign his soul to eternal wandering torment."

Oh boy. Ari's shoulders hunched. It wasn't the gruesomeness of the threat, she'd heard a lot worse from Mike.

No, it was the way the chained man said it, as a foregone conclusion. He meant every word, and it sounded like he grimly enjoyed the idea as well.

"Our lady is weary," he continued. "Tomorrow we ride for the Mere. Be ready."

That apparently finished up the meeting, though it did exactly nothing for Ari's new questions. The guys stirred, exchanging glances, more than one touching rapier-hilt; Hannixe rose immediately to collect Ari's goblet, then led her upstairs, chivvying softly like a mother with a tired toddler.

Which was a relief, since Ari could use some time alone to think. Unfortunately, despite her need for even a few minutes' worth of brooding, exhaustion won.

It wasn't even a contest.

22

ENOUGH

WHATEVER WAS IN THEIR 'GREATER DRINK' DIDN'T ERASE THE need for sleep, and may have even contained a mild sedative. The mattress was just firm enough, the linens wonderfully clean. There were no pillows but several soft bolsters, both round and square—and Ari didn't realize she'd probably stolen Hannixe's bed until she woke in slow stages, sprawled flat instead of curled into a tight protective ball.

She hadn't slept so well since before her marriage; thankfully, there were no dreams. Just an endless, velvety restorative unconsciousness, then opening her eyes to see heavy black timbers sectioning off white plaster ceiling, the room unfamiliar but brimful with a silence somehow comforting instead of isolating, the sense of other breathing, living creatures nearby.

There was a window, the shutters closed and barred—probably because of those robot things and other dangers, Ari realized, stirring under heavy blankets, both dense-woven wool and lighter comforters filled with something that felt analogous to down. A golden orb in its branching holder next to the door brightened as she moved.

Tesla would love that. Was it technology or magic? She lay motionless for a few moments considering the difference before consigning it once more to the realm of useless questions.

Whoever painted this room would use oils to capture the rich vivid tints, working fast and layering to give an impression of the bedstead's wood grain and thickly whitewashed stone wall. The cloth on the bed would be the bigger problem, time to show off technical skill with wrinkles and folds. Maybe the angle from the doorway, framing the tumbled covers, an edge of the highly carved wardrobe, its wood fragrant like cedar but blue-toned and closely grained.

A soft silver gleam came from the necklace; light as a whisper, it hadn't disturbed her at all. The shift was surprisingly comfortable as a nightgown, and since she'd seen Hannixe deal with the laces it wasn't difficult to get herself back into the underlayers and outer dress with its seed pearls and heavy flow.

There was no sign of her jeans, boots, flannel button-up, or anything else. Which should have disturbed her more, and Ari wouldn't have minded a mirror.

Or maybe she would have, since she felt awkward and ridiculous even with nobody around to see. Thankfully her hair wasn't too tangled, just a few incipient knots easily parting under tentative fingertips. The slippers were no trouble, and the most surprising thing was the faint lingering taste of spice in her mouth instead of morning-breath.

All in all, this was surprisingly comfortable. Maybe they'd let her abdicate peacefully once this Bright King guy was dealt with, and she could rent a small abandoned house?

It was a lovely thought. She padded past the tiled room holding the bathtub, dark and empty, and slipped down the stairs.

Except for the clothing, it could have been the aftermath of a particularly successful party. The fire was low, and Keners was propped against the knee-high hearth with Hannixe cuddled to his chest, both deeply asleep. Even unconscious, he cradled the grey-haired woman tenderly, and her profile in repose would have tempted Botticelli to reach for his sketchbook.

The rest of the guys were sprawled wherever they could find room—Darjeth on a bench, one hand hanging limply like David's Marat in the bath; Sarle, arms crossed and hat pulled low, reclining in a chair with his booted toes pointed in a V; Naithor under the big butcherblock table. Jazarl was in the same chair he'd taken last night, arms also crossed over his chest and head resting against its wing. Alzarien was propped in a defensible corner near the hearth and Majan lay along the wall near the stairs, hat over his face and his booted ankles crossed. Only Hannixe had a blanket, heavy, brightly patterned wool tucked solicitously around her.

The front door was open, and a tall spike-clad shadow stood on the stone step just outside, limned in violet-grey dawnlight. He didn't move as Ari approached, but she figured he was aware nonetheless.

Her hypothesis was verified when she was less than five feet away and he turned his head slightly, chin almost touching heavy steel gorget. The invisible static of his attention settled upon her.

Ari swallowed, nervously. But he simply moved aside on the step, noiseless despite the amount of metal he carried. Cool fresh air enfolded her as she crossed the threshold, and she might have gone a little farther if his left arm hadn't raised, hand loose, to bar passage.

Okay. She probably shouldn't be wandering outside in slippers anyway, even if the garden's stone paths were immaculate. Ari hugged herself, cupping her elbows. "Hello." Thankfully, the word didn't quiver; they didn't seem to have an equivalent to *good morning*. At least, the invisible translator couldn't supply one.

"My lady." Quiet, so as not to disturb the sleepers. "Are you well?"

Haven't slept like that in ages. Maybe ever. She nodded. "Are you?"

That earned her a long, considering sideways look. "Of course. How can I be otherwise, with my lady returned?"

You really shouldn't say things like that. Ari hoped that was enough in the morning pleasantries department. This was a golden opportunity to find out a few more details, if he'd cooperate. "We should talk."

"Certainly." But he didn't move; apparently he was really going to make her work for it.

"Privately, I mean." The blush was back, creeping up her neck, but maybe he wouldn't see it in soft indistinct predawn.

"They will not hear. But..." He indicated the garden with a slight twitch of a gauntlet. "So long as you stay close, my lady."

She was already nervous enough to shudder, and scanned the mist clinging to neighboring houses, the road's glistening surface. Heavy dew coated bushes and flowers, glittered on the white-painted fence and the archway's tangled vines. "I thought those clockwork things didn't come here."

"They may be tempted." He didn't move, looming patiently on the step. "But 'tis not just that, my kindness. I once failed to guard you closely enough, and the result was disastrous. I will never make that mistake again."

Oh, for God's sake. Ari gathered every bit of courage she had, ignoring the tiny shrieking voice of cowardice. It might be a bad move to have this particular conversation now, sure.

But by Jesus and gin—as Mom used to say—Ariadne was tired of lying, of covering up with a mumbled *it was an accident*, smiling when Wanda Lee started in again, of attempting to soothe Mike's moods, of constant agonizing indecision. This guy was the power behind the throne, so arriving at some kind of agreement was necessary.

It might even help her survive this and retire, which sounded like a *great* idea.

"I'm really not what you think." Ari had said it before, but now she had the chance to make the statement stick. "Your moon-lady."

"My lady Moon." Not quite a correction, and at least he didn't seem angry. Maybe he'd expected her to begin bargaining for a political arrangement sooner. He gazed at the road, impersonal, his profile sharp.

"Yes. That." Ari's fingers bit her elbows, squeezing hard. The bruises on her arms were nearly gone, the 'greater drink' doing a lot of work she'd probably ruin. "But I'm just a mortal, right? I was running away and I landed here, maybe through one of the Bright King's doors you were talking about, and I—"

"Do you think Hannixe would break her long silence for a stray mortal? Do you think my sword would recognize you or the Golden seek you out, were you not more than you seem?" He wasn't staring at the road anymore. Instead, he turned, and that scorch-hot gaze pinned her. "You purified a poison-pool near the Keep, as well. More than that, *I know you*, no matter what shape you wear. Did you think I would not?"

The wall of metal came closer, but Ari didn't flinch. She couldn't, too busy staring at his eyes. They were the same as in those awful nightmares, but he wasn't wrapped in a mound of chains anymore.

He wasn't talking like a savvy political manipulator either. No, his tone was almost ragged, and the intensity of his expression was a shock. What if he was a fanatic? What if he really believed she was...

That's ridiculous, Ari. And yet, the face in her dreams was an incontrovertible fact. What explanation or theory could fit?

Guessing correctly once when it counted was useless if she couldn't continue the trend.

He bent slightly, iron still soundless though the chains draping his arms swayed. "The same," he murmured, and his breath held the same spice-tang as last night's strange drink. "Your eyes, in your quiet and your speaking, but more than that. Since the moment I first saw you amid flowers on the heath while your companions fled in terror, I have known what you are."

Um. Her brain seized up again. *Come on, Ari. Don't be stupid. Do something.*

But what? The sense of helplessness wasn't like waiting for Mike to go off again or yet another session of not living up to her mother-in-law's standards. Instead of breathless tension it was endless falling, but that wasn't quite right either.

Like flying. That was it, the imagined rush of wind under feathered wings or the stomach-flutter when a plane bounced on a pocket of warm air.

His lips moved slightly, as if wanting to say more. But he stopped, those eyes darkly incandescent and the rest of him a haze of dangerous warmth, an unfamiliar sensation filling Ari from slipper-soles to scalp.

"I..." A tiny, helpless whisper. She was failing miserably at negotiation. "I don't know what to do."

His chin dipped incrementally, the merest suggestion of a nod. "You have freed me, and brought hope to your companions. You are alive, and before me again." His mouth curved up at either corner, just a fraction. "It is... enough."

Nothing is ever enough. The crashing realization that she was making a gigantic fool of herself pushed Ari back a step, nearly tripping on the threshold.

His right gauntlet shot out, closing with that same exquisite care around her arm. A brief, steadying touch, but it burned all the way through her, and when he let go she was almost bereft. A susurration of waking went through the room behind her, cloth moving and the sighing of a deep yawn.

The chained man turned back to his vigil. His broad black-armored back was stiff, but something in his stance said it wasn't anger.

She couldn't find the word for his body language, which was dangerous—anticipating someone else's mood was the only way to be even halfway safe. Plus, Ari realized, she'd lost the chance to make her case.

Now, in fact, she couldn't even remember what her case *was.*

A crimson furnace on the horizon said dawn was underway instead of merely nigh, and there were three new equines grouped with the others outside the garden fence, stamping and making horsey sounds. Two were grey, one dark and one much paler, and the third was cream-colored with a flowing mane and tail, its tack adorned with silver discs. Hannixe regarded the beasts somberly as Keners closed the gate; the house was buttoned up tight and looked forlorn now, as if it sensed abandonment.

"They are tame enough," the Grey Lady murmured. Her elbow brushed Ari's arm, comfortingly close. "But I have not ridden in some while."

"Yesterday was my first time." It was a lot easier to talk to another woman; Ari's fingers moved uneasily over pale cloth. Hannixe had produced this sleeved mantle—clearly cut to accommodate the dress—from somewhere, and fussed with the large draping hood while Ari tried it on. "I'm surprised I didn't fall off."

"We shall n-no doubt go at an easy pace; 'twill be difficult to fall." She was trying to be comforting, maybe; Hannixe smoothed a fold of her own rain-colored cloak. "And our lord prince is not likely to select a beast so ungrateful as to inconvenience his lady."

If you say so. "He seems very..."

"Grim?" The other woman's dark eyes gleamed as she glanced swiftly aside, the corners of her mouth tilting up. "He was passing sober before, indeed, but now..."

"He's very thorough," Ari said. It was difficult not to smile, and she was deeply glad for another girl in the group. In fact, Hannixe reminded her of a college friend, cheerful brunette Annelise, who had moved to Massachusetts the year after graduation. "And sort of..." *Repressed.* There was a term in their language, but Ari wasn't sure it had the right overtones.

"Difficult to say, is it not?" Hannixe's laugh, low and sweet, brought a glance from Keners, who was busy checking the tack on the new grey equines. He smiled before turning back to his work, the stripe at his temple flushing as mist thinned further and ruddy light crept between houses. "Many called him cheerless before, though you found much comfort in... but forgive me, I should not speak of such things."

It would have been nice to get more context, but Ari was uneasy with any mention of 'before'. The urge to look over her shoulder to see who they were really talking about grew more pronounced each time.

Jazarl and the chained man were in conference at the head of the group, where the big black equine stood patient, tail flicking irregularly. The blue-haired man nodded, conveying the impression of a respectful bow, and swung away, gesturing to his fellows. "To horse," he called, and the chained man moved along the fence, bearing down on the women.

Keners reached them first, his dark grey half-cloak dotted with mist. "May I have the honour, my lady Hannixe?"

"Of a certainty." Her cheeks turned pink; the fresh color was even prettier though her eyes were still red-rimmed. The damage did indeed look permanent. *With my queen gone, all I could do was weep*, she said, matter-of-factly, while braiding Ari's hair with swift grace. *Hand me that r-ribbon, if it please you... oh, very lovely indeed.*

"My lady Ari." The chained man arrived, the metal on his boots making faint sounds against paving—he was back to advertising his movements. "We are ready, when it pleases you to mount."

Great. Now she had to struggle into the saddle wearing this getup. There was plenty of material to cover everything even if Hannixe hadn't done something to make the skirt divided, frowning at cloth while that strange unsound of magic or a different technology brushed the air.

Thankfully, it was easy—one foot in the cupped cradle of the chained man's armored hands, a moment of effort, and Ari found herself atop the white equine as if she'd been performing the movement for years. He even guided her toes into the stirrup, and she found the one on the other side with a glance. *Okay. Great. I can do this*. Ari gathered the reins, concentrating hard and biting her lip.

Keners performed the same service for Hannixe before swinging into the saddle of the slightly darker dappled grey. The chained man looked up at Ari for a moment, and from this angle she could see an edge of soft black cloth below the lip of his gorget.

What was he wearing under all that iron?

He nodded, briskly, and moved away. A moment later he was in the saddle as well. Hannixe's equine stepped close to Ari's, and the entire group set off. Majan and Alzarien vanished into the thinning mist ahead at a trot, but the others arranged themselves around the two women at an amble. Darjeth's grin was visible even under the shadow of his hat.

Ari gripped the reins hard, hoping she wasn't going to embarrass herself. The white equine's rolling gait was reasonably easy, she supposed, and maybe they could find more magic pondwater for any blisters that might occur.

Did these people get blisters? If they were aliens maybe they wouldn't, but...

Another day full of dangerous questions stretched before her. The mist thinned still further, and as the last few houses receded they turned off the road, onto rolling grassland.

23

FAIRYLAND RULES

IF SHE THOUGHT OF THIS AS A ROAD TRIP, ARI DISCOVERED IT became possible to enjoy a horseback hike. It was certainly faster than walking. She watched Hannixe carefully, copying the other woman's sway in the saddle, holding reins in the same fashion.

Fringes of woodland cut across grassy undulations, their shadows cool and inviting. Grass touched the equines' bellies in places so the entire group looked like bobbing swimmers, and a tang of mint rode the soft sweet breeze when juicy blades were crushed under shod hooves.

The chained man was a black blot at the head of the group, and Jazarl's men took turns splitting off in pairs ahead and behind, vanishing almost as soon as they left despite the paucity of hiding places. Keners joined Majan halfway through the morning, with a single burning glance at Hannixe, and she sighed as he faded from view.

"He worries," she said, softly. "But this is much safer than the Road, or the lands near the Keep. Now that you have the Carcanet, of course, there is far less danger."

The necklace, hidden under Ari's mantle, gave another soft reassuring pulse of warmth. It seemed almost alive, or maybe she was just uncomfortable thinking about the other woman who had worn it.

Their queen, their Moon.

Hannixe apparently expected a reply, so Ari cleared her throat. "It's very light." She watched the chained man crest a slight hill, his dark head turning as he scanned the grass ocean, the thickening archipelagos of woods both evergreen and deciduous.

"For you, yes. Another attempting its use would not find it so." Hannixe seemed part of her horse's rhythm; its hide almost exactly matched her cloak. "Look, *geserin*. They gave the village its name." She pointed at a mound of bushes loaded with small white flowers.

"*Geserin*," Ari echoed, attempting to place the accent correctly. The other woman was full of plant trivia; if she wasn't a botanist, she gave a damn good impression of one.

"Just so. They are used to flavor certain tinctures, and give a sweet scent to bedding." The breeze teased at Hannixe's grey mane, lifting curls and bringing a becoming flush to her soft cheeks. She glanced sideways, as if gauging Ari's reaction. "Little medicinal benefit, but each bloom has its place."

Here was another chance to make an ally. At least Ari could feel good about that. "You know a lot of plants."

"Never enough, though I thank you for the compliment." A slight drooping motion, giving the impression of a curtsy even while in the saddle. "Herbs do not wholly make a healer, for all they help immensely. And you have ever loved flowers—I should ask, my lady Ari, do you like them now?"

"Flowers are good." So far, she was doing reasonably well. At least she wasn't embarrassing herself. "And it's just Ari, please. *My lady* sounds a little... formal." A subtle social gambit, asking to be upgraded from stranger to acquaintance. It took time, even if the other person was amenable.

"Ah, it is our habit." Hannixe's smile was a wonder. If Burne-

Jones saw her he might well expire on the spot, or start painting a slightly less sacred triptych. "But I will address as it pleases you."

That was even more encouraging. "Can I ask... the Moon-lady, your queen. What was her name?"

"Your name is Ari, is it not? Ariadne." Hannixe tested the word, and now she was attempting to mimic Ari's accent instead of the other way 'round. "'Tis beautiful."

"No, I mean before." *When your queen was strangled.* No wonder they didn't want to talk about it; the event seemed traumatic as fuck. Now they were on their way to the Mere, maybe for some ceremony or to meet other resistance fighters; Ari had to find out what would be expected of her. "The misfortune."

"I cannot say." Hannixe sobered. "The grief, the pain—it was too much, you understand. The shock when *he* found you on the shore of the Mere killed a great many of us."

"Us?" Ari took a deep breath, reshuffling her list of theories and questions. Maybe the name thing obeyed ancestor-worship rules, or fairytale ones?

Which was a sobering thought. Especially its corollary—*which* set of laws, precisely? Were all fairytales about this planet with its red giant sun and scarless, plate-dish moon, or were there others in the universe just waiting for people to happen onto them?

"Your companions, my lady. Some from the Whispering, others from the mortal realm." Hannixe glanced to her right; Sarle was riding there, but too far away to hear the conversation.

Grass rippled in vast sea-patterns, and the sheer seamless reality of this place hit Ari again. If this was Tir nan Og or a different dimension instead of a separate planet, was her own world zooming ahead on fast-forward without her?

Being tossed back into her own dimension as a Rip van Winkle sounded distinctly unappetizing. But maybe the statute of limitations would have run out?

It was a consideration. She couldn't even wonder about this Whispering thing yet; maybe it came after the Mere.

"My lady?" Hannixe, anxious now. "You seem troubled. Perhaps I should speak less."

Oh, crap. "No, not at all. I like it. The men, they're not very communicative." Of course, being chased by big horned robots didn't leave a lot of time for heart-to-hearts.

"In truth it is a relief to have my voice once more. I s-simply could not speak, with you gone. But now you are here, and it is..." The grey-haired woman tilted her head, beaming mistily in Ari's direction; her voice had smoothed amazingly and the stutter was all but gone. "It is very good."

Did Hannixe think Ari was amnesiac? No, because the queen had been murdered. Maybe it really was a reincarnation thing, or a succession—*the King is dead, long live the King,* or something similar? Was any mortal who fell through the door nominated for the position? But the chained man seemed to operate under the same assumptions, acting like no random passerby could have yanked the sword out of its yielding prison and also attributing drinkable pond-water to Ari personally.

They were all assigning an awful lot of competence and importance to a 'stray mortal' who was simply stumbling through increasingly outlandish scenarios, hoping not to trip too badly.

Whatever reply Ari might have made was lost in a coughing growl to the left; it sounded disturbingly close. Ari stiffened, and the white equine's ears pricked.

"'Tis only a *kitha*-cat hunting," Hannixe soothed. "They will not dare attack mounted riders, especially with our prince nearby."

That's great. Still, Ari kept a sharp lookout. The landscape was pretty, certainly, but the reminder that she didn't know even half the dangers here was a slap of icy water, as if she'd overslept on a day Wanda Lee had plans.

Their group contracted, the men's equines pressing closer, and stayed that way as the red sun mounted higher. Hannixe pointed out other plants; their names slipped right through Ari's head and vanished. The biggest question was what she was supposed to do at this Mere, followed closely by the sickening feeling that the Bright King might have something awful planned for whoever still resisted him. If Ari had any brain-cycles left over she could also wonder about those mortal doors, fairyland rules, and how she would get home.

Unless, of course, she didn't *want* to. How reasonable was it to hope she could stay? No cop or judge would find her here—but the 'faithless accursed' and his robots, not to mention the 'restless dead', might.

There was never really any escape, Ariadne knew. Not for people like her.

A dark line lingered on the horizon for a long while, then crept steadily closer. Ari eyed this new development nervously, and was relieved when Hannixe let fall that it was forest, not some fun geographical feature like the Breach.

At the first short halt Ari watched as Hannixe dismounted and found, much to her relief, that she'd guessed how to perform the maneuver reasonably correctly. The Grey Lady clearly expected the Fox to assist her, but that also meant Ari had to half-fall from the white equine's back into the chained man's hands. Each time he caught her with no apparent effort and she landed soft as a whisper, but continued success didn't make it less unnerving.

Especially considering the way his hands lingered on her waist before he stepped away.

The growling things weren't the only inhabitants of the grass- lands. Ari spotted bigger game, like long-legged brown animals shaped somewhere between mules and deer, browsing singly or in loose groups. Leaping not-antelopes moved in flocks like dolphins, their horns bright blue dabs and their tails white rabbity cottonpuffs. Birds suspiciously like hawks floated on ther- mals, the smaller brown or blue-and-white feathered things keeping close to the ground while predator-shadows drifted overhead.

The white-flowering bushes were joined by purple blooms bearing a resemblance to lupines, splashes of crimson near-poppies, tall spiky things akin to black sunflowers, and thistle-like spires with wicked prickles as well as seedpod burrs the size of her thumb.

It would suck to fall into a bed of those. So far there didn't seem to be any poison ivy, so that was a blessing. But an occasional blurring buzz like rattlesnakes came from one side or the other, and each time it did Hannixe glanced in that direction with a look of mild concern until the noise faded.

Still, the stops were welcome. At least Ari didn't seem to be developing blisters, and the white equine wasn't upset at its rider's lack of expertise.

"Too quiet." Jazarl shook his head, waving aside the offered canteen. None of the guys seemed to want a drink, though Hannixe took a mouthful and Ari at least three gulps—not meaning to be greedy, but it tasted wonderful.

A dull faraway ache from unaccustomed exercise retreated under the cool flow. She could only imagine what it would feel like without the pondwater.

"Our enemy is no doubt watching the Road." Keners squinted, staring into the distance; he accepted the canteen from Hannixe and capped it by touch, with an efficient twist. "He would not expect us to brave the Poisonwood from this angle."

Poison wood? Nobody mentioned that bit before. Maybe it was a figure of speech, but she couldn't be that lucky. Ari suppressed a shudder; Hannixe's shoulder pressed against hers. The other woman seemed to find closeness comforting, and Ari had to admit she didn't mind.

"He may have gathered forces to strike Gesthel." Darjeth was keeping watch in another direction; his tone was soft, calculating. "Expecting us to bring our lady Moon to her handmaiden, and hoping to..." He trailed off, thoughtfully.

"We have done what we can to confuse the trail." Alzarien pushed his hat up, rubbing at his forehead. The red tips to his eyebrows and lashes matched a shadow of stubble on cheeks and chin. "And no doubt the Fox left a few gifts in the village."

"In the surrounding fields as well, as is my habit." Keners shrugged. "The Golden are not particularly intelligent. Though stubborn, I shall grant them that."

"Do you think perhaps the faithless accursed would leave the Mirrored City and ride for the village?" Sarle did not quite hunch defensively, but he did lean slightly back on his heels as the chained man's gaze settled upon him. "It must be asked, my lord prince. He will want to... make certain, whether he intends to acquire or to..." The sentence petered out, and the stocky man looked away.

A thick, uncomfortable silence descended.

"Acquire?" Ari sounded small and deeply unnerved, even to herself.

"He declared himself king of the Underdark." Majan's hair ruffled as a breeze swept past, sighing in the grass; he replaced his hat with a swift habitual motion. "But as the Blight spread, he could not cleanse the Mere or bring those surviving of the Keep to his service without force and the contagion of his curst Law. The villagers left or were taken by infection; there is nothing for him to rule. Though treacherous, he is not stupid. Murder achieved him nothing; he may now seek instead to kidnap."

Now Ari was wondering just who had lived in the abandoned village—and they talked like there had been more than one hamlet, too. What kind of infrastructure did this place have? Did the queen make decisions about sewage, real estate zoning, property taxes? Were there foreign affairs? Other heads of state? Ministers and spies?

Nobody mentioned neighboring countries.

"The Golden were indeed pursuing her," Jazarl weighed in. "But we have seen none of the rotting filth save the one detachment upon the Road."

"Passing back and forth, as if to net a fine catch." Naithor nodded, but he was pale under his tan and very deliberately did not look at the chained man.

Who stood near Ari, staring past the equines. Though his expression hadn't changed, set and closed, an invisible roil of fury spread from him. The chains hanging from his arms moved uneasily; the ones wrapping his legs and torso gave sinuous twitches. Even Hannixe regarded him nervously, and glanced at Ari as if she should know what to do.

Was there a universe in which she wouldn't be called on to soothe angry men? It didn't seem possible.

"Well, he hasn't caught us yet." She tried to make her tone pragmatic, calming, and inoffensive all at once, but probably only succeeded in sounding nervous. "And once we reach this Mere, we're safe, right?" It came out as *correct*, perhaps not with the shade of meaning she wanted.

The chained man looked down at her, and the deep staticky unsound of rage drained away all at once. "You are already safe, my lady."

Am I? It was a dizzying change, anger vanishing as if it had never existed. Was he just good at hiding it? Mike had been, at first; she now studied this man, who was far more dangerous than her husband had ever been.

Ex-husband. Any way you sliced it the divorce was final, and if she was dumped back in her own mortal world at least she'd never have to deal with him again. A small mercy, but also an utter relief. Even the guilt of pulling the trigger was eclipsed by that consolation. Which probably just showed what an awful person she was, but at the moment Ari didn't care as much as she should.

She realized she was staring up at the chained man, that dark feverish gaze locked with her own.

Behind his screen of indifference and the sense of barely controlled, murderous power, something else lurked. It peered at her, cocking its sleek dark head, and the pale smear at the bottom of each pupil-well was her own face, reflected in tiny, astonishing detail. For a moment nothing else existed, Ariadne and this nameless man stranded in a blank wilderness.

"Of course," he said softly, as if she had spoken. "Do you doubt it?"

What? "No," Ari heard herself reply, hoping it was what he wanted to hear. "Not really."

"Good." The barest hint of a smile touched his mouth, there and gone in a moment like lightning.

The rest of the world rushed back, a wheel of color and sensation, and she was abruptly aware of standing in the middle of a group, Jazarl's men looking away with faultless politeness, Hannixe studying Ari's profile anxiously and Keners watching the grey-haired woman, a leather canteen dangling from his left hand.

"We shall reach the Poisonwood soon," the chained man continued, turning to gaze at the dark line in the distance. "Stay close, and use the greatest of care."

24

POISONWOOD, CUPBEARER

THERE WERE NO ANALOGUES TO THESE TREES IN ARI'S experience. Most looked vaguely succulent, their fleshy bark deadly, leprous pale; spines tipped with reddish ichor festooned the taller while the shorter bore crazycrack-quilted channels full of nasty resinous flow. Many were weighed down with clusters of maroon foliage—some like maples, others fernlike, still others deeply notched in parallel like oak leaves. There were tall black evergreens, their swollen needles dropping with tiny ugly *plops* when the breeze rose, and gnarled shrubs with bright, violently orange or jaundiced berries peeping through yellow-spotted leaves. Fungal growths clustered among and on fallen logs, giving off a faint eerie luminescence even during daylight, and spiny clumps of sword-shaped stuff like nightmarish aloe vera curled its blackened tips, sending up little puffs of steam wherever red sunlight striped its hide.

"All very poisonous." Hannixe was clearly thrilled. "Though some few may be used in small amounts for certain cures. There is nothing so vile but that it cannot serve the Moon, my lady, and... oh, look, see there, those very white waxen berries? They are called *beautiful stars*, and very poisonous though a syrup made with them and *sagradahl* leaves may induce rest without pain for those most grievously wounded—"

"Soft, my lady." Amusement lit Keners's sharp face. "I do not think our queen wishes to know every venom in the wood."

Ari was just glad she hadn't woken up here. A *naryin*-filled clearing was probably the best place she could have landed, a piece of luck she didn't deserve but was grateful for nonetheless.

"But 'tis so interesting." The Grey Lady glanced anxiously at Ari. "Forgive me, my lady. Relief makes me giddy."

"I like the study of plants." Ari meant to say 'botany', but their term was longer. The invisible translator had barely any lag now, and she had the strange sensation of almost *thinking* in that rolling, fluidly accented tongue.

If she'd majored in linguistics, would she have met Mike in that Renaissance to Modern Art class he'd admitted to taking because he thought it was an easy pass? Would she have married him, or someone else? Mom always said thinking about what might have been could drive a person insane, so it was best not to.

The chained man said a door would open for this queen of theirs, but clearly their opponent could make a few as well. What if any random mortal could stumble through one of the Bright King's entrances, and the resistance simply nominated the first person to show up as some kind of royalty? Historically that sort of thing ended with a sacrifice, didn't it? But that didn't explain the dreams.

Nothing really explained the dreams. Or, more precisely, nothing Ari was willing to contemplate at the moment.

Hannixe pointed out a few more plants after that, but lapsed into silence as afternoon wore on. An acrid edge of rot and nastiness rose from the Poisonwood's floor along with thin noisome steam and curls of outright smoke. The vegetation cringed away from the chained man's mount, leaving a wide blackened track for the rest of them to troop along.

Ari belatedly realized the scorched area was slowly recovering behind them. Swollen-headed fungal things released bursts of greenish spores, branches uncurling, the blackened bits dropping with heavy, nasty wet sounds as fresh growth swelled to take its place. The rushing, creaking sound of repair was very much like that of the forest near the Keep except for an unpleasant sliding edge, like bloated wet fingers rubbing together.

The group halted near sundown, gloaming thickening between trees, stripes of phosphorescence brightening on certain plants. Tiny flickers like lightning bugs gathered in clouds amid the canopy, their swooping near-random patterns nauseating to watch.

A long rectangle of slick white stone shimmered through the undergrowth, pillars marching at its margins. The roof, steeply pitched and pierce-carved, was of the same material, and the whole thing floated like a dream, its edges sharp and distinct as the road's. Equine hooves made soft musical sounds as the beasts stepped onto what seemed like marble floor between pairs of carved columns, and though Jazarl and his men looked pleased, Hannixe frowned.

"It's so different." She peered in every direction, twisting in the saddle. "This must be the Small Pavilion, so the Mere is that way. But... oh, the groves of shanbark are gone, and the *naryin*. Once these woods were full of song, and the *cres*-moss made for lovely pillows. And the paths were of white stone—but where are they?"

So this Mere was close by, and Ari still didn't have a clue what the approaching ceremony entailed. She saw nothing but shadows, faint nasty glimmers from fungus or glowing insects, and the steamsmoke rising as the chained man's passage through the Poisonwood healed over. Maybe 'healing' was too strong a term— the forest oozed to cover the scar, soft and repulsive, full of slow toxic pleasure.

A chill walked down her back. This place's foul, expectant near-silence felt very much like the house on Hardison Hill, actually, and the old breathless tension gripped her middle.

The chained man lifted her down from the saddle as usual, but did not move away once he had set her carefully on both feet; the slippers were holding up surprisingly well, even with metal stirrups rubbing against embroidery.

"Do not wander," he murmured, his breath touching her hair. "I did not think the rot had spread so far, nor burrowed so deep."

That's hardly comforting. Still, the heat and bulk of him felt strangely protective. Ari turned, once again nearly trapped between him and an equine; he seemed to like doing that. Instead of anxiety at being so close to a big male, a curious, utterly ridiculous sense of safety poured through her, dispelling all unease for a single heart-stopping moment.

It couldn't last. Ari's shoulders tensed, wanting to creep up to her ears. *Come on, give me a hint.* "What happens next?" It was ludicrous, she should've been trying to slip away, restoring a modicum of personal space, instead of freezing.

"Your Cupbearer will find us, I think." He glanced aside, checking their surroundings. "Jazarl tells me she roams this place at will, too canny for the traitor's abominations to catch."

Sounds like another Keners. "And the Mere?"

"It may wait another night for your attention, my lady." A slight edge of humor tinted the words. "Come. Let me show you something small, which may amuse you."

Jazarl and his men set about tending the equines, Hannixe lingered at the edge of the marble floor, peering at the woods. Keners hovered nearby, clearly hoping she wasn't about to take a stroll.

Which left Ari walking next to the chained man, the heavy sway of her skirts mimicking saddle-rhythm, the equine's rocking gait lingering in her legs.

In the pavilion's center a white stone dish easily six feet across rose upon a plinth, looking for all the world like an oversize epergne. Carving rioted over the stem, figures on horseback leaping and cavorting, but the bowl was decorated only with fruit and leaves, greenery frozen in stone.

It looked far healthier than the current flora, that was for damn sure.

The chained man held out a hand, armored fingers flicking once. A spark bloomed in the bowl's bleached, pristine depth, underlighting a shimmer like summer heat over pavement; a slight coughing noise, and a ball of blue fire appeared. Its top stretched upward, tapering to ever-shifting points, and it produced a lot of light for such a tiny blaze.

"No need for wood," the chained man said. "You said it would be a shame to burn the *kaloidyei* and shanbark, so the Pavilions, greater and smaller, were raised and are lit in this fashion."

Oh. "She," Ari said, and could have kicked herself.

That got a reaction. The chained man's hand dropped, and he turned to focus fully on her. "What?"

"*She* said it. Not me." It definitely wasn't the time for this conversation. Of course, there was never going to be a good moment, and Ari needed to know if this entire thing was going to end with some kind of Wicker Man episode. Whatever she was supposed to do at this Mere would likely be unpleasant, and she was on pins and needles waiting for it.

"Ah." No trace of anger, audible or visible; the chained man simply nodded as if he'd expected her reaction. Of course, if he could bury rage so deep even Ari's finely tuned antennae couldn't pick it up, she was probably—as Mike would say—cruising for a real bruising. "You are the same as ever, to us. Does it disturb you?"

That's one word for it. Ari wanted to step away, but his gauntlet shot out and braceleted her wrist, warm and irresistible.

She froze. "I really do want to help you." Ari stared at the blue flame, shadows bringing the carvings to flickering life. Were they actually moving, fueled by magic or tech? Maybe it was just a giant gaslamp.

Wouldn't *that* be hilarious.

"*All* of you," she continued quietly, hoping to keep this discussion private. "But if I was... what you think, wouldn't some of this be familiar?"

"Can you say it is not?" Iron-clad fingers tensed, though they didn't squeeze. "Is nothing in our company of any comfort? I would have thought your closest and most honoured handmaiden, at least, would meet with your approval."

Bad move, Ari. How could she explain this was better than whatever waited for her back home, and yet more terrifying than Mike's hands on her throat?

At some point in her marriage she had understood he would eventually kill her, and accepted as much with a variety of fatalistic fatigue. It was one thing to anticipate that everyday danger; what human female could avoid it? The statistics were clear, soaking every moment spent in society.

But if she lost this detail-saturated, dangerous, lovely world, finding herself once more blinking and dazed at the verge of a summerstorm landslide or staggering away from the smoking Oldsmobile on a winding road, the police cruiser squealing to a stop, its lights stab-flashing...

Two deeply conflicting urges, fighting over one lone, very confused woman. And right on time, the fact of the goddamn dreams reared its ugly head. Brothers Grimm had never covered *this* nonsense; Lord Dunsany might've but Ari had moved away from literature and into visual arts before she got to him.

"I..." Words failed her. Before she could find another way to stick her foot in her mouth, though, a new voice rang from the far, shadowed end of the pavilion.

"By silver, there are equines." A figure in midnight-blue velvet, the skirt hemmed higher than Hannixe's—mid-shin, instead of ankle—and a pair of glove-soft indigo leather boots moving underneath, resolved out of flickering gloom. Hazel eyes, thickly lashed, peered at the blue flame; a flash of mahogany skin showed, and very white teeth. "And... no. It cannot... it is. You..."

The woman halted, her skirts swirling for a moment. One hand flew to her mouth, the backs of the fingers touching her lips, a gesture familiar from time spent with Hannixe. A complex mass of dark braids wrapped in a coronet about her head, the rest pouring behind her shoulders, nearly to her knees. She made a soft, inarticulate sound, then flew across the intervening space, bursting into the rapidly expanding sphere of foxfire-blue illumination.

The new arrival flung her arms about Ari just as the Grey Lady had, hugging breathlessly tight. "No," she chanted, in a clear soft soprano. "No, no no. Oh, no. Oh, my lady, my lady. I knew you would not leave us, not forever. Oh, by silver, by silver and Moon, my lady..."

Then she burst into tears, laughing at the same time. Ari, her wrist caught in gauntlet-fingers and the rest of her nearly crushed in a stranger's arms, tried patting the young woman's back with her free hand.

This, then, was Leshe, and she treated Hannixe to a furiously tight embrace as well. The two women looked vaguely similar, just as the men all did—something in the shape of their cheekbones and large beautiful eyes, not to mention the vibrant velvet of their flawless skin.

Ari was feeling distinctly outclassed, but that was nothing new.

"It has been so long," Leshe said, dashing at her tear-spotted cheeks with quick butterfly motions. "And there are terrible things in the woods, it has all changed. You!" She spotted Sarle next, and made a beeline for him, running toe-first like a ballerina temporarily brought to earth. "I have not seen you for mortal ages, but the Moon returned a few nights ago and I thought you would visit at last."

"Forgive me, I could not arrive earlier." The stocky man opened his arms for a hug; a gleam on his own stubbled cheek was lost as he hunched to rest his forehead against hers. "Perhaps what I bring will grant me some lee."

"Silly." Her motion stilled for a few moments, and the young woman took a deep breath. "I would forgive you just for appearing. It has been a little lonely, with no-one to talk to save Keners every once in a while. And is there an equine for me?"

"Soft, little sister. All in good time." Sarle held her shoulders; the two of them made another Pre-Raphaelite illustration lit with blue glow, pale columns shimmering gently in the background, Majan and Darjeth to one side, Jazarl on the other holding something to an equine's sensitive nose, palm and fingers flat as the beast nibbled at a treat.

Leshe's greetings to the others were more restrained, but with everyone grinning so broadly it was a happy picture indeed. Ari's cheeks felt strange; she hadn't smiled like this for a long while. Sure, she wasn't one of them, but anyone could feel happy for other people's joy.

The chained man's shadow nearly swallowed hers, since he loomed at her shoulder. Spiked and sharp that darkness hovered, and hers had an odd refraction at its heart, a soft silver glimmer. It could have been the blue flame catching a stray gleam from his armor or a piece of tack, but the white-gemmed necklace hidden under Ari's cloak pulsed again, its warmth spreading in hazy rings.

Finally, Leshe turned away from Naithor and hurried back over glowing marble, heedless-quick. "I hid the Cup," she said, nearly skidding to a stop, her dark hair swaying. "But when the Moon rose again, I retrieved it. We are going to the Mere, yes? And then that awful Ternek—"

"Do not speak that name." Sharp and swift, the chained man's command made the blue flame waver for a moment, flattening in its bowl. "Our lady queen requires rest. There is clean water for you, and you may make merry as you please with the other companions

—but softly, and do not mention the faithless accursed so lightly. You are granted much since our lady finds your antics amusing, but blasphemy I will not brook."

So that was indeed the Bright King's name—Ari vaguely remembered a previous mention. She bookmarked the fact with careful mental effort, a curious momentary chill slipping down her back.

Leshe turned somber, nodded swiftly, and sank into a twin of Hannixe's curtsey. "Your pardon, my lord prince. I am simply so happy." Her hazel gaze turned to Ari, and a tremulous smile bloomed afresh. "I am sorry, my queen. I would not cause you pain for anything."

"No need." Now Ari was repeating the chained man's phrasing, and she almost flinched at the echo; the Carcanet pulsed again. She quelled the urge to take a step sideways, putting herself between him and Leshe; it probably wouldn't end well. "Really. Everything's all right."

"Your accent is strange." Leshe cocked her graceful, braid-crowned head. "But your eyes are the same, and... yes, you *feel* the same, as well. Here." Her hands rose, graceful birds, and when they parted a bright star flamed for a moment, snuffed almost as soon as it was born. "See? I guarded it well, my lady, as I was bid."

She had produced a cup of dark wood—a goblet, similar in shape to the two at Hannixe's house and the carved fire-bowl. Its sides were satin-smooth, but along the rim a thin line of silver seemed to flow in a lazy circle.

No, the silver *was* moving. Ari stared at the slight motion, trying to decide if her eyes were fooled by the blue light or by Leshe's moving closer, toes pointed out and her steps soundless-soft.

The young woman offered her treasure with both hands, and Ari took the cup. Warm as the Carcanet, carved wood nearly alive against her touch, stretching under her fingertips like a cat enjoying its beloved human's petting.

The rim gave another flash, silver flaring with pale fire. Ari nearly dropped the thing, and the chained man's warmth touched her shoulder as he leaned close.

"And so." Soft, and intimate. "Doubt yourself if you wish, my lady Ariadne. But do not expect us to do the same."

25

BLUE LIGHT, RED BLOOD

THE EQUINES' SADDLE-BLANKETS WERE THIN BUT SURPRISINGLY cushiony, and the stone floor merely chill instead of outright cold. Ari expected to have trouble relaxing, but the moment she stretched out, her head pillowed on her arm and Hannixe drawing the pale mantle over her, the world vanished.

Eyes bulging and her tongue clumsy-swollen, lungs burning, the need for oxygen blotting out even the pain as he squeezed, *Ari's chapped lips twitching.*

Please, Mike, please don't. *The words dammed up in her chest, the horrible silence broken only by his panting breaths. An equally terrible warm looseness near her crotch—had she peed herself?*

Cold metal against her fingers. Her hands squeezed too, desperately. A bucking jolt, like a terrified animal trapped between them squirming furiously for escape. Mike's lips skinned back, his teeth gleaming, Jim Beam heavy on his breath. If he lit a match and exhaled he could probably produce a fireball; the gun made another convulsive movement.

His grip slackened. A thin thread of copper-tinged air slid down her throat; she choked afresh.

Another shot. Mike staggered back a single step, his hands falling away. Ari's sock feet hit hardwood, and the gun went off again. That time she heard it, muffled thunder striking her ears almost before the muzzleflash lightning. The .38 leapt like a scared cat, and its next dry bark pushed Mike back another pace. Ari's shoulders pressed against the cracked, full-length mirror, the edge of its frame digging into her left triceps, and finally she dragged in a single glorious breath. A wad of nasty metallic wetness caught at the back of her palate—she retched, and the gun went off once more.

Maybe she could have stopped there. But panic and fury were twin snakes inside her, and both struck at the same moment. The last shot caught him high in the chest, a bloody hole opening like magic, and then the gun gave only a series of dry clicks while he folded down, limp as a doll, and thudded onto hardwood, blue eyes wide and still glaring, terribly empty.

Blue light, red blood. Like the flashing in the rearview as the Oldsmobile's engine finally gave out, steam billowing, and icy white headlights sliced a soft summer evening, searching for her...

"Peace, my kindness." A rumble filled her ear, unforgiving metal pressed against her cheek. "I am here."

Ari froze, heart hammering, breath trapped against a rancid throat-clot.

Iron cradled her, warm as flesh; she blinked, and a hot tear trickled down her cheek. He knelt on slick white stone, his arms locked around her, and the humming sense of power like a drowsing transformer on a hot summer day vibrated through her own bones. Chains hung quiescent from rerebrace and vambrace; though she'd seen the metal tentacles punch right through shining oversized robots no sharp spike of fear bloomed inside her.

Was this what it felt like, wearing armor all the time? Maybe he didn't *want* to take it off; having that kind of protection between a fragile body and an uncaring, violent world sounded flat-out marvelous. He held very still, sharp points and edges brushing her dress.

Nighttime hush filled the pavilion. The Poisonwood murmured under a light breeze; the blue light was soft and indirect instead of bright enough to read by.

It comes with a dimmer switch, for your convenience. The thought was blessedly rational, entirely sane, and even faintly amused. Ari dragged spicemusk-tinted air into her lungs and sagged with relief.

"Peace," he repeated, and the rumble was his voice, resonating in chest and breastplate both. The word was soft and beautiful in their language, and Ariadne never wanted to leave.

She wanted to stay there, safely enclosed, and just fucking *rest*. Not for long—a few seconds, a minute, an eternity. Both her own reality and this savage wonderland were goddamn exhausting.

But survival required continual alertness, constant effort. "I'm all right." The words quivered, Ari suddenly nine and terrified again, shaking in her mother's arms after night terrors.

"Are you?" The chained man didn't move. "I should have guessed this place would stir old hurts. Forgive me."

I was about due for a nightmare anyway. At least it hadn't been one of her usual bad dreams, even if she woke to a familiar near-haggard face hovering over her.

She'd traded one set of horrors for another. Was it possible to tell which collection was better, or at least fractionally less dangerous? "It's not your fault," she managed, each word a bare dry husk even in their beautiful rolling language.

Because none of this was his doing. That was the hell of it, Ari knew—plenty of adulthood was finding out nobody was responsible for certain events, and those who actually did hideous things never felt guilty about it.

"Lenient as always." His gauntlet twitched, as if he wanted to pat her back. "Lie down, my kindness. Rest."

I don't think I can. And what was that title, *my kindness?* Some kind of mistranslation, maybe, because Ari didn't feel particularly kind.

She couldn't even forgive herself.

Yet another day of weirdness loomed. The darkness seemed midnight-ish, even if her circadian rhythm was shot all to hell. "The others?"

"All weary, and safely abed." The deep thrum of his voice was almost too comforting. "I took the watch."

You know, I don't think I've even seen you nap. "When do you sleep?"

"I have had enough of torpor." The way he said it, flat and businesslike, was chilling. "Only when the traitor is punished, the final fetter broken, the Keep cleansed, and my lady safely in her bower will I rest, and not before."

That's one hell of a shopping list. Ari stiffened slightly. His arms loosened, setting her free. She could settle on the rumpled blankets, tug at her skirts—the material had bunched, of course, since she wasn't graceful as Hannixe or used to handling so much fabric—and push her hair back. Braids and curls slipped between her fingers without tangle or knot, and the thought of a whole line of Grey Lady haircare products as well as Greater Drink carbonated beverages was bleakly funny.

The chained man remained kneeling, his shadowed gaze trained on her. No longer so gaunt or pale, he still carried an uncomfortable, unblinking intensity. Yet the feeling was almost friendly after so much time spent in its vicinity, and it was hard to be anything other than relieved he was nearby in case some of those clockworks —or worse—showed up.

The large ceremonial goblet rested near the head of her impromptu bed, its silver rim still shifting slowly, sinuously. Ari bit her lip, rubbed her palms together briefly, and scraped her courage into a reasonably neat pile. "I have to do something with that next, don't I."

"Simply bring the Cup to the Mere. All else will follow." At least he sounded certain.

Somehow she doubted it was so easy. Was she supposed to pull some further Arthurian trick to follow up getting his sword free? Would he be quietly disappointed if it didn't work? Or would that hot, implacable gaze rest on her for a single moment before a chain snaked out, quick as a whipcrack, and...

Huh. Oddly, she couldn't imagine dying like that, even if it might be relatively quick and painless. Her brain simply refused, maybe because too much terror had soaked into the grey matter already. "How far away is it? The Mere."

"A short walk." His head tilted slightly. "I sense it would please my lady to accomplish this task sooner rather than later."

No time like the present had been one of Mom's favorite sayings, along with *look on the bright side*, not to mention *Jesus and gin*. "I don't want them to see me fail." She probably shouldn't have been so honest, but there was no help for it now.

"Ah." He offered his hand once more, the same cupped palm and steady look. "I will tell you something as we walk, then. Come, my lady Ariadne. Let us better understand each other."

26

TOOK, AND KEPT

The others were indeed asleep, most of Jazarl's men draped on stone as if it were comfortable, Hannixe wrapped in her cloak and Keners's arms, Leshe sitting propped against a pillar, head tipped back and fingers loose in her velvet-clad lap. Sarle was stretched out next to the Cupbearer, his hat pulled low and his hands clasped on his chest as if snoozing after a heavy lunch. Only the Grey Lady stirred as they passed, the chained man's boots deadly quiet and Ari's slippers hardly less so.

Stepping off the pale marble took a great deal of courage, but her companion's gauntlet was reassuringly warm and he turned, slightly, as if to steady her down a stair. She could remember Mike doing the same thing while exiting a restaurant one rainy autumn night, and a swift piercing pain went through her heart. The Cup dangled in her free hand, brushing her skirt.

Swollen, poisonous vegetation cringed away from the chained man, puffs of acrid smoke rising and flattening, glowing fungi shriveling. He moved carefully, one slow step at a time, and was silent until the pavilion had receded a good distance, glimmering dreamily through heavy undergrowth. Even the Carcanet's pale gleam was lost in thick gloom, and finally the chained man spoke again, soft and reflective, as if to himself.

"I was hunting." His slow, even tread was easy to keep up with, and somehow he avoided rocks and fallen debris that might trip a night-blind companion. "That day, I rode in pursuit of something which could kill me."

What an opener. But this was a road trip after all, Ari figured, and it was easier to approach certain subjects sideways, especially if you were busy looking ahead and didn't have to make eye contact with a fellow passenger. "Why?"

A short, disbelieving sound—after a moment, Ari realized he'd laughed, though not the bitter little bark he'd used in the cobbled bailey. This time the amusement was softer, yet just as deeply pained.

"Worlds were conquered, power assured. What else was left?" He guided her around a clump of orange-berried bushes, their branches shriveling as the edge of his personal space approached. "My coursing led across a field of flowers, and mortals fled before me—all save one. Perhaps she meant to protect the other girls; it was their custom to gather the blooms upon certain days, for good luck in marriage. Or perhaps she was simply too afraid to move." He inhaled sharply, as if he'd stepped on something unpleasant, but the steady forward motion did not cease. "Even when my mount reared she stood still, gazing at me, her arms full of white cups and petals."

The image was vivid—chained man on giant black equine, a girl on a plain of bright flowers, a blue sky with pale, scudding clouds. If Wyeth had ever painted fantasy illustrations, he might have captured the tableau.

"Perhaps I was angry at being balked," the chained man continued, aiming them between two massive spike-festooned trees. A dip between the black-barked columns held some approximation of a path, probably the kind of false trail common to any wooded area. You could get turned around easily in thick forest like this, thinking you were on track until nature's impersonal cruelty caught up. "Or perhaps I knew, though I would not admit... It was a moment's work to take her up. I put you upon my saddle, and we were in Underdark before you could draw breath to scream—not that you did. You were still clutching the flowers when I drew rein, very near where the Keep is now."

Her. I get it, he's talking about her. "She was a... a mortal?" The word felt funny in Ari's mouth.

"Indeed." A short silence, while he turned again to steady her; a slight slope ran downward between thornbushes, their spikes glistening with tarry resin. "I took you, and I kept you. Wonders and amusements I have made in apology, and companions brought or awakened to ease your loneliness. I judged it safer for none to guess the truth and it did not matter in any wise, for what is mine belongs to you. The faithless accursed laid his filthy hands upon you because he thought to steal what you never asked for. What was *forced* upon you."

Oh boy. So the Moon lady really had been a figurehead, and the palace coup hadn't gone entirely as the Bright King planned. "But why did everything... They said everyone died, and the mortal doors closed and everything?" Ari's fingers tightened on the Cup's stem, satiny wood solidly, oddly reassuring.

"'Twas not your passing but my grief which struck them down, my kindness. I set aside my sword, for what use was it then? And I let the traitor's Golden fetter me, as I did not care to resist with my lady gone; the Underdark has festered and turned to blight in your absence. It mattered less than naught, and yet..."

This is absolutely nuts. What would he do if Ari dug in her heels right now? She'd been half believing some crazy bullshit about being a reincarnated fairy queen, but in the end she was just shoddy imitation.

It hurt. At least she hadn't thrown herself at him, that would have been truly embarrassing. But they were heading for this Mere, she was going to fail a crucial test, and then what?

Landslide? Jail cell? Hospital bed? Rip van Winkle in some unimaginable mortal future, longing for a return to Tir nan Og's alien foliage, breathless violence, heartbreaking beauty?

"You doubt what you are," he continued, measured and implacable. "No matter. I learned something in those fetters, my lady Ariadne. I am not the worst of hunters, and I thought only one single prey had ever escaped my riding. Yet I did not fail that day upon the heath; I claimed what I had sought. Chained and grieving I yet lived, therefore you would return at least once, no matter how long the journey. So I waited."

The trees thinned, drawing away. Moonlight fell through a gap; a clearing was coming up.

What the hell? Trying to parse this while navigating a poisoned forest in the dead of night could give a girl a migraine. "I thought you said you were hunting—"

"What else can you be?" The chained man halted, and his free hand came up, indicating the vista. Fluid rippled, the sound of wavelets on a smooth shore. Ari peered around his armored bulk. Her scalp crawled, individual hairs attempting to rise. The sensation slid down her back, her arms, spilled over her legs, and no magical drink could dispel it. Neither could the warm pulsing of the Carcanet, gathering fallen silvery moonlight and returning it with a vengeance. "Behold, the Blood Mere."

27

A GAME WE PLAYED

NOT QUITE LARGE ENOUGH TO BE A LAKE BUT CERTAINLY FAR TOO big for a pond, the Mere's surface rippled uneasily. The bright white stainless moon had just crested a shadow-line of bulging, misshapen trees on the far shore and its reflection turned sanguine; the fluid was red.

It wasn't water. A distinct copper-laden smell reached Ari on the soft, playful breeze, and she almost choked. It filled her head like a nosebleed, heavy and trickling; she might have tried to stumble backward, turn and run, if not for her fingers trapped in the chained man's gauntlet.

Her other hand dangled, the Cup much heavier now, its wood pulsing-alive. Or maybe that was Ari's imagination, although why she should worry about more fantasizing with all this going on was beyond her. The spectacle was a nightmare even Bosch or Goya would have had a hard time capturing; any of the Surrealists would have raced to get the vision down before it faded. Maybe Frazetta or Jeffrey Catherine Jones could do it justice; Ari wondered if fantasy illustrators ever caught glimpses of this place and simply transcribed the vistas wholesale.

Undergrowth petered out in long scraggles; bare black earth sloped down to meet tiny questing waves. Dirt gave under her slippers, dry and crumbling; while the magical drinks might save her from throwing up properly, the blocking effect only made nausea worse.

Moonlight soaked the Mere's surface, small bubbles and curls of steam rising where bright reflection touched. The fluid was a different red than the tired, swollen sun, and Ari wondered why this mad planet's nightly satellite bore no pockmarks. Was there a shortage of comets or space debris in certain corners of the universe?

The shivers had Ari again, hard and fast. The smell was just plain awful, for all it was fresh instead of rotting. Was the earth itself bleeding? Or was this a pocket dimension, no real planetary laws to obey despite each day's apparent rising and setting?

Silence, except for kitten-playful ripples mouthing bare blasted shore and the bubbling farther out where moonlight touched, cool light stirring the surface. The Carcanet was almost scorching now; the Cup gave a little twitch, an impatient animal wanting attention.

The chained man said nothing. Maybe he was disappointed, or perhaps he liked scaring her? Had any other poor idiots fallen into this horrible, violent, lovely place and been brought here to fail?

Leshe *lived* in this awful forest. No wonder she was so happy to see other people; Ari tried to imagine sleeping in toxic bushes, smelling this coppery reek, knowing that somewhere in the woods lurked a lake of...

Oh, God. "I can't," she said, miserably aware of the words trembling. Being forced over a bridge made of alien dinosaur bones was one thing, fine, okay. But this... "I won't. Please. Don't make me go near that."

I really am a coward.

"You must bring the Cup to the Mere." The chained man stared at the not-water, and his gauntlet tightened on her hand. Not enough to hurt, certainly enough to threaten. "I would not ask, were it unnecessary. I do not enjoy this place as it is, and no doubt you are... unnerved. This is where it happened, after all."

I really did not need to know that. "Where that guy, that Ternek—"

He inhaled sharply as if struck, air slipping past his teeth with a hiss.

"I'm sorry." Ari stepped away, nervously, her arm stretched between them since he wouldn't let go. "I'm so sorry. Please don't be angry."

She could occasionally mitigate Mike's rage. This guy was a far different proposition.

The chained man stood for a few long moments, still staring at the Mere. "Your companions fear me." A muscle flickered in his cheek. "And well they should. But you? No."

Sorry, that ship has sailed. Ari let out a shaky breath. "Did *she?*"

"At first, yes." His shoulders slumped, spiked pauldrons moving just a few degrees. Strange, how that was enough to change a large figure's entire outline, expressing resignation or even sadness. "It took time to... reassure you. I look forward to repeating the act, so many times as necessary. But the Mere must be purified, my lady Ariadne. Please."

Oh, for fuck's sake. Ari tugged against his hold, barely caring if an edge sliced her fingers or wrist. Arterial bleeding would end all this madness in a hot minute or two. "If nothing happens, will you send me home? Or..."

"Home?" Now he looked at her, and his expression seemed honestly baffled. "The Keep is not yet fully cleansed, my lady."

"No, I mean back. To the... to the mortal world." *How am I even saying this?*

"You mean to attempt flight? I suppose I cannot blame you." Half the chained man's mouth curled up, a bitter-edged smile. "That was a game we played, as well. Several times."

I'm tired of games. Ari pulled against his grasp, more firmly this time. Eventually he'd have to release her, or the gauntlet would slice her like deli meat and make everything else about this nonsense academic. "Let go."

Amazingly, he did. She nearly staggered, and all but cowered when his hand shot out to brace her afresh.

He froze.

Ari drew herself up. "It's not that I don't like you." The old cliché—*it's not you, it's me*, and hoping the guy wouldn't go off the deep end when you deployed it. "I just... I'm not what you think. I'm just Ari, and you don't know what happened. What I did."

Was she really going to confess to murder in front of a man locked in fairytale armor? Jesus and gin.

"Do you think it matters? I have not asked what you suffered in the mortal realm, yet I can guess. And those suppositions are bleak indeed." He shrugged, armor moving far more fluidly than metal should. "There is time enough to address vengeance for your mistreatment after this is finished. But it *must be done*, my lady. Would you like me to beg?"

"I..." If she kept refusing, he would probably drag her shoreward and push her in. Ari shuddered at the thought; it was always fractionally better to approach a horror under her own power than be violently coerced. Her gorge rose. It was difficult to force words past the obstruction. "I just have to take the Cup down there?"

He paused, as if surprised. "I would suggest filling it."

Oh, God. Was she going to have to *touch* that lapping, deadly mess? Of course, and she was wearing white. This place wasn't content to terrify the shit out of her with ginormous skeletons, horned robots, and 'restless dead', it also had to *embarrass*, like forgetting a tampon the day of an important presentation.

Hannixe was probably full of helpful advice about cramps. Assuming these alien folk ever had them.

"Fine," Ari said, and maybe the invisible translator didn't know quite how to process the word because it came out in quivering, brittle English. She had a choice, though it wasn't much of one; if she was going to fail, maybe she could do it with a little dignity instead of being dragged like a reluctant puppy. "Just fine."

She lifted her chin and set off reluctantly downhill, her skirts whispering, slippers crunching on dry powdery earth.

The Cup's pulsing intensified, a cut artery synchronized with waves of despairing revulsion. The wooden goblet was warm as the damn necklace now, just on the edge of uncomfortable scorching. The big perfect moon's reflection bubble-steamed, more than half its bulk above the treetops on the Mere's far margin, and the smell was thicker and more sickening with every step.

It really did remind her of nosebleeds, especially the few times Mike had forgotten to be discreet and popped her right in the face. Behind the memory was a reassuring catechism—no matter what else happened, she would never have to deal with him again.

Or would she? Once you accepted alternate dimensions, different planets, or fairyland, time travel wasn't so outlandish.

I'd rather die. Well, she might get her wish.

She'd already done far more than she ever thought possible— shooting her husband, dragging a sword out of clinging rock, coming up with a correct hypothesis or two, and not going completely insane with fear on a bridge made of extraterrestrial or eldritch vertebrae. This was small beer, this was nothing.

Hold that thought. Pretend it's a beating. Just disconnect and get through.

Easier said than done. Her breath came in short rasping sips. The ground really was crunchy, like dry cinders. Her footsteps made tiny chewing noises; Hannixe's borrowed shoes were going to be filthy at the end of this.

Oh well.

She didn't realize the chained man was right behind her until his gauntlet closed over her shoulder, warningly. "Close enough, my lady."

Ari nearly started out of her skin. Did he think she'd run away? "I can't reach from here." *I'm a lot shorter than you, and I don't have fancy tentacle chains.*

"Take care." The words were a deep, warning growl.

You want me to do this, let me goddamn well do *it.* She swallowed an uncharacteristic but highly bracing flare of annoyance and decided not to bend over; she'd probably tip headfirst into the... the pool.

The Blood Mere.

So she was forced to step a little closer before sinking into an clumsy crouch, one hand attempting to keep the dress's hem out of softly moving fluid. A different, dozy heat rose from the Mere's surface; the smell was everywhere, dyeing the darkness a rusted vermilion. The moon's reflection was a bloated, gory semicircle. Veils of steam twisted, tiny screaming faces peering out of the vapor.

Imagination or reality? Either way it was deeply creepifying. Her heart kept leaping into her throat, splashing back into her stomach, and repeating the acrobatics. Her arms prickled, goose-flesh attempting to break free.

She gripped the Cup's stem, hoping to fill it without getting any on her fingers. Was he going to drink whatever she dredged up? Ari's stomach tightened even harder, fighting both the evening's last shot of clear pondwater and the Carcanet's soothing, irregular pulses.

Lower, lower. She had her balance, and hopefully his knee wouldn't nudge her. Mike might do that, tipping her right into a pile of something noxious.

It was just a joke, Ari. Lighten up. Funny how the 'jokes' never involved his embarrassment, only hers. And his goddamn mother, cawing with laughter while Earl gave one of his occasional, skeletal grins.

Ari sucked in a breath, leaned a little further. The Cup's rim tilted, brightening as it caught stray moonlight. Swelling and thinning, the silver chasing sped its rotation. It really did look snakelike, and she hoped he didn't expect *her* to drink anything from it.

Her left foot slipped. Ari teetered, and the thought—*of course, I'm going to fall in*—died amid a white glare.

The Cup's rim met a heavy, cloying surface. A hiss of steam, a flash lasting much longer than lightning should, a soft painless jolt up her arm. Her eyelids fluttered, but the light did not wane or flicker; it poured through her, a vast sweet unsound like a train's thundering passage married to a choir lingering upon the last swelling note of an Agnus Dei.

A sensation of falling swallowed her whole. Yet the drop was arrested, the jolt tightening every nerve and vein, and she was yanked breathlessly upward, collapsing against warm metal.

The Cup's contents scattered, flashing silver. The Mere flamed with pale radiance; a great soughing, tossing wind poured over the poisoned forest. Branches thrashed, trunks groaning, needles and leaves and cactus-spines torn free.

Oh hell. Ari kept her eyes squeezed shut, but it was no use. The light was *inside*, not bothering to go through her lids or even her optic nerves. Doors opened along internal halls, a dizzying sense of looking across every blessed year of her existence—that was what they meant, she realized, when they said *my life flashed before me.*

As soon as it arrived it was gone, and she sagged. The whirlwind passed through toxic trees and poisonous undergrowth, spreading in concentric rings. But she was prisoned in metal-sheathed arms, and his chin rested atop her tumbled curls—Hannixe's work with braid and ribbon was sadly damaged now, Ari thought, and blinked.

What the hell was that?

"The Mere is renewed." His voice sliced through the storm, quiet and sure. "Do you doubt now, Ariadne?"

28

NATURE OF PERCEPTION

DAWN FOUND THE DEADLY FOREST SWATHED IN CLINGING, greasy fog. Creaks and sighs raced through the trees; Leshe stood at the very edge of the stone floor, staring intently at a wall of white vapor as she held the Cup to her chest.

She could keep it, so far as Ari was concerned. Never touching the damned thing again seemed like a *great* strategy. Blue flame in the large stone dish paled bit by bit as daylight mounted.

Hannixe's fingers moved in Ari's hair. "Perhaps resting would have been better," she said, anxiously.

Ari hunched, hugging her velvet-covered knees. Of course the sudden storm had awakened everyone, but she barely felt any breeze while tucked under the chained man's arm as he shepherded her back to the pavilion—where Hannixe was wringing her hands, Leshe round-eyed and clutching at the other woman, and the guys stood tense and braced, ready for the worst with rapiers drawn.

Just as when it happened, Hannixe had sobbed, while she and Leshe threw their arms around Ari. The chained man let this happen, clearly consigning her to the women, and the guys sheepishly put their blades away—Keners last of all. It took a while to calm the Grey Lady down, and honestly Ari was glad because while she was focusing on someone else, her own unsteady hands and roiling stomach could be ignored.

Pretty soon she was going to have to seriously rethink a few basic assumptions about her role in all this, and Ari wasn't looking forward to the event.

"The Golden corrode swiftly in the Poisonwood," Jazarl said, his hand resting on the hilt at his belt. "But if that protection fades…"

"'Tis not them I worry about, but the restless dead." Keners's nose wrinkled. "Perhaps the traitor has found Gesthel abandoned, and he will not overlook a tumult near the Mere."

Ari shuddered at the mention of the lake. It was clean, cool water now, so clear the sandy bottom could be seen—and how about *that*, friends and neighbors? The reek of fresh blood was gone. So was the persistent toxic heaviness in crowded, poisonous vegetation. The creak-cracking sounds rising in waves all about the pavilion as dawn strengthened were like the forest around the Keep as it grew in fast-forward.

Do you doubt now, Ariadne?

It was like a trick question on the nature of perception administered by a particularly snotty philosophy professor. If everyone but Ari believed she was a reincarnated fairy queen, were they right or was she? The fact that inanimate objects seemed to agree with the prevailing sentiment couldn't be ignored, either.

Was she a changeling? Was there a mortal Ari waking up in a landslide, the cops on her trail? She should've been overjoyed at a minor success, but it only made the anxiety worse.

"How long until the Conjunction?" Darjeth wanted to know.

"Some short while." The chained man said it like calendar days and timetables were annoyances best ignored. "When our lady Moon is rested, we shall leave for the Blight and the Mirrored City. He built it at the entrance to the Whispering, more fool he." Grim amusement tinted his tone.

Ari hoped she wasn't supposed to do something terrifying at

this 'Blight' as well, or the 'Whispering'. Would there be an infinity of progressively more difficult, horrifying tests—an escalating fairy-tale curve? The consequences of inevitably bombing an exam were unimaginably unpleasant.

"There." Hannixe had finished her ministrations; without a mirror Ari couldn't see the result, but that didn't matter. "How lovely. And the color, like *sapha* bark. Soon it will be longer, and we will have such pleasant times choosing ribbons."

Ari finally stirred, pulling the pale mantle—Hannixe had insisted on bundling her back into it—closer. "What's the Conjunction?"

"They do not happen often. The Moon moves before the sun; all grows hushed and the Whispering is open to any who have taken the greater drink. Normally only you and our lord prince may enter that place."

An eclipse, okay. The Whispering, though. Sounds grim. "What's there?"

"Indeed I do not know, it is a sacred place only you and the prince may enter. Many among your companions are awakened within before being brought to the Keep. I was, though I do not remember the event. None do." Hannixe settled next to Ari on the folded blanket, reaching for a canteen. "Here, take a mouthful. The Mere is cleansed, soon the traitor and his Blight will be dealt with and we may return to the Keep. Then there will be great celebration. Perhaps we will dance—do you still enjoy dancing?"

I doubt you guys will set up a mosh pit. Ari's waltz or foxtrot was deeply substandard at best. "Dancing is nice," she agreed, carefully, and weighed the canteen. Not a lot of water left, and no more bottles of that 'greater drink'.

"And we shall go riding in the mortal realm, to rescue more companions." Hannixe's relief was plain; she took the canteen back, uncapped the top as if for a child, and offered it again with a grin.

"That's right, you said they don't all come from the Whispering place." The water was cool, and soothed Ari's stomach. The variance between physical well-being induced by their magic drinks and the constant anxiety failing to find an echo in her body was almost worse than simply being sick with fear.

"Oh, no." Hannixe laughed as if the suggestion was hilarious. "When you have a mind we go riding. Leshe adores such things, and when we find a mortal with your mark we take them up."

"If the traitor has gone forth among his servants the contagion will be strong." Majan's expression suggested he disliked raising the issue, but since nobody else would, he was nominated. "Should not our ladies be held in some safeness?"

"Where is one to be found?" Darjeth's sarcasm was gone, and so was his amusement. He glanced at the fog outside the pavilion, a quick catlike motion; his pale hair was slicked back and his blue eyes narrowed.

"The Blight shall spread no more since the Mere is renewed, and the restless dead are only dangerous while I remain fettered." The chained man's gaze rested on Ari; even at this distance it was a palpable weight. "When my lady Moon and I confront the faithless accursed during the Conjunction, I shall be freed. He will rue uttering such a foolish curse; he did not compass her return."

Wait a minute. Blinding realization burst inside Ari's head as she re-capped the canteen. So she was supposed to face down this Bright King? It was a condition of getting the chains off?

That *definitely* explained why the chained man was so eager to have her performing errands. He just needed someone to stand in for this Moon-queen of his. Maybe once it was done he'd be grateful and send her back through a door to the mortal world? Or these people would let her stay in a little cottage somewhere, with pearl-cabbages and a flower garden.

Which would be nice, but Ari wished he'd just told her so outright instead of all this nonsense about heaths and blossoms, hunting and games.

Now everyone was looking at her except Leshe, who examined the forest instead, dark braids rippling down her back. Hannixe's mane was astounding, but the other woman's looked like a solid century of growth with nary a split end.

"My lord prince," Jazarl said, carefully, "perhaps our queen should not be forced to endure the Blight or the traitor's presence. Surely we may simply deal with him in a manner befitting, without troubling her more."

Thank you. Ari's gaze met his, and the blue-haired man straightened slightly. It was nice to know her careful attempts at finding allies had borne at least partial fruit.

"Unfortunately, that is the condition of release." The chained man might have said more, but Leshe stiffened and whirled, blue velvet skirts belling.

"'Ware," she hissed, a low fierce warning. "Movement in the woods, and 'tis not friendly."

Nobody argued. Keners immediately broke away from the group of men, bearing down on Hannixe. The Grey Lady rose, bending to catch Ari's hand and draw her upright. Darjeth and Alzarien ran for the equines; Majan, Naithor, Jazarl and Sarle drew rapiers, the sound of edged metal leaving sheaths dismally familiar by this point.

The canteen dropped from Ari's nerveless fingers; Hannixe caught it, hustling her for the equines as Keners hovered, rapier-hilt gleaming and his head up, scanning the fog. The pale streak at his temple glowed, and he steered his lady for her dappled grey mount the moment she let go of Ari's arm.

The white equine stood stock-still, ears back and dark eyes ringed, its lip lifting to show those *definitely* non-herbivore teeth. Ari had to put her foot in the chained man's cupped hands yet again, hauling herself into the saddle. She gathered the reins, and the chained man's grasp found her ankle. He looked up, and the metal-clad fingers tightened.

It was probably a warning, like Mike staring across a crowded room, cautioning her not to say anything to tarnish his public image, not to talk too long to another man, not to laugh too loudly or spill anything. *Don't fuck this up.*

Now she was wishing she'd gone back to sleep after the nightmare, but at least the Mere was dealt with. She should've known even worse was around the corner.

"Do not worry," he said, his tone slicing through the confusion of others mounting, Leshe hopping neatly into a saddle and Sarle swinging up behind her. Everyone except Ari knew exactly what to do. "Your work is done, my kindness. Simply let me finish this, and all will be well."

Oh, yeah. Sure. Ari nodded, and didn't bother replying.

There was no point.

29

SELF-DEFENSE

RED DAYLIGHT BURNED, PICKING AT THE FOG'S SCAB-EDGES. THE Poisonwood stretched, crackled, creaked, and squeaked. Ari caught glimpses of trees thickening, losing their spines, and bushes shaking off pendulous berries as their branches shifted shape. Mushrooms shriveled, deliquescing swiftly; the black sunflowers crumbled, seeds puffing into bursts of ash before they hit the ground.

The entire place was morphing, and she was almost glad for the thinning screen of mist. Seeing the woods around the Keep growing in fast-forward was one thing, akin to watching a timelapse in a nature documentary. This was... something else, and she didn't like it.

At all.

Maybe Hannixe agreed. The Grey Lady didn't point out new species of flora or talk about tinctures and pastes. She rode close to Ari, her hood thrown back and ashen mane bobbing as she scanned what could be seen of the forest. Keners and Sarle led the way, Leshe before Sarle in the saddle, occasionally pointing in one direction or another. They accepted direction without question, sometimes steering away from what she indicated, other times turning immediately at her urging.

The chained man's black equine was just behind Ari's, and she felt his scrutiny. Her back ran with harsh tingling gooseflesh, her breath turning short when the sounds around them crested. She couldn't decide what was worse, the mutating vegetation or that little phrase they tossed around so casually.

Restless dead. Those horrible moans, the damp slap-padding footsteps, and that other extremely concerning term, *contagion.* Not to mention *blight.*

At least the falling leaves, branches, and other crap avoided their group, though sizable boughs frequently thudded down to one side or the other. The equines laid their ears back and snorted at the noise, but did not prance; they were tense and alert as their riders.

Ari's fingers were cold. The chill crept up her arms, and her toes were numb as well. Maybe it was the constant stress, or the knowledge that she was just an appliance. The chained man wanted out of his tin can, and that was understandable.

I just wish he hadn't said all that stuff. Thank heaven she hadn't reciprocated, or made a bigger fool of herself. There was that to be grateful for, at least.

If she was eventually sent back home—assuming she wasn't a changeling—it was time to start thinking of how to cope with the cops and the Hardisons. Ari might be able to make a case for self-defense even without the bruises, unless her injuries returned when she did? If the media got interested—or a savvy public defender—she had a good chance at manslaughter instead of murder charges. Of course Mike's parents had a lot of money, but that wasn't everything, right?

That was if she stayed to face the music. If she could deal with lakes of blood and giant, shiny horned robots, maybe crossing state lines and starting over again wasn't such a big deal. Maybe she could even emigrate, putting an international border between her and the entire awful mess.

Ari straightened in the saddle, pushing her shoulders back. The deep piercing chill was new, at least since her arrival. It could be purely psychological, she supposed. A fresh breeze brushed her cheeks, slid away to dance in the speaking forest, and the mist shredded.

The trees no longer wept red resin or thick black tar. Some of the poisonous things Hannixe had pointed out lingered, true, but they looked far less virulent as they jostled with other flora. All in all the place looked a lot healthier now, and that was good because—

"*Allalai!*" Majan yelled, and his mount gave a high shrill shriek. "'*Ware, they come!*"

The things boiled out of the forest, and a scream tore from Ari's throat.

The worst wasn't the smell, overpowering as the stink of the Blood Mere but hitting the nose differently, sending atavistic pin-prickles over her skin—every living being knows death when they scent it. Nor was it the hanging flesh overgrown with metallic excrescences and widening, weeping sores, though the sight was far more terrible than any Last Judgment painting or special effect on a high-definition screen. Nor the way they moved, twitch-jerking, sometimes dropping to run on all fours, slim moving pistons and tiny sharp-edged gearwheels tearing at flayed muscles.

No, the worst thing about the Bright King's other servants was their rolling, empty, cobweb-filmed eyes, bulging with horror. And the sounds.

Palms and soles swollen, fingers and toes receding, they made soft slapping noises while running crabwise; their jaws worked endlessly, champing and dripping yellowish foam. Little piping cries issued from shredded throats, whistles and chuffs when they were moving at speed. And they moaned, too—like damned souls, those terrible, chilling cries she'd heard while huddling among Jazarl's men.

Ari's mount screamed as well, Hannixe's rearing. Jazarl gave a short sharp shout which might have been an obscenity. Naithor's equine lashed out with a back hoof, catching one of the things in the chest and flinging it against a swiftly growing tree with a wet, sickening thud.

The things massed like flies, swarming, and no few turned their heads blindly in Ari's direction as her equine stood trembling and sweating. The chained man said something, a low imperative command; dull-black metal snakes shot in every direction, finding their targets unerringly. The splorches were deeply nauseating, and the way rotten flesh exploded into metal-starred chunks even worse. Alzarien avoided a splatter, leaning back in the saddle, and the flash of disgust married to a moment of fear on his sharp-featured face spoke volumes.

Another scream—Leshe, huddled before Sarle in the saddle as his rapier swung, lopping off an undead creature's bumbling, questing hand. The chains sang, snaking through cringing air, and Ari's mount decided enough was enough.

The white equine bolted. For a terrifying moment the world was cockeye and Ari knew she was going to fall, tumbling over frantically working hindquarters. But her hands were tangled in the reins and her knees clamped, stirrups pinching slipper-clad feet unmercifully. She managed to hunch forward, cowering against the massive creature's neck.

Bugling in terror, the equine shot into the forest. All a rider could do was hold on, and hope for the best.

30

UP TO THE TASK

CLINGING TO LEATHER STRAPS, FLYING MANE STINGING HER FACE and hands, Ari was too busy to scream, pray, faint, *or* wonder. The equine bunched and released under her, a giant spring pulsing in terrified rhythm, and she no sooner reached some kind of equilibrium than the beast shifted direction with a jolt that threatened to send her tumbling. A gathering, a sudden weightlessness, and they were airborne, the creature floating over a half-seen fallen log.

I hope you know what you're doing, honey. The poor animal had endured enough, and frankly so had she.

Grasping fog-fingers receded, shafts of red sunlight piercing the canopy and strobe-flickering to either side. The equine's gallop smoothed, though the creature plainly had no intention of stopping, and Ari found she could cling to the reins a little more firmly, leaning into a rhythm now bearing less panic and more purpose.

Zombies. Jesus. But the metal lodged inside their muscles, pistons and gearwheels working in dead flesh, *that* was a new one. Were they mutating into the big golden robots, or failed experiments?

This Ternek guy's probably real fun at parties. His name sent a shiver down her back, or maybe that was just the current situation shaking her like a small stuffed toy in a dog's jaws. The Bright King had strangled a woman in order to take a throne, and he somehow created murderous supersize robots as well as ambulatory corpses.

The chained man, though terrifying in his own right, was looking better all the time. Certainly far more restrained.

Trees flashed by on either side. Undergrowth waved as they passed. The forest was settling, the bright warnings of *hi, I'm poisonous* becoming far fewer and eventually rare indeed. Straight grey trunk-columns mixed with pale-barked, crimson-leaved trees, a sprinkling of evergreens thickened, and the equine settled into a canter.

Well, *settled* was a relative term. Ari's heart pounded nearly in time to hoofbeats, breath thick in her throat, and she felt like a violently shaken soda can. Stealing quick glances left and right, she decided they were indeed out of the Poisonwood, but didn't dare risk attempting to stop the poor beast.

It seemed to take forever before the equine slowed further. Craggy hills reared on either side, hemming them in, the forest rioting upslope and down. A moving glitter to Ari's left was a stream, glimpsed and gone. Her back was sore, the feeling attempting to break through a screen of analgesic from magic pondwater, and she wondered again if the liquid merely masked sensation instead of doing any real healing.

But it had made her bruises and cuts shrink, hadn't it? Her legs were numb; she didn't even want to think about getting out of the saddle.

The white equine's canter melded into a trot, its hooves no longer throwing up great clods of earth. Then a walk, plodding, its ears pointed forward and Ari able to move cautiously, looking around in more than small sipping glances.

Thinning trees, hills now higher but also drawing away. The shrubs and ferns were half-familiar, more closely akin to those around the Keep. The rock was dark grey instead of black with mica speckles, great rounded lichen-clad boulders thrusting through the earth's skin. The white equine was working downhill; Ari glimpsed ochre and amber in the near distance, more undulating grassland in yellow tones instead of green.

Maybe that would be good for her mount, even if its teeth weren't that of a grazing critter. And Ari had to think about the saddle now; she'd watched the guys strap tack on the horselike beasts more than once. Maybe she could reverse the process.

She didn't think it possible that anyone had followed their wild career. Her heart pounded in her ears so hard she wouldn't have heard if they had; her throat was full of thin hot sourness. If she was now on her own, she could at least unsaddle the white beast tonight, hoping it wouldn't take a chunk out of her with those sharp carnivore fangs.

But then what? Walk? She doubted she could get a saddle back *on* the big animal, especially if it took exception to the process. Should she try to find this Blight or Mirrored City, hope that the chained man or Jazarl's guys could track her? Cast around for a 'door' to the mortal realm, hop through, and see what the hell? Of course, she had no idea what any doorway would look like, since she'd been knocked out by landslide on her way here.

Or maybe she was dead in her own world, and would start to rot the moment she passed through? Now *there* was a wonderful thought. She didn't know nearly enough about the terms and conditions of this bullshit. The reflex of planning ahead, thinking through contingencies, trying to cover every angle had gotten her through living in the house on Hardison Hill, but in the end she'd still been surprised by Mike's...

What on God's green earth had set him off? Her brain was leaping around like a ferret on crack, Jesus and gin. She had to *think*.

The white equine stopped, ears flicking. Ari swayed, cessation of motion nearly knocking her from the saddle as all the shakes and jolts had failed to; the Carcanet was warm, nestling against her skin like a small frightened animal. She freed a cramped, trembling hand, red marks creasing her palm and fingers, and patted her mount's lathered neck. "Easy," she managed, in a trembling approximation of their rolling, beautiful language. "Easy, big fella. Or are you a missus?" English words salted her croon; she didn't have to worry about being overheard.

"That was awful," she continued. "But I think we lost 'em. You did good, you know that? I was scared too."

It was so much easier talking to an animal, even one with sharp hooves, pointed teeth, and a few hundred pounds' worth of muscle on her. The equine's ears swiveled, and she thought it was probably waiting for direction, some sign that its rider knew what the hell to do.

She had to figure this out, not just for herself but for this poor creature. As usual, Ari doubted she was up to the task.

A headshake and a horsey snort, mane flying, and the equine took a step. Then another, more tentative than she'd thought such a heavy critter could be. Its ears swiveled again, and Ari held her breath.

She heard it too. Hoofbeats.

So she wasn't alone after all.

The pale dappled grey burst from a screen of foliage, Hannixe on its back moving with natural grace. She spotted Ari, and even at a distance her relief was plainly visible. Ashen hair a banner, skirts floating, she aimed her equine in their direction and managed to slow the beast, leaning back, reins stretched taut.

Not only that, but Keners was right behind her, bending low over the neck of his slightly darker mount. The streak at his temple glowed, and Ari realized the sun was high and the angle of light said *late afternoon*. When had that happened?

Then Darjeth appeared, clinging to the saddle of his chestnut. He sagged, and Ari's heart lodged in her throat.

He looked hurt. Or sick. They were all so graceful and healthy, it was a shock to see.

"My lady!" Hannixe, calling breathlessly. She leaned back a little further and her equine obeyed, coming to a halt precisely at Ari's side. The white beast made a sound that had to be a greeting, tail flicking, and Ari realized she was both hopelessly rumpled *and* happy to see at least quasi-familiar faces.

"Hannixe." Her lips shaped the word, silently. *Oh, hey. I'm so glad to see you, even if I was ready to do all this alone.*

Well, *ready* might be an overstatement. But still.

"Are you hurt? Let me look at you." The grey-haired woman freed one hand from the reins, reaching out; Ari's own fingers lifted, questing blindly. "By silver, I am glad to have kept you in sight. You ride well."

Liar. But she meant it kindly, Ari decided. Her voice wouldn't quite work, despite being perfectly usable a few seconds ago.

"Have a care, Hannixe." Keners arrived on the Grey Lady's other side, his equine stopping on a dime. "Come, just downslope; we may halt, and rest the mounts. I like not to be so easily seen upon a ridgetop."

Darjeth's mount clipclopped up, forging past them. The blond man was pale, and great clear drops of sweat stood out on his forehead. "Thank the Moon," he said, shortly. "We have outpaced both help and harm; let us take some rest and counsel."

"Are you all right?" Ari's fingers finally found Hannixe's, tangled together briefly before separating. The contact was powerfully soothing. "The others?"

"They were in battle, last I glimpsed." Darjeth sagged, wincing. "Do not fear for them overmuch, my lady. Our lord prince is with them, and that counts for a great deal."

"Oh, aye." Keners made a chirruping noise, and the equines began moving as a pack, picking their way downhill. "Yet until he is fully free, contagion is a risk. Still, he—"

"Hush." Hannixe sounded stern, for once. "Of course he will be well, and our other companions too. Perhaps they are already upon our trail, though 'twill be difficult with the forest shifting through renewal."

Yeah, let's hope for the best. Mom would be proud of her for even thinking it. Ari arranged her reins, though the horselike thing was deciding where to go and she was simply a relieved passenger. "Darjeth? Are you all right?"

"Well enough, my lady Ari." His grin was a shadow of its former self, and he held one elbow stiffly clamped to his side. "Though perhaps not for long. Safety is of more import, let us seek what shelter we may."

❧ 31 ❧

YET MORE LOSS

THEY HALTED SOME DISTANCE DOWN THE HILL. ARI FOUND SHE could half jump, half fall out of the saddle while Keners was busy helping Hannixe and Darjeth struggling with his own dismount. The blond man hit the ground hard, staggered, and his chestnut equine gave a restless tail-flicker.

"What is it?" Hannixe bustled to his side, though Keners looked like he wanted to restrain her. "Darjeth?"

"Not much," he said, and caught the chestnut's reins with a wince. "Not so wide as the Keep's door, but deep enough. I have some time before it becomes serious."

Bright red spattered his side, his leather jerkin and blousy shirt bearing a ragged slash. Keners dealt with the equines while Hannixe and Ari helped the blond man to sit on a boulder; carefully, the grey-haired woman folded blood-drenched cloth aside, hissing quietly through her teeth as she saw the wound. Ari wondered briefly that these attractive, graceful creatures bled the same way she did.

It hadn't seemed possible.

The edges of the slice were blackened, veinlike branches spreading. "A claw-touch, not a bite." Darjeth craned to look down, eyeing the cut as if it belonged to someone else. "The same happened to my husband not long after the misfortune, and I was forced to grant him peace as it spread. I have some little time before I must ask a friend for a likewise service."

Oh. The words sank in, and Ari shivered with a mix of sudden comprehension and sympathy. *Oh, no.*

"Some *athelen*, or *estel*-leaf," Hannixe said. "Keners, will you find—"

"Soft, my lady." Keners was busy with Ari's equine. "The beasts have been ridden hard, grant me but a moment to tend them."

"Your waterskin," Hannixe said, urgently. Darjeth handed over his leather canteen; she shook it, and her expression grew grave. "I must make certain, this is from near the Keep, aye? Purified by our lady Moon herself?"

Ari stared at the wound, her own ribs aching in response. Her fingers curled into fists, released—she was useless, unless Hannixe needed a thoroughly uneducated assistant.

"Of a certainty. There was not time to fill it at the Mere, more's the pity." Darjeth kept his arm lifted awkwardly, sweat-darkened blond tendrils clinging to his forehead. "You should keep it for your use and hers, though. Don't waste the gift on me."

"'Tis no waste," the Grey Lady snapped, and busied herself with uncapping, then dribbling a little on the slice.

The water foamed immediately, like peroxide on a lanced boil. Darjeth's head tipped back, teeth bared and eyes half-lidded; he looked like he wanted to swear and only refrained by sheer force of will.

Ari winced again, shivering even harder—Mike always thought her empathy was stupid and hilarious, putting on horror movies just to see her squirm. Hannixe poured a little more; the bubbling intensified. Darjeth's eyelids fluttered, his lashes pale at the base, darkening at the tips.

Keners finished with their mounts and approached, hand

resting on rapier-hilt. "Behold the mark of the faithless accursed," he muttered grimly, no doubt for Ari's edification. "It will spread until the metal shows, and then he will be the Bright King's creature."

"I will endure," the blond man hissed. "And I will never bend to the traitor's foul Law. *Ever.*"

"It's an infection, right?" Ari looked from one man to the other, then at Hannixe, whose mouth turned down as she cleansed the slice. Foam receded, dripping down his jerkin, dyeing the leather dark. "There has to be something, some medicine, that will—"

"Oh, aye." Hannixe exhaled softly, and peered at the foam. "There are ways to slow it and those faithful to the Moon may resist for some short while. But the only true cure is the Bright King's death. Look, clean water has arrested the rot."

Bright King's death. Okay. She didn't see how such a small band of resistance fighters could pull that off, but there wasn't much of a choice. "And that's what the..." She almost said *the chained man*, but that probably wasn't proper etiquette. "The prince. He can do that, so long as we reach this Bright King during the Conjunction? When is that?"

If anyone was capable of making all this stop, it was *him*. Or at least, so Ari had to hope.

"Tomorrow, our lord prince said. He did not wish to say in your hearing, my queen, thinking you would worry as the time grew short." Darjeth shrugged, relaxing slightly as the bubbling ceased. He lowered his bent arm a bit, and peered up at her. "But he will be riding in search of you. He will not waste a single moment in confronting the traitor if your safety is in question."

Ari's gaze met Hannixe's. The Grey Lady's large dark eyes were sad, and full of pleading. She clearly expected her ersatz bestie to have some kind of plan, but Ari's poor overworked brain was all but producing steam through her ears at the moment.

Too bad, Ariadne. Deal. "You know how to treat it. Right?" It came out as *correct*, again, but Hannixe nodded.

"I can slow the rot, especially with your aid." At least she sounded certain.

"The Conjunction tomorrow, all right." *Very well*, the invisible translator supplied. "And the... the Mirrored City?" The syllables were strange and slippery in her mouth. "In the Blight? How far away is that?"

"A hard ride across the edge of the Dry Sea and then through much of the Blight itself." Keners half-turned to examine their mounts, then swung back to keep an eye on Darjeth. "The Road will be watched. Three days at least, unless our prince is with us to urge the equines along."

Hannixe perked up. "Or unless we go through the—"

"No," Keners and Darjeth said, in unison. The chorus was actually kind of funny, though Ari didn't feel like laughing.

Not in the least. She looked around almost wildly, as if she might suddenly find a first-aid kit or emergency room, a bandage, something, *anything*. Nothing but hills, trees, and grass, a violet sky and a huge exhausted sun the color of the Blood Mere.

"The Spires," Hannixe continued, brightening. The double flush of activity and hope suited her, and those dark eyes nearly sparkled. "They stand between the Dry Sea and the Blight; we must be near one of the entrances. A day at most, and if our lord prince is riding upon our trail—"

"*No*, Hannixe." Keners was having none of this. "I will not risk you, and our lord prince will be wroth if our lady Moon is endangered."

"And I would not have either you *or* our queen risk yourselves in such fashion." Darjeth twisted to examine the wound again, tweezing aside bloody cloth and leather; the edges of the slice were red and raw as supermarket meat, but the spreading black vein-fingers were smaller and now the injury did not bleed or froth.

Guess chivalry really isn't dead. Ari straightened and turned away, took a step. Another. She tipped her head back, staring at the sky; purple-tinted clouds hung in layers. Above a far horizon the moon lingered, a drained, perfect disc in daytime. Yet more astronomical weirdness, though she'd seen the satellite of her own home planet do the same. There was an old rhyme about it, too. *And waning half the midnight knows*, that was all she could remember at the moment.

Goddammit, Ari. Poetry won't help now. Think of something.

"The prince will follow," Hannixe insisted, stubbornly. "Or he will move along the Road to assail the Mirrored City, thinking our lady taken by the traitor. Either way he cannot fault us for seeking to save a companion in need. Nor could I do less."

"All those mortal years you did not speak, and now you are commanding." Darjeth's laugh was nearly bitter as the chained man's. "No, my dear Grey Lady. I would not ask it of you."

"Indeed you did not," she shot back. "'Tis our lady queen's will we are to work, not mine or yours. So much has been taken from us, and she is to bear yet more loss?"

"Hannixe—" Keners tried again.

Come on, Ari. What were the options? She had to think, and it was difficult with them yammering away.

"And others of our number may well be suffering the same," Hannixe continued. "Even our lord prince himself, since he is not fully proof against the contagion while he wears the last fetter. He said as much, do you not remember?"

She had a point, Ari admitted silently. Those things with their naked, bloated feet and swollen discolored hands, the weird buried metal bits in their rotting flesh, their chewing jaws...

Another galvanic shudder went through her. The zombies apparently only had to claw at someone or bite them to infect, but they used the word *contagion* as well. What if it was a virus, or bacteria?

Hannixe continued, her voice fading behind the rushing in Ari's ears. Disassociating now wouldn't do any good; the coping mechanism was only useful in certain situations. She struggled to push it away, to *think* through the noise, tempted to simply sink down onto long grass and curl into a little ball, covering her head and hoping for the best.

The *real* reincarnation of their fairy queen probably wouldn't be having any of this discussion bullshit. Or maybe she would, nobody said a lot about her particular preferences.

Even if Ari was simply a second-rate copy, she could still do some good. She quelled another shiver, trying once more to shove the rushing noise and trauma detachment aside—there had been so many zombies, an entire Thriller flashmob.

How many of their group were now wounded? Or that horrible word, *bitten?* The chained man had armor, sure, but he wasn't immune. What if he got sick?

What if he got *worse* than infected?

No. The outside world spilled back in through her eyes, her ears. At first a trickle, but then a flood. Ari found she could push the disassociation away with a wringing internal effort.

"I do not doubt your courage, my love." Keners's tone was soft, reasonable, almost tender. "But the hazard is far too great."

Darjeth wisely kept his mouth shut.

Ari was pretty sure this place would end up killing her—if it wasn't the robots it was the zombies, if it wasn't either it was the wildlife, and if all that didn't manage the job this Bright King would probably get his hands on her.

If the resistance won somehow, the chained man would send her home once she wasn't useful anymore. She couldn't stay, so what did it matter?

But that was no way to live. She could have just let Mike finish strangling her instead of lashing out in self-defense, and the truth was she'd known what was going to happen well before she scrambled for the nightstand. The realization had arrived the moment she saw his face, heard that awful, uncharacteristic silence.

Ari had made up her mind to at least *try* surviving. Which carried its own questions—and consequences.

Did she want to be like Mike and his parents, cruel and selfish, or did she want to be like Mom, like the Ari she'd been before marriage? Her ex-husband mocked her habit of giving change to beggars or trying to help strays and wounded animals; *every man for himself* was a Hardison family motto.

Her mother's was closer to *it takes a village*, and Ari's... well, *help where you can* was preferable to just about anything else. Otherwise she might have left the chained man in the Keep, his sword stuck in that chunk of rock and the rest of him in an iron burrito.

How would things have turned out in that case? Probably much, much worse. Even if the chained man only cared about getting unleashed or the shadow of his dead queen, he had still rescued both Ari and Jazarl's men, and was doing his best to protect them.

"It makes no difference." The words came out in English, not their lovely lilting tongue. "So I might as well."

A long pause, wind breathing softly through forest lungs. The wheat-colored grassland beyond rippled, individual blades bending under an invisible caress. Each one was weak, endlessly frail, but together...

"My lady?" Hannixe, tentatively.

Ari turned back to her companions. They watched her anxiously, even Darjeth, and a weight settled on her shoulders. The feeling was familiar, almost like coming home.

"Which way?" Her face felt strange, but at least the invisible translator was still functioning. "The Mirrored City, which way is it?"

It was Darjeth who answered. "By which route, my lady?"

"The short one." Ari regarded him steadily, daring him to debate. "The one that takes a day." *Which should get us there in time for this Conjunction-eclipse thing.* If she'd known time was so precious, she certainly *would* have worried; maybe the chained man had indeed been trying to do her a solid.

It was entirely like him, she decided.

"The Spires." Hannixe's eyes shone now, fresh hope igniting in their depths. "A brief ride across the margin of the Dry Sea will bring us to an entrance, and from there—"

"My lady queen." Keners wasn't giving up without argument. "It is *dangerous*. The faithless accursed will be watching, and—"

Good. "Well, if he's busy looking for us, the prince will have an easier time getting to him." She hoped she sounded far more certain than she felt. "Hannixe, how often do we have to treat Darjeth's wound?"

"When it pains him." The other woman lifted the canteen thoughtfully, weighing what remained of its contents. "Or perhaps we should leave him and Keners here, and ride swift as—"

"I think not." The Fox outright bristled, but he didn't lift a hand or move menacingly toward Hannixe. "You cannot ask that of me."

"Nor of me." Darjeth rose, wincing. "So long as I remain myself, my lady queen, I am at your disposal. Though should I become otherwise, I will ask my friend the Fox for one last favour."

"And I shall grant it." Keners's glower was nearly as fierce as the chained man's. "If it must be done, then let us begin."

"Wait." Hannixe bent, and began fussing with her skirts. Fabric tore, a sharp businesslike sound. "We must bind the wound, or it will reopen as we ride."

Well. That went way easier than I expected. Now Ari only had to deal with the crushing suspicion that she was making the wrong call.

It was too late. Hannixe ripped strips from her grey dress, though both she and Darjeth gave horrified refusals when Ari suggested giving a little of her own clothing to the cause. Keners hurried back to the equines, and Ari ended up taking charge of the canteen. Maybe they could find some more water along the way, and she could see if an imitation of their queen was good enough. She could argue the Cup had been responsible for the Mere's cleansing, but there was the second pond in the forest near the Keep and Sarle acting as if it had burned him before she touched it.

Ari could at least try, and if it worked, great. If not, she'd figure out something else.

First, though, she had to struggle into the saddle by herself.

32

NEAR UNNOTICED

THE DRY SEA BORE A CLOSE RESEMBLANCE TO PRAIRIE, YELLOW grass dotted with mats of smoke-colored flowers on low, creeping ochre shrubs, all rippling with a noise like the ocean on a rocky shore. The palette was pure Wyeth, but the light deep and liquid as Vermeer, the colors thick and beautiful as van Gogh's wheatfields. There was no hint of mint to this foliage, a sweetish smell like dried apples rising instead, and Ari's fingers tingled. Touching a stirrup or other piece of metal tack didn't quite create sparks, but did produce a brief thrill along the nerves; strands of hair not trapped in braids briefly lifting on an invisible current.

The equines were tired, but plodded along willingly enough. Ari worried about fodder—whatever critters with teeth like that would eat—but she figured Keners knew what he was doing.

Though the warmth was springlike instead of summery, the distance held shimmering heat-ripples. Shadows danced through them—more of the almost-antelopes and pale shadows Hannixe said were *shakren.*

"Like the equines, only smaller, and the color of your mount. They bear a single horn." She tapped at her forehead with graceful fingertips. "Curved, almost as a bow. The grass-pards hunt them, and the windsnakes."

"Foul-tempered beasts," Keners added, shortly. "They should not trouble us." Still, a vertical line lingered between his dark eyebrows, and he scanned their surroundings ceaselessly.

Each time they halted Darjeth tried to help Ari with dismounting, but she managed to reach the ground herself without too much trouble. Getting back *up* was the problem, but fortunately the blond man's side held up admirably and he could give her ten fingers. His own mounting was a little less elegant than usual, and each stop meant another session with the canteen. The foam wasn't so bad as the first time and the angry dark branchmarks didn't spread; he took each treatment like a champ.

He didn't even swear, though he gritted teeth hard enough to crack. A real gentleman all 'round.

So was Keners. He didn't try to make Hannixe pay for over-riding him, so far as Ari could tell. Instead, he focused on keeping the equines tended, but Ari didn't miss how he hovered over the Grey Lady at each stop, rapier handy and his pale gaze resting speculatively on Darjeth.

Hannixe found a few low-growing plants with pungent silvery leaves, and when crushed and applied to the wound they seemed to ease the pain. But the level in the canteen dropped steadily, and the Dry Sea was living up to its name.

The sun sank, and just as it was halfway below the horizon—the moon hanging nearby seeming almost as swollen—they reached the Spires.

Towering stacks of glossy black stone spread in a wall, thin crimson veins throbbing near their fang-points. Wind from the Dry Sea poured past, moaning only a little less eerily than the Breach. Ari eyed this new geological monstrosity nervously.

No artist she'd ever studied could truly capture this, though she was sure more than a few would love to try. At least its geometry was reasonably natural instead of alien, and didn't give her the willies to the same degree as the bone-bridge.

Keners became even more stiffly vigilant, riding first in front, then behind; Darjeth stayed to Ari's left, equally watchful. Hannixe drooped in the saddle, braiding together strings of silvery shrubbery for later use.

They turned along the spike-wall, jog-trotting with black stone to their left for a long while. Finally, just before the day died completely, a single gap yawned. A listing, weathered wooden post stood just to one side of the aperture, and Keners called a halt.

"A guide," he said, indicating the pillar. "Destroyed, of course, but…"

Darjeth's breathing was ragged as Hannixe changed the poultice. She dabbed more crushed leaves on the slice, frowning in the bloody light of sunset. "Is it very bad?"

"Not so much. I simply cannot dance at the moment." He gave a tight smile, but his forehead was damp, his cheeks hollow-gaunt as the chained man's had been at first.

Ari peered at the wooden guidepost. A length of rusted chain fell from an eyelet carved in its top and trailed across dusty gravel, vanishing into the gravel-floored cleft between two massive, glossy spires. The rock towers looked very sharp, and the combing windsong mounted as evening rose. "A guide?"

"Gaps are few, and at some there are guides. Before the misfortune, all one had to do was follow a chain in order to arrive safely." Keners frowned, staring into the gap. "I had hoped the renewal would bring them to some kind of repair."

Huh. Ari stepped closer, studying the wood's grain, the thick rust on the chain. It looked ancient, many links rotten enough to snap under their own weight.

"Perhaps enough remains of this one, and we can feel our way through." Hannixe shook out a fresh scrap of fabric and bent once more, accomplishing a neat compression bandage with a few swift movements. Darjeth obeyed her slight prodding, lifting his arm and twisting to grant her greater access—but slowly, his teeth bared in a grimace.

"Unlikely." Keners shook his head, examining the chain as well. "If we step into a false passage we may well wander starving for a hundred mortal years. That is, if the windsnakes do not descend. They would not approach the chain, but if 'tis broken or we stray, they will feast well." He glanced at Ari, pale eyes narrowed, and the message was clear.

This is a really bad idea.

"Well, you are canny enough to elude both the Golden and the restless dead." The Grey Lady straightened, stretching and shaking her hands briskly. "Finding the way should be little trouble for you, no?"

"If my lady asks it, I will do all I can." The Fox didn't sound happy about the notion. "Even in darkness."

"There is no hope," Darjeth said, clamping his arm against the bandage and sagging atop his rounded grey boulder-seat. "You have done all that is possible, Hannixe—you and our lady queen. Perhaps you should simply leave me, and withdraw to some safety."

Like hell I will. Ari bit her lower lip, gently; the torc with its white jewel warmed against her breastbone, safely tucked under her mantle. The forest had healed itself in fast-forward, the Mere had turned to clean water. It was ridiculous, but maybe...

She stepped closer to the post. It trembled slightly, but that could have been the wind.

"Be careful," Keners said. "My lady queen, do not—"

Ari's fingers met dry, rough wood. *Please. I'm doing the best I can here.*

For a moment nothing happened, and she felt utterly ridiculous. Evening breeze mounted, the Spires keening, and the sound went right through her head like the grinding shatter of a car accident.

An image of the chained man rose in Ari's head, sharp and vivid. Head cocked as he rode, he stared at some point past her, the big black equine shaking its mane impatiently. Splinters quivered under her fingertips, sharp edges jabbing. Metal crackled and rang, drowning out the wind's voice.

Do you doubt now, Ariadne?

She snatched her hand back, her entire arm tingling as if waking from nerve compression. The wooden post stood straight and tall now, sleek and darkly varnished; a last gleam of blood-red sunset passed down the dull iron chain, snaking whole and untarnished into the gap. Pebbles shifted, gravel settling, and somewhere in the distance a low rolling growl like thunder echoed.

"By silver." Keners sounded wondering, and not a little awestruck.

Darjeth did, too. "I have heard that before; 'tis our lord prince's displeasure. I think he has ascertained our aim."

I certainly hope so. "He'll follow us?" Ari couldn't squash the thin thread of hope blooming in her chest. She turned to Hannixe and the guys, shaking out her hand. The buzzing in her fingers wouldn't abate.

"I think it likely he feared you taken, and was already riding hard through the Blight to attack the Mirrored City." Hannixe shivered, cupping her elbows in her palms, hugging herself very much as Ari habitually did. "The traitor will be so busy with that event, we shall pass near unnoticed."

"Good." Ari hoped it didn't mean the chained man was angry at *her.* But if she was going to get a beating—or worse—she'd damn well better make it worth the price.

Like filching cash from Wanda Lee's purse to add to her getaway fund or fleeing from a big white house where her ex-husband's body lay on hardwood, some things just had to be done.

"Keners," she continued, "how are the equines?"

"Strong enough for one last effort." There was a new note in the Fox's tone, suspiciously like respect. "As am I, and my friend Darjeth."

"I am ready." Hannixe helped the blond man to his feet. "Let us make what speed we may."

🜲 33 🜲

EXPECTING VISITORS

HEADS DOWN, HOOVES CLICKING ON SHARDS OF BLACK GRAVEL, the equines walked. The chain to their left scintillated at irregular intervals, a blood-red glow tightening each link as it passed. Which was disconcerting, true, but no more so than anything else in this place. The route twisted, hairpinned, and zigzagged between spires, and Ari was soon hopelessly turned around. Each passageway looked identical, especially in the dark—sheer obsidian sides vanishing overhead, passageways branching on either side, a few stars glimmering between crowded fangpoints, sharp-glinting pebbles underfoot, the dry wind singing, musical creaks, and occasional violent shatterings in the distance.

"Glassfalls." Darjeth roused enough to explain, when the first sound of breakage gave Ari a violent start. "The Spires sometimes break, my lady, but the guide will keep us from such danger."

She hoped he was right. Imagining vast sheets of glossy, razor-edged stone calving off glacier-style was terrifying.

Their halts were brief, and Ari was glad of the starry darkness when she had to somehow haul herself onto the white equine once more; at least nobody could clearly witness her lack of grace. The moon didn't rise far, lingering near the horizon, and wondering about whatever fucked-up astronomical rhythm this place had was a waste of energy.

Sometimes you just had to go with the weirdness. She was getting a lifetime's worth of experience in *that* department.

Occasionally deeper shadows flitted overhead, long sinuous shapes with frilled wings blotting out the stars. "Windsnakes," Keners said softly during a short break, when he noticed her staring nervously upward. "So long as we stay near the guide, they are little danger. They have learned to fear it, and taught their brood to do so as well."

Which was great, but Ari still flinched each time she noticed the drift-fluttering shadows. And when the sound of giant black-glass sheets hitting the ground vibrated underfoot, as well. Some were too near for any comfort.

Darjeth didn't complain, but his breathing grew shallow and getting him out of the saddle took all three of his companions. He apologized for the trouble each time—until he didn't, barely conscious, his eyes nearly closed. Hannixe's heart-shaped face grew grave in the gloom, and she applied the last of the poultice herbs to his wound in a thick paste made with a scant dribble of canteen water.

Keners often sniffed the breeze wandering through the Spires, tense and alert, the streak at his temple glowing. With his sharp nose and quick movements, he did indeed look the fox they named him.

The night wore on. Ari's throat ached, but she waved aside the canteen each time Hannixe offered. "Save it for Darjeth," she said, finally, and the Grey Lady nodded.

She didn't drink either, and the long considering look she shared with Ari felt like an old friend's. The chain made a low metallic noise, tightening as another brief crimson pulse passed through; Keners helped his lady mount, then cupped his hands to help Ari as well. "Up," he said, softly. "Morn comes, my queen. Take heart."

The last stretch seemed to take forever, the chain doubling and twisting between sharp-edged folds. The crashing of calved glass-sheets intensified, some shatteringly close, and the chain's pulses grew more frequent. The frilled, sinuous flying shadows lingered; Ari glimpsed the glitter of eyes on a few of them, alight with pale blue foxfire very like the Small Pavilion's lamp-flame.

Then she realized she could see Keners's equine in front of her, and Darjeth's beside him. Hannixe to her right was visible instead of a mere indistinct shadow, and the pale smears clutching her own reins were Ari's aching hands, glowing in the dim grey of approaching dawn.

The Spires sang a long, low mournful note. Keners pulled rein, his head up, and Darjeth's equine followed suit. The blond man slumped in the saddle, either not noticing the lack of movement or too exhausted to care.

"Never the same way twice," the Fox said. "And we have moved slowly indeed. Yet..."

Ari peered past him. The chain reached a tall wooden post past the final obsidian skyscraper to their left, an iron snake rising to terminate in another carved eyelet. Just beyond, a long bare slope full of scattered glass-gleaming pebbles and other small gravel ran downhill to an amber-tinted ribbon—the Road, it looked like, led even here. Its auriferous gleam cut through a flat landscape reduced to greyscale rendering, all color drained. Indistinct and arid, the plain looked... unhealthy.

Drained, she thought. *Sucked dry*.

A line of whitish glow along the horizon showed where the sun was struggling up; the moon hung low too, huge in perspective though no less perfect and unstained.

"Is that..." Ari shivered.

"The Conjunction is nigh," Hannixe confirmed. "There lies the Mirrored City, home of the Bright King and source of his Blight."

It was difficult to tear her gaze from the dawn, but as Ari focused she saw a vast vengeful glitter at the Road's northern terminus. High mercury-colored walls restrained a swelling bulge of reflective surfaces full of what little illumination empty sky and depleted plain could manage. Come actual daylight the entire thing would no doubt flame like an infected blister; she blinked several times, trying to make sense of the shapes in the middle distance.

"And there," Keners added, "the army of the faithless accursed. He is expecting visitors, it seems."

The Fox was right. Rank upon rank of Golden stood before the bright-polished walls, their horned heads swiveling. Between their neatly regimented squares other shapes cringed and writhed, moving restlessly; plaintive moans lingered just at the edge of hearing. Ari sensed the wet nasty slapping of their swollen paws, though the susurration was too far away to be truly audible. The plain was crawling with all manner of sickening shapes, and Ari was suddenly, nauseatingly certain she had made the wrong decision, that Darjeth was going to die and the monsters below were about to notice three intruders on a hill, charging up to welcome their enemies in a gleaming, rotting wave.

A rim of fire touched the edge of the world, its angry flush breaking bland uncolor. The vast crunches of glassrock shattering from the Spires ceased for a breathless moment as the guide-chain ran with bright crimson. Another rumble of thunder sounded, though the sky was innocent of any cloud; the scree on the slope moved uneasily, like a pan of popcorn kernels in hot oil just before the real fun begins.

"Is that the Conjunction?" Ari whispered.

"No." Keners shook his dark head and glanced to their right, the stripe at his temple flickering. "'Tis rage, my lady queen, that of your first companion. Naught rouses it but a threat to his lady, and any true knight shares the feeling."

Oh. Ari shifted in the saddle, feeling disheveled, aching, worn out.

And very, very frightened.

The sun's first limb boiled free, sky-lakes bursting into flame.

Rumbling increased, stones on the slope pop-jumping wildly though none approached their small group, and the Spires suddenly shrieked as a cold gust blew through the entire collection of polished obsidian fangs. The road blazed bright gold, bloody streaks crackling along its flow, and the sound of galloping hooves shook cringing air.

Another red gleam appeared opposite the Mirrored City, the space where the Road vanished alive with glitters of lightning. The hoof-growl crested, and so did the thunder.

In the distance, amid fresh wavering heatshimmer, the chained man appeared.

❧ 34 ❧

THE REAPING

A SHOUT ROSE FROM THE BRIGHT KING'S ARMY, THE GOLDENS' *metallic bugle-blares mixing with piping, forlorn moans from the ravening restless dead. No doubt the cry was massive, for the bright walls of the Mirrored City flexed and trembled at its throbbing.*

Yet the hellish din was drowned in thunder. Down the Road the Underdark's first knight rode, his steed's footfalls reverberating to the very depths of his kingdom. Swept in his wake were half a dozen companions, their eyes agleam with fevered power, clinging to the reins of snarling, bare-fanged equines. None had elected to stay behind, though the risk of hearts bursting or bones shredding during wild career was very real; to their queen's defense they rode, the Cupbearer and those who had remained in the woods near the Keep to harry the traitor's forces, those who waited faithfully for they knew not what.

In that waiting, they would not bend to the Bright King's corrupt Law. Another allegiance held them; the usurper's fury at intransigence could overwhelm with death and rot, but not force true obedience. Even the corpses of his enemies could only be puppet-pulled, mindless meat married to metal.

None would serve him willing.

The Sun leapt upward, its face the color of fresh blood. As daylight mounted the Bright King's army surged forward, a flood of clockwork horrors and masses of sickening ghouls. Yet the prince did not halt, did not slow. Swift as doom, relentless as death, his companions formed a wedge, and the prince's sword held aloft was a flaming column.

As the day's red eye separated from horizon-line, a small group crashed into a swelling horde. Stabs of lightning spread, chain-leaping from one abomination to the next; the rapiers of the faithful burned with renewed force. Screaming undead, teeth bared and foam spattering, were granted peace. Smoke gouted upward; the sound of cavalry impact was swallowed in terrible, furious vibration.

Black iron snakes rayed in every direction, ripping through entire ranks of the accursed. The carnage was unspeakable, and if upon the nearby hill-side a lady turned away from such a view, 'twas only natural. Gobbets of rotting flesh flew high and shattered metal hulks were tossed like straws in a hurricane, for in extremity even a fetter may be turned to a weapon. The bedlam intensified, yet still vanished into that fathomless hive-hum of pure rage threading through every part of the Underdark, from the shore of the wine-dark Dreaming Sea to the Spires, from the Whispering to the Hollow Cliffs, from the floor of the Breach to the tallest spire of the Keep, where a single bloody glitter burst into life after so long in dark abeyance. From the Mere to the Lonely Mountain every beast cowered, even the fearless pards and the wolves of the Cloudrush, for a greater predator was snarling.

Through the ranks of the Bright King's servants the storm winnowed, and none escaped the reaping.

Before the Moon's edge first caressed the Sun's, the work was done. A battlefield smoked with desolation, no restless dead or Golden remaining. Piles of rotting ghast mixed with shattered high-horned helms and punctured breastplates lay heaped before tall walls of frozen quicksilver; pistons and gearwheels, cogs and gobbets of quivering, contagious corpse lay heaped together, sponge-rotten skulls and shorn metal limbs strewn in a vast carpet. Only the Road was free of wrack, for it burned every foul thing set upon it to nothingness.

Straight through vast carnage the Road ran, and with it the prince. To the great gate of the Mirrored City he passed, its glass flaming with morn-

ing. The chains hanging from him flexed and drove forward as the Moon drifted across her consort's face; a great hushed gloom fell upon smoking, shattered wasteland.

Thrice they battered, those chains bent to purpose deep and vicious. Cracks spiderwebbed the gates upon the first blow, slivers rained down upon the second, and upon the third a vast crumbling noise of breakage almost managed to rival the deep vibrating hum of his fury.

Almost.

The wall was breached, the Mirrored City open. Yet he did not surge forward. The Moon hid half the Sun's face, and from a hill to the side of the battlefield a single lone gleam showed, pale and perfect—the Carcanet, its light briefly piercing cloth.

Only then did the prince hesitate. For from the Spires, his lady came riding.

THE MIRRORED CITY

THE MOMENT THEIR THE EQUINES REACHED THE ROAD'S FLAMING golden surface, the cloud of rot and burning oil faded, replaced by a smoke-sweet, musky perfume.

Getting there, however, required threading between hills and piles of shattered robots or quick-rotting zombies; more than once Ari almost retched. Maybe some of the greater drink lingered, proofing her against the worst nausea. Darjeth swayed in the saddle, greenish-pale. Hannixe pressed her hand over mouth and nose, blinking furiously as her great dark eyes welled with tears.

Keners leaned aside a few times, his gorge plainly rising, but none of them outright vomited. Which was, so far as Ari was concerned, a victory as well.

And to think she'd been worried about the chained man facing all those monsters. Still, the Bright King could have something worse in reserve.

Her stomach didn't settle as their weary equines trotted up the road, heading for the massive hole torn in the Mirrored City's wall. She had no idea where so much glass could be found or made, but it coated every surface—mostly in giant sheets, though plenty of the buildings beyond were covered in mosaic-chips of variable size. On a clear summer day it probably glowed fit to give any onlooker a migraine, and she wondered who in the hell would want to live like this.

The rumble-thunder underground was so thick it was like silence. The moon was two-thirds across the sun's face, every shadow scalloped, and though she knew not to look at any eclipse unless you wanted to lose your retinas the temptation was well-nigh unbearable. The Carcanet throbbed steadily, heat spreading through her a little further with each wave.

Her heart leapt into her throat as she counted her companions, none missing—Jazarl, his hair purplish in the red-dyed gloom; Alzarien with a makeshift bandage around his upper arm and his dark eyes gleaming furiously; Sarle's brown equine hovering protectively close to Leshe's new mount. The mahogany-skinned woman in the middle of the group brightened as she saw Hannixe and Ari, opened her mouth as if to greet them, but subsided, her hands tightening on the reins as she glanced at the black-armored man who faced the shattered gate, his back to the rest of the world and the chains draped on his frame moving slowly, seaweed fronds caught in a slow irresistible current.

Majan nodded at Keners, his pale hair taking on a cupric cast to match Alzarien's. Naithor, leaning on his saddle-horn, studied Darjeth, and the relief crossing his tanned face was transparent.

Oh, thank God. Ari tried to pull the reins, but the white equine had ideas of its own. It paced through the group until it reached the black one, and the chains parted to let it through. *Oh no. This... Wow. Good God.*

Smoke rose in veils and eddies, columns and whale-spouts. There were hundreds of bodies and shattered robots piled against the walls on either side, spatters of effluvia and reddish oil-ichor painted nearly to the glass-sheathed battlements. Distorted reflections twisted in the mirrors' depths.

It hadn't taken very long at all. The wreckage was not nearly so terrifying as the fact that the one who made it had refrained until this particular moment.

What else could he do?

Ari's pulse hammered. Her breath caught, her fingers trembled. The chained man's profile, icy and remote, changed slightly. There were thready, leaden vein-fingers crawling up his throat, cupping his cheeks, but they cringed away from the sheer savage wrath burning behind his expression.

So he'd been infected after all. He turned his head, with terrible slowness. That feverish gaze finally met hers, each dark eye holding a bright silvery crescent as the Conjunction progressed.

The eclipse was nearly total.

"Ariadne," he said. "Are you hurt?"

Uh, I should be asking you that. She shook her head. "N-no." *But you... you're...* The words trembled, locked behind her lips, and with them lurked the ghost of a name. Maybe it was his, remembered or newly found; it certainly suited him.

Her throat refused to work properly. So did her tongue. Ari simply watched him, holding that terrible gaze until it softened— not much, a few degrees.

Yet it was enough. The terrible threadlike branchings moving through his skin darkened briefly, gaining a millimeter, and halted.

"Come," he said, finally. "One last matter, my lady. And then..."

Then what? She didn't want to ask. He was probably going to send her home. After all this, a jail cell or court hearings might be a relief. At least he'd be cured, and Darjeth too.

Fine. Let's get it over with.

As if she'd spoken, the prince gathered his reins and turned to face the gate. His equine stepped forward, and glass cracked all along the Mirrored City's walls, rays of breakage spreading with small creak-flexing noises. The deep furious thunder muted some-what, but did not cease.

He rode through the gate, and her mount kept pace. Behind them, the faithful followed.

Built in layers marching up a sharp slope, streets laid ruler-straight despite the nod to medieval defense, every lane and alley was cobbled with fist-sized dollops of clear glass. Mirrors clothed each wall and door, the entire pile a vitreous-coated mockery of Gaudi's architectural genius. For all the glass there were no windows; nobody lived here. Bare and sterile, the Mirrored City mounted to a pile of glittering reflection in the shape of a castle, crouching just below the vast hill's crown.

It would be easy to get lost in endless reflections, Ari thought, but the chained man's shadow sent webbed cracks through every surface it touched, robbed shining sheets of the power to misdirect. The cobbled road sought to twist, but the black equine's hooves radiated dark fractures as well.

In the smoking umbra of a prince's passage, his companions were kept safe.

As full eclipse was reached, the citadel at the city's crest loomed before them. It did not reflect their strained faces or Ari's dishevelment, the chained man's set expression or Leshe's bright eyes, the stripe in Keners's hair or Hannixe's pale hands. Instead, the mirrors were full of racing stormclouds underlit by bright diamond seams of lightning, and Ari caught glimpses of tossing branches, a landslide scar on an overgrown hillside, a burst of white engine steam turning to gouts of oily smoke, the fierce orange and yellow smear of a burning black Oldsmobile.

Her throat ached fiercely. So did the rest of her.

The Bright King's stronghold was a copy of the Keep, the moat a dry crevice lined with upthrusting shards of broken mirror, a drawbridge of clear glass shuddering as the chained man dismounted at its lip.

He paced to the side of Ari's mount, and raised his gauntleted hands.

She could have fallen out of the saddle herself, she supposed.

Yet she let him lift her down, gently, her slippers touching slick hard cobbles butterfly-soft. His gauntlets were warm even through her dress's and mantle's layers, releasing gently. He stepped away and paused, looking down at her as she turned from the white equine's shadowed flank. The shadowy threads reaching up his cheeks had not moved, and the pale glowing crescents caught in his pupils blazed.

His name rose again, battering at the obstruction in her throat. She shook her head, and found she was trembling afresh. Waves of shivers passed through her, hot and cold.

He moved, but only to offer his arm. Ari took it, gazing steadily up at him—the last time she'd performed this particular motion had been at her wedding.

Oh, God. The sound of the others dismounting was lost in stillness, the vibration of rage withdrawn yet still vast, underlaying every thought.

The chained man said nothing, setting off over the drawbridge. Ari found she could keep up with him, leaning on warm steady metal. None of the others followed, nor did they speak. They stood with the equines and watched as Ari and their prince moved, step by step, into the Bright King's fortress.

❧ 36 ❧

GLASS CASTLE

HE SEEMED TO KNOW WHERE HE WAS GOING. ARI CLUNG TO THE chained man's arm, hoping she wasn't about to commit some kind of embarrassing blunder. Even that constant fear felt worn and threadbare at the edges, a pain so familiar it was almost comforting.

Whatever was going to happen now was utterly beyond her control. It probably always had been.

This cobbled bailey was a copy of the Keep's, except the doors on its far end were empty arches, their throats full of dry, drowsing reflection. The colonnade along the right side was full of soft nasty noises. She was suddenly certain that space was where the zombies came from, since the quiet slithering sounds lurking in its gloom were very akin to the padding of their flayed, tumid paws.

The long low building on the left held a rosy mirroring of flame inside its doorways and reverberated with the ghost of hideous hammering. The mental image of a hellish assembly line, robots slammed together piece by piece until bright horned helms were lowered over shrieking metallic faces frozen in agony, was so clear and distinct she faltered, her shoulder pressing against the chained man's armored arm.

Finally, as if compelled by the movement, he spoke. "Peace, my lady." Just the same as always, and none of his armor-spikes did more than gently scratch her mantle's sleeve. The edge of his spice-musk scent held a hint of cleansing, purging flame. "Just a few more steps."

And then what? But she couldn't ask, not least because she was half afraid the answer would be far worse than any terrible, suspicious anticipation.

They passed through the largest archway, into the Keep proper. The wall-mirrors ran with lethargic, infected glow, cracks spreading from the chained man's reflection; the ceiling was a mosaic and the floor dusky glass. No slivers popped free, the edifice holding together despite fierce vibration, and she wondered how long it would take this place to fall apart. What animals would poke through the dusty shards once it did, searching for shelter or a meal? Or would they avoid its corpse as they did its barren, glittering glory?

There were no birds here, no not-possums, none of the small sounds of woodland or urban wildlife. Not even rats would inhabit this dump, she thought, and another wave of great gripping shakes passed through her, as if she was crouched against a bathroom door while Mike kicked the other side. *You better come out, Ari. You hear me? Come the fuck out, I wanna talk to you...*

Endlessly reflected hallways and glass-clothed rooms flowered around them, creaking cracks accompanying each measured footfall. The light became low, brownish, and she sensed the eclipse was near its midpoint now.

A pair of huge doors, thick glass beveled and cut in strange whirling patterns, reared atop three wide, shallow steps of smoky bubble-streaked glazing. The chained man glanced down at her, his eyebrows slightly lifted, and Ari found she could decipher the look with no trouble at all, even through the rising threads of contagion clasping his face.

As if she knew him—or at least, part of her did. Fear evaporated, his presence suddenly a deep inalienable comfort.

He's here. Nothing can hurt me.

Ridiculous. Utterly bonkers. And yet, she found she could believe.

His boot landed on the first step, and the doors shattered inward with a titanic jolt. Shrapnel whickered as it flew; Ari climbed the stairs at his side, for once certain no sharp edge could touch her.

A vast hall lay beyond, full of whispers and strange directionless sepia light. The clouded floor cracked in great spirals, fissures radiating from the chained man, and Ari's eyelids fluttered. At the far end a strange cascading glitter winked back, its colorless shining too bright for gloom-adapted pupils. It hurt to look; she squeezed her eyes shut and leaned on the chained man's arm. The Carcanet's heat intensified, its heartbeat evening into a steady flow.

Step. Another step. A long chain of soft, relentless footfalls. Her slippers found nothing but level ground, and the armored arm under her hands was steady. He led her carefully, and when he stopped she did too, the darkness behind her lids still deep-soft and utterly comforting.

"Look at her," the chained man said, and his voice was terrible. It boomed through the entire citadel, floated across the drawbridge, whistled past the small group huddled there, and caromed over the Mirrored City as the entire shining excrescence lay supine.

The hush afterward was vast and shadowy, full of dry rushing flame to match a hint of smoke in the chained man's scent.

He spoke again. "Look at me." Again the words roared, and mirrored towers shattered. Great shards and slivers plummeted, crashing on cobbled thoroughfares like the Spires' eternal crumbling. Glazed walls heaved and buckled, and even the sun blinked for a moment as the chained man's fury reached apogee.

Ari found she could open her eyes again. The headache-inducing glow at the far end of the hall had shrunk, and now she saw a half-familiar shape—the Bright King, slumped upon a giant, twisted throne of corrugated glass.

Her heart gave a wrenching, wringing leap.

The chained man spoke for the third time. "Look at us," he said, softly. The words reverberated as the others had, and outside the glass castle the entire city shuddered, its remaining towers sway-cracking.

No. It can't... no. Bile whipped the back of her throat, and Ari longed to scream.

Because she *recognized* him.

Hunched in a suit of polished armor shaped very much in imitation of the chained man's, his lips pulled back in a hateful grimace and his blue eyes rolling, Mike Hardison stiffened, and screamed.

KIND AS EVER

THE CRY WAS ONE SHE KNEW INTIMATELY. DEEP AND GRINDING, it was the sound her husband produced when he was too angry for words, and the congested rage on his face was hatefully routine as well. Ari's knees buckled. The metal under her palms softened, crumpling as well, and for a moment she thought she had, with hysterical strength, put a dent in blackened iron.

The Bright King surged from his throne, snatching up a long heavy blade resting against its trembling, splintering side. His armored boots were polished to shining; his spurs struck white sparks from the rivening floor. "*NOOOOOOO,*" he screamed as he flung himself toward her; she could only watch, the dry clicks of an empty revolver filling her head, a reek of gunpowder and blood in her nose, her bruised throat throbbing, and small blood vessels bursting in her eyes, glaring red petechiae she'd glimpsed in the Oldsmobile's rearview mirror.

Little branching threads, red instead of black. Had the clear, clean pondwater soothed those wounds as well?

The chained man stepped forward, her hands falling from his arm. The shadows on his cheeks retreated, infection burned to nothingness in a furnace of renewal. Iron cracked, clatter-clanging on quaking glass tiles. Underneath, he wore dusty black—linen shirt, velvet tunic, breeches like his forest knights, and functional dark leather boots like Keners's. He stepped out of the chains and they fell, wriggling, their small hissing chimes lost in the tumult.

Yet the Bright King did not slow. Frozen, Ari watched death approach at a run, and the sound of shattering was the full-length mirror on the bedroom wall when Mike threw her against it, small slices on the back of her head clotting up swiftly while she drove from the house on Hardison Hill; the noise he now made was full of her husband's last rattling exhalation as he thudded to the hardwood, his T-shirt full of bloody holes.

Clunk. The clamor stopped, sliced in half. The chained man—he wasn't chained anymore—made a slight dismissive movement, both massive spiked gauntlets falling in spent petal-pieces.

Invisible force slammed into the Bright King, tossing him aside like a discarded doll. He flew, his sword's heavy straight blade—a copy of the chained man's, though lacking the wickedly taloned quillons—scintillating once before it landed and corkscrewed, blackening like paper in a fire.

He hit the already-cracked wall with a sickening crunch and Ari swayed on nerveless feet, her hands finding each other, clasping hard at the low V-point of her gown's waist. Her mantle's hem fluttered on a gentle, dusty breeze.

The Bright King slid down from the dent, landing with a heavy, horrible thump. Now she could see his face was a little sharper than Mike's, lacking the blur of too many nights spent downing shots of Beam at the Kittykat Klub, and his bright blue eyes weren't bloodshot. Nor did his nose have the slight bump from a touch football injury in high school, and no wheat-colored stubble roughened his cheeks.

Still, the resemblance was goddamn uncanny. Ari found she could breathe again. Cool air freighted with a faint tinge of musk and spice wrapped around her, filled her lungs. Shards fell from the ceiling, grinding to smaller splinters in midair, shattering further into deadly needles as they hit the floor, yet none came near her. Safe in an invisible, protective bubble, she examined Ternek, the faithless accursed.

The prince's shoulders moved, a rolling motion as the last of his armor melted away. The chains slithered together, roll-melding into a single cable, a sinuous dull-black length rasping dryly as it curved for the fallen traitor.

Who coughed, a bubble of bright blood bursting on his lips. "You," he husked, staring at Ari. "I killed you."

Did you? Ari's fingers knotted together so hard they hurt, a bright spike of pain through the layers of magical pondwater, the greater drink, and the prince's unseen aegis. "I repaid the favour," she heard herself say, softly, in the lovely, mellifluous language of this place. "We are quits in that, at least."

The Bright King's teeth were grimed with blood. Slivers of glass festooned his golden hair. He stared at her as if she'd spoken in English, or some other foreign tongue. The black iron snake slid between shattered mirror-fangs, its front end drawing up like a cobra's questing head, muscular ripples running down its sides.

The prince waited, his silence almost like a living thing. Finally, he made a small shrugging movement, graceful and light. The ruins of armor settled into immobility on the floor at his booted feet, a discarded skin.

"My lady Moon." Each word was a caress. "Tell me your mercy does not extend to this, your once-companion. All you must do is turn away, and consign him to my vengeance."

"No." That spurred Ternek to motion. He twitched, battered armor squeak-crumpling. Giant dents and pleats marred the bright metal; now he was the one trapped in an unforgiving carapace. "Please." The half-familiar blue eyes widened, and he strained as if to lift an arm, once-bright metal creaking as the limb trapped inside struggled for release. "*Please*, no. I am sorry, I beg forgiveness. You are merciful, my lady Moon, please do not let him—"

"What will happen?" Ari's voice was husky as Hannixe's in the village. The urge to cough mounted, as if she were still bruised from Mike's strangling fingers. The Carcanet's warmth pushed at the sensation, forcing it back bit by bit. "Afterward, I mean."

"We shall rejoin your faithful, and ride by easy stages to the Keep." The prince, chained no more, turned to gaze at her. His smile was no longer bitter. In fact, if he looked like this more often —interested, soft, expectant—nobody would ever fear him again. "We shall take up our old amusements, or new ones if you prefer; more companions will arrive when you wish for them. In some few mortal years none will recall this traitor's name or his cursèd face, though I shall never leave my kindness unguarded again. I suppose that might count as remembrance, but I doubt it."

Not quite what I meant. "You won't..." *You won't send me back? I can stay?* Would she sound like a needy little bitch—one of Mike's favorite epithets, come to think of it—if she asked?

"Ariadne." The way he pronounced her name was flat-out indecent. The chained-no-more reached out, and his fingers touched hers. A brief brush, bare flesh meeting for an instant, but it sent a scorch-thrill all through her. "Do you still doubt?"

"P-p-please," Ternek stammered. "Please, m-mercy..."

"All you must do is turn away," the prince continued, taking no more notice than of a buzzing fly at a picnic.

Turn away. It sounded so simple.

I wish I could. Ari swallowed, hard. If she didn't do what he wanted, he probably *would* send her back, which meant a lifetime spent running and looking over her shoulder if she was lucky.

If she wasn't, a jail cell was the best she could expect. The Carcanet burned at her breastbone, and she would miss that pulsing fire, the sense of deep inarguable comfort.

It wasn't the only thing she'd long for. "I can't," she said, heavily. "I'm sorry."

The prince stirred; Ari stiffened, bracing herself. He took a single step toward her, eclipsing the sight of the fallen traitor. A stupid, paltry, futile little kingdom built on murder and suffering, now reduced to splinters.

"Merciful as ever," the prince murmured, and lifted a hand. Ari flinched, but his fingertips merely stroked her cheek. He smoothed away the hot, swelling teardrop she hadn't even been aware of, and smiled once more. "Very well."

Ternek screamed. The cries rose in paroxysms of terror, far worse than the Goldens' clanking or the moaning of the restless dead.

Ari wanted to look past the shadow before her, but his touch on her face was warm and forgiving, and he did not move. Metal rasped, slithered, punctured. A hiss, a rattle, a grinding of glass, a sound like landslides tearing apart hills on a storm-lashed summer evening.

A final cracking, as of a giant mirror splitting in half, and the cries cut off, cleanly.

"There." The prince leaned down, and his lips met her forehead. A different heat than the Carcanet's spilled down Ari's back, curled low in her belly. "Do not be alarmed, my kindness; he yet lives. The mortal realm may have the accursed, and he will linger a long while there."

Oh. Was he going to send her back now, too? Ari nodded, bracing herself.

When the prince stepped away, there was nothing but an empty suit of battered tin armor slumped against a cracked, dusty mirror. The two reflective halves above a discarded metal jumble didn't show the throne room.

Instead, they were full of blue-and-red lights, the orange smear of a burning black car, and a blond man with his hands raised, his mouth a rictus and a flash of lightning glinting on two officers' raised guns.

What the hell? Ari watched, oddly detached, as if a true-crime episode was playing on a TV trapped behind a store window. The officers trained their pistols on the blond man, and when the lightning flashed again his shadow was malformed, as if wrapped in a giant snake's dull black length.

A jolt went through the glass castle, from the depths where the restless dead were married to contagion and the hopeless to polished metal, cresting at the highest needle-spire which now began to crumble. The prince chained-no-more slipped his arm around Ari's waist and bore her swiftly through the ruin; she sagged in his grasp, her hands creeping up to clasp behind his neck.

❧ 38 ❧

GRACE, EARNED

THE MIRRORED CITY SANK SLOWLY INTO A VAST YAWNING chasm, towers toppling and walls grinding to powder as the Moon slipped fully from her consort's embrace. A day could pass swiftly, watching such a spectacle.

By late afternoon the corpses of the Bright King's servants had been swallowed whole, tumbling into the earth's embrace, and the rumbling receded as if to a distant seashore. A vast pillar-cloud of dust rose before thinning rapidly, shredded by clean moving air. At sunset a bare earthen plain stood where once the drained, colorless Blight had spread, and the Spires sang a mournful note as they witnessed the change.

The Road still passed through, its golden glimmer unaltered. A high sharp-featured line of purple peaks lurked at the revealed horizon, a single diamond star winking from its tallest summit. "What's that?" Ari wondered, and shook her head.

She hadn't meant to speak.

"The Whispering." The prince beside her, no longer in dull dark armor but linen, leather, and velvet, regarded the faraway gleam. "We shall visit it soon enough, never fear."

Behind them equines stamped and chuffed, well pleased to be resting with their fellows. Jazarl and Darjeth—the latter's wound healing swiftly since the Bright King's infection was now wholly purged—exchanged tales in a low murmur. A small ring of black stones from the Spires' feet surrounded a bright blue flame, crackling merrily without visible fuel as Hannixe sat watching, her head resting upon Keners's shoulder. Occasionally the Fox bent to press his lips against her temple, and each time she smiled.

Leshe moved among the equines with Sarle, her questions light and rapid, his answers lower, more considered. Alzarien stretched out, propped against a saddle, his arm healing as well and his hat pulled low as he contemplated the blue flames. Majan examined arrows one by one before sliding them into a quiver, for he wished to be prepared upon the journey to the Keep.

Though there was little danger, Naithor pointed out, with their queen returned and their lord prince unfettered. Majan agreed with a nod, and handed over a handful of arrows for the bronze-haired man to inspect as well .

Ari's arms did not quite ache, though she hugged herself hard as she watched evening gloom rise in waves, more stars peering through indigo veils. The prince chained-no-more stood close, the edge of his body's heat deeply comforting.

How long would that last, though?

"Is it a door to the mortal world?" *I have to know.* She held herself stiffly, tense and ready. The others were too far away to hear, but she felt their worried glances. The Carcanet's warmth was friendly; she tried not to feel it, imagining how they would ask her to give the jewel back.

"After a fashion." He turned slightly, and his gaze was a weight as well. "Did that realm treat you so well you long to return, then? Or do you wish to..."

She squeezed a little tighter, holding herself together. "I just want to know." *You have what you needed. Am I going back or staying here?*

"The Underdark will be fully healed anon." He made a slight, dismissive motion, as if it didn't matter. "Soon enough a door may be found wherever we please. I would, though..."

"You would what?"

Another small, restless movement. It ended with his arm touching her shoulder again, the lightest of pressures; there was no spiked iron between them but the habit of space remained. It would probably take some time to fade, Ari thought, just like she would continue to flinch at the sound of breaking glass or any series of dry, heavy clicks.

For a long, long while.

"I would have you stay," the prince said, finally. "What must I do, to earn that grace?"

"Oh." *That's... not what I expected.* Ari's arms loosened. Finally, she could take a deep breath. Her skirts moved, a soft friendly whisper. Deep dark relief filled her like the warmth of a magic drink, like the sound of freedom through car windows as a trap receded in the distance, like air reaching starving lungs.

"Ariadne." His hand found her elbow, cupping gently. "I warn you, I will not... You have sought escape before. If that game pleases you, I will play again. As many times as it takes."

Well, that's probably not healthy, but... She tipped her head back, gazed briefly at the stars, and brought her chin back down, that faraway silver glitter atop the mountains finding an answering pulse in the Carcanet. "All you had to do was ask."

"Stay. Please." He paused. "Will you?"

Ari's mouth felt odd, because she was smiling. She turned to a prince chained-no-more, rising on tiptoes, her hand braced on his arm. Muscle was hard and warm under a velvet sleeve, and he leaned into her touch.

The name finally came free. He bent more than willingly, and she whispered in his ear.

He nodded. "At last," he said, softly, and his arms closed around her. Their companions looked away, amused or simply polite, as the Moon kissed her lover at the edge of a freshly healed blight.

And all of Underdark sighed with the evening breeze.

finis

ACKNOWLEDGMENTS

Many thanks are due to my beta readers J. Dunkle, K. J. Walker, and Kassandra A., for convincing me to go ahead. And as usual, much gratefulness goes to my writing partner Mel Sterling for all the regular reasons, to Skyla Dawn Cameron for everything beautiful, and to my children for giving me a reason to survive as well as putting up with me.

Last but certainly not least, I thank you, my beloved Readers. Let me show my gratitude in the way we both like best, by telling you yet another tale...

Soon.

ABOUT THE AUTHOR

Lilith Saintcrow lives in Vancouver, Washington, with her children, dogs, cat, and a library for wayward texts.